SO-AYI-450

*For Tony + Jean —
with the hope you*

Scandal

A Novel

by

Gwen Davis

*enjoy it, + find your
room. + Everything else
you're looking for.*

TELEMACHUS
PRESS

If you purchased this book without a cover you should be aware that this book is stolen property. It was reported as "unsold and destroyed" to the publisher and neither the author nor the publisher has received any payment for this "stripped book."

This book is a work of fiction. Names, characters, places and incidents are either the product of the author's imagination or are used fictitiously. Any resemblance to actual persons, living or dead, or to actual events or locales is entirely coincidental.

Scandal
Copyright © 2011 by Gwen Davis. All rights reserved, including the right to reproduce this book, or portions thereof, in any form. No part of this text may be reproduced, transmitted, downloaded, decompiled, reverse engineered, or stored in or introduced into any information storage and retrieval system, in any form or by any means, whether electronic or mechanical without the express written permission of the author. The scanning, uploading, and distribution of this book via the Internet or via any other means without the permission of the publisher is illegal and punishable by law. Please purchase only authorized electronic editions and do not participate in or encourage electronic piracy of copyrighted materials.

The publisher does not have any control over and does not assume any responsibility for author or third-party websites or their content.

Cover Designed by Joel Iskowitz

Cover Art:
Copyright © Joel Iskowitz

Published by Telemachus Press, LLC
http://www.telemachuspress.com

ISBN: 978-1-937698-45-4 (eBook)
ISBN: 978-1-937698-46-1 (Paperback)

Version 2011.12.18

Printed in the United States of America

10 9 8 7 6 5 4 3 2 1

For Mimi, who opened the door,
and for Denise, who said "Come in,"
and for the gods of Bali, who still have their Magic.

If a person gets caught by ambition only
when in a group, you could say that it was
a collective shadow.
Sometimes you feel quite all right within,
but you can come into a group where the devil
is loose and get quite disturbed ...
On the other hand, we could say that as long
as such collective demons get us, we
must have a little bit of them in us.

M-L. von Franz, <u>Shadow and Evil in Fairytales</u>

Scandal

CHAPTER ONE

WHEN I FIRST was at UCLA I knew this crazy old man, well into his nineties, Samson de Brier, who said he had been the lover of Andre Gide. Andre Gide, for God's sake. But I loved knowing someone in Hollywood who knew (or said he knew) a true intellectual, a Nobel-prize winning Existentialist. As high-toned as that sounded, Samson still took great pleasure from collecting old movie magazines, Photoplay, Modern Screen, glossy mags from those really splendid early days. I took him out to dinner a couple of times, frail and failing as he was, so he left them to me. You know, the kind when Joan Crawford was young and a bathing beauty and so was Douglas Fairbanks, Jr. and they ruined each other's lives for a while but it doesn't say stuff like that. It's a treasure trove, really, what Samson left me, along with some stories about the young and beautiful Marlon Brando who used to stop by Samson's house and fuck his agent's wife. The agent dumped his wife but kept Marlon Brando. I love Hollywood.

So I have these magazines with pictures in them of Karen Engel, who's in the suite on the third floor here at the hotel, when she was a toddler, the beautiful child of beautiful parents, her father who ran a studio, and her mother who was a siren of the time. Then I have the issue bordered in black where her mother committed suicide, and five-year-old Karen was the one to find her with her throat slashed. Not exactly an enchanted childhood. None of these kids had it easy as many psycho wards could attest. But they were all dressed well, at least for the publicity shots.

Tolstoy wrote that happy families are all alike, but I don't think there are too many happy families in Beverly Hills. Maybe the Iranians who came here when the Shah fell, but who knows what goes on in their houses. The native residents, as far as I can tell, have just as many confused secrets as those 19th century Russians. Children on cocaine, husbands on their secretaries, the only part of that never--changing story being that often now the secretaries are men.

The hotel I manage has only 51 rooms, so Rock bands don't stay here, as we don't offer enough space for mayhem. But there is usually a young movie star, or a young man who doesn't know why he isn't a movie star. When Rita checked in, and I saw through her disguise, trying to hide her remarkable eyes, I guess she figured the hotel was as good a place as any to hook up with someone, maybe get a Green card.

"Rita Favorita" the Italian papers christened her in the hot course of the scandal. The rest of the European papers picked up the name. This hotel is the rare high-end/low-key one in Beverly Hills, so people who come here are generally not annoyed by the paparazzi. Mostly they're saving their flashbulbs and buzz-buzzy ways ("Zeta! Zeta!" they yell, trying to get the subject to turn her head) for outside the Beverly Hills Hotel, the forecourt of the Peninsula, the Montage, or the Regency Wilshire where the movie of 'Pretty Woman' was set. Rita would make the current female 'stars' seem homely, or at least sexless. Eyes like hers leveled at the right guy (or the wrong one) last time just broke up a popular

Hollywood couple. This time they nearly brought down an entire country.

The lucky thing for a European who's been in a scandal is they can be pretty anonymous here. Nobody in the States pays much attention to what happens in other countries. This still may have the attitude that it's the greatest country in the world, in spite of everything that's going on, but it does believe it's the only one that matters, so most people pay zero attention to what goes on elsewhere except when elsewhere is exploding.

I myself have a subscription to 'Hello!' so keep track of European gossip, because our clientele is in good part foreign, so I like to stay on top of who's in those glossy pages. Rita had the cover and a big spread, if you'll excuse the expression, in several issues. Her real name, as I remember, is Elisa, but that doesn't rhyme with anything but Pisa, and she's from Rome. So Rita Favorita she will stay.

Her disguise is kind of amateurish for a professional. Sunglasses, a wig, too much make-up over her tan: she would probably have a fake mustache if she were a guy. The face behind it is diamond-shaped, pointy-chinned, little-girlish. For some reason that pleases me, as it allows me to imagine she isn't quite the whore the Italians branded her. I try not to read too much into first impressions, but you learn how to spot things without even lifting your eyes when you are managing a hotel, like a candle-bulb that's burnt out in a chandelier.

Her sunglasses are thick dark horn-rims with crystals all around them. The blonde is an obvious wig, hiding her notorious red hair, which gave the papers even more ammunition, not to mention labels. Red. Rosso. Slut. The name of the hottest pussy porn-site. Not that I myself indulge. I just happened to hit on it by accident checking out a Bruce Willis movie. The web can lead to unexpected adventures, but who has time for them when you're managing a hotel.

I am not yet what I consider middle aged, forty, so I have risen pretty high considering how competitive the hospitality business is, and that it really isn't anymore about hospitality, but like everything else has become about the bottom line. That makes me sad but then there is a lot about the world that makes me sad. I won't dwell on that because it's my job to keep a cheerful façade like the hotel has, bright lights shining. So if anyone asks me how I am, I always say "Never better."

Truth is people don't want to know if you have anything really wrong in your life because they are so worried about themselves. When you're concerned or anxious about the impression you might be making on someone else you don't have to be, because they are concerned with the impression they are making on you. What people like to fixate on, as it distracts them from having to face what is true or false or empty in their own lives, is gossip about shiny people. So it's kind of an unexpected bonanza, Rita Favorita coming to my hotel.

In spite of all the accusations, there is something innocent about her. But life is hard. Increasingly hard. Like generations long before her, she might have made the mistake of thinking it would be easier in America. Money growing on trees and the rest of it. But it's just as tough here now as in the rest of the so-called civilized world, unless you are heartless or in the financial game, not necessarily in that order. Still, it's a place where a looker, built, as they used to say, like a brick shithouse, can use traditional tricks to reach her goals. Never falling completely to earth, even with stilettos on. Or maybe especially. One of the videos on the porn site was that very thin, long stiletto heel forking a guy's crotch till he got hard and the woman blew him. I didn't hang around but I couldn't help seeing. I am not the kind of man who delights in that sort of thing, riveting as it might be for the moment you chance on it. But as I am not in politics, it is hard to be comfortable with being a bit pervy.

After her involvement with the saggy old prime minister, sunbathing naked on his yacht, I'd bet Rita would welcome a change of pace. In a perfect world, which this isn't, but it must seem pretty new and glitzy when you're coming from the Coliseum, he would have to be attractive. Maybe she wouldn't insist on handsome. After all, this is Brad Pitt territory and good-looking after a while becomes dull. I've noticed that from the men accompanying the cookie-cutter types you see hanging around the counters at Neiman Marcus a couple of blocks away from here, waiting for the sales when $7000 bags are marked down to $4000. Not that I like to judge, but who are these people, so extravagant even in hard times? Most of them with perfect features, the men as well as the women, as if there was plastic surgery envy. After a while it's like a cartoon, as though they've all been to the clinic across the street from here where many of our clients go to repair before they restore in our comparative quietude.

Whatever man Favorita targeted she would probably prefer him tall. She is an impressive height, one of those big-boned girls, but ultra-feminine, with sensational tits. Those, too, made several front covers, and went viral, as they say, on the Internet. I like that expression because it makes the Internet sound a lot like a disease, which I think it may be. Maybe she came here hoping to impress her knockers in the cement in front of Grauman's, the way they should have had Marilyn Monroe and Jane Russell do instead of their hands and feet.

"May I have a credit card?" the receptionist at the front desk asks. He is Willie, good-hearted, twenty-three, a little dull, just doing his job, not even really looking at her.

"Mi dispiacce..." Rita says. "I am not having. Only cash."

She pulls out a bundle of notes that would, as they used to say, choke a horse. There were horses once in Beverly Hills, galloping along the track that ran on Santa Monica Boulevard down to the ocean, when the movie business was just beginning, but they are long gone, along with people that carry that much cash. There is still a dirt path alongside the gardens that border Beverly Hills, between the plants and the boulevard, and every once in a while in the early morning silence, I can hear the echo of those hoofs galloping towards the sea.

One of the things I was considering doing for my thesis if I had stayed in school was a history of Hollywood. The origins of the business, how it took off and grew mighty after those little Jews from Chicago stole the whole process from Edison, is past fascinating. The way the studios got started and the American Dream migrated into movie houses, where people could lose themselves in the darkness, and feel comforted. Even if they couldn't get what that dream had been in the beginning, that everyone could become whatever they wanted, they could still imagine they were friends with those figures on the screen, and were part of their lives and stories, and so forget the hard reality outside.

There's that great line from 'Sunset Boulevard,' "Just us, the cameras, and those wonderful people out there in the dark" We can't all be Gloria Swanson, but we can be and are the people out there in the dark, and it is a relief, especially in bad times, to think we are wonderful.

Rita Favorita is standing with that roll of bills. Willie the receptionist looks uncomfortable, so even though I don't like to interfere with my employees, make them feel they are doing less than a great job, I step in. "How long are you planning to stay?" I ask her.

"I... no sure."

Her room is three-hundred eighty a day, plus tax, so I have her lay down two thousand, which she does without turning a hair, red or otherwise. Then I explain she will have to put down another five hundred to cover her extras, food in the restaurant, beauty parlor downstairs, a personal trainer we call in for residents who want to make serious use of the basement gym, a masseuse, the mini-bar in her room. Again, that bothers her not at all. I explain in very slow gentle sentences, which is my way, that when the two thousand is used up, and the cash for the incidentals, I will have to ask her for another deposit. She looks at me very hard, struggling to understand every word I am saying. But apparently taking in the essential part, she says, with that accent, "No worries." Obviously one of her ... what shall I call them? ... associates? ... was Irish or Australian, where all anguish is met with 'No worries.'

"My father was Italian," I say, hoping to make her feel a little bit at home. Usually when I have a repeat guest I send them a small basket of flowers on their arrival, with a note: 'Welcome home.' In a world where so many feel displaced you'd be surprised how much return business that gets you. Even if they hadn't planned on coming back soon, they do. "Mi papa."

She smiles. The teeth behind the glossy, full lips do not match the rest of it. They are a child's teeth. Tiny. The front two overlap, come forward a little, so the tip of her tongue catches in the right over left, and I can see the sharp point at the corner of her overlapping tooth. A little like a stiletto heel?

"Mi papa was American," she says. "Not enough to make me a..." She struggles for the word, her long-fingernailed, well-manicured tanned hand twirling the air, as if she would change it to another channel where the answer is.

"Citizen?" I offer.

"Si. Has to be my mamma." She looks genuinely disappointed, not just with the immigration rule, but also possibly with her father, for marrying her mother without thinking ahead. Assuming her father actually married her mother. From the scurrilous reports in the European press, she was likely turned out before she was ten, so what kind of background could she have come from?

At this moment the elevator near the front desk squeaks to a halt, and Karen Engel opens the inside gate, one of those brass things on hinges that take forever. The elevator, an old-style French one, brought from the Grand Hotel de Quiberon in Brittany, helps add to the antique feeling of this place. Our guests seem to enjoy that Old World atmosphere. To add to the feeling of colorful antiquity, we even have an old-fashioned switchboard, with keys and holes they plug into, bought by the management at auction. It works to a degree, but mainly it's there for interesting show, so guests can feel timeless, a part of a vanished era that everyone imagines was better.

The walls here are Venetian plaster, with a hand-waxed shiny eggshell finish, hung with old photos. Some are daguerrotypes, the beanfields that were once Beverly Hills. Some show the more glamorous vanished past, people crossing on ocean liners, royals getting out of limousines. Mme. Engel herself would have an antique feeling had she not stayed so impressively in shape, her body, at least in clothes, the same as when she was as famous as any woman in America, or maybe the world.

Her face, of course, does not look the same as it did then. It has obviously had a number of assists. She is booked here for six weeks, so I guess she has come here for a lift from the doctors who work out of the clinic across the street. For all the convenience of this location, it is also strangely secluded. After the stitches are out, women can hide here and Arnica and Vitamin E away the bruising. You get to know things like that as a manager across from a plastic surgery hospital, when you have to send the bellman out to the pharmacy, to bring back stuff that heals. At least on the surface.

The other one who's here strictly for plastic surgery is the poor bastard in 408. He was in a terrible accident off the highway in Malibu that killed his wife, and burned 40% of his body and face. The burn clinic part of his recovery was pretty much over four months ago, but they've been doing a series of grafts across the street. The hospital bookkeeper stops here for a drink at the end of her day, and although she is discreet to a point she has told me a little about him that adds to what I know myself. He is very closed, like his door always is. He takes his meals in his room, sending the hotel limo driver for bottles of pomegranate vodka. That seems to me not so much the act of a drunkard as a lonely man who doesn't like what's in his mini-bar.

Of course he doesn't want to be seen, with his whole face and neck covered in bandages. He goes out in the daytime only to consult with the doctors at the hospital. I am not old enough to remember Claude Rains, but the Contessa who comes at Christmas to visit her great-grandchildren, bumped into him once in the hall and told me it was like seeing 'The Invisible Man.' She was too well-mannered to scream, but it did make her hold her heart.

There is one other old royal, a Marquesa who is a longtime resident of the hotel. She has a little white dog that she comes

*down twice a day to walk, something the dog does with more ease
and panache than she does. One has the feeling the dog is keeping
her alive.*

*"Did my letter come?" Karen Engel says softly, stopping by
the reception desk. She seems unaware of Rita Favorita, staring at
her with that look the young reserve for those they know they have
seen but can't remember exactly where. But since Rita is in
Hollywood, or its priciest vicinity, she seems to get that Karen is a
movie star, and appears appropriately wide-eyed. With those eyes.
Pale green, with specks of gold. Luminous.*

*"The mail isn't in yet," says Naomi, the other receptionist,
reaching for the ringing phone.*

*There is something curiously touching about Engel, a woman
who still waits for an actual letter, with all that the world has done
to amp up communication and make it less meaningful. The post
offices here are in as much money trouble as any other business,
so a lot of the branches have closed, and there's no more Special
Delivery. I guess whoever sent her the letter she is waiting so
breathlessly for either didn't want to attract too much attention to
it by sending it Express, or was too stingy to pay the tariff.*

*'Hotel Royale,'" Naomi says into the receiver. "How may I
help you?" She covers the mouthpiece, smiles at Engel. "I'll send
up your mail the minute it comes."*

*"Thank you." Engel goes out towards the garage, where her
Lamberghini is parked. It is apparently all she has kept besides the
'Madame' from her last husband, Hendrik Bos, the Dutch
billionaire dumped by the communications company he founded
when they discovered his hand in the till. Rich people. They can't
seem to get enough. Once that particular scandal erupted, he
disappeared completely, with several more hundreds of millions of
other people's money. There are lawsuits against him from all over*

the world, investors who thought he was giving them trading tips when in hard fact he was giving them the shaft. I wonder if the letter she is waiting for is from him, but I let that query go, even in my head, because if curiosity killed the cat, it certainly would get rid of a hotel manager. Discretion is not the better part of valor in a hotel: it is what keeps you your job. All the harder because a manager who seems amiable becomes a kind of housemother in the eyes of long time guests and staff so they tell you everything.

It is lucky for me that Samson is long gone, because it would be a mighty temptation to share all the inside info with him, and probably would have kept him alive for another hundred years. If he knew who was hiding out in the secret, fairly inaccessible room, fourth floor rear, it might even bring him back from the Beyond.

421 is as close as the hotel comes to having a 'safe room,' one of those in-house hide-outs that the very rich or the very paranoid have in their mansions, that no one can get into unless they have a key or are invited. It is my understanding that Allegra de Sevigny has one in her house, journalist though she purports to be, climber that she actually is. If she only knew who has taken sanctuary here, she would give her right arm, and several dinner parties. His door is right by the stairs that no one ever uses, so even his food can be brought in without anyone's seeing. Burgers and fries.

We offer free limousine service to places in the vicinity, a white Rolls Royce so guests can imagine they are in one of the better hotels in Hong Kong, where they line the entrances as if there had never been a handover to the Communists. But Mme. Engel obviously prefers her own wheels. It is fascinating to watch her leave a room. Her walk seems fluid. She has obviously been exercising. Her pants are stylish and what's in them is still pretty impressive.

The fading celebrity having left the lobby, I am free to turn my attention to the newly glossy one. Besides the Louis Vuitton luggage the bellman brought in on a trolley, Favorita carries a small brown leather notebook. That also looks Italian, a leather tie around it, with one of those little gold angels they stamp on things in Italy, putti, they are called, as I remember. Those tiny cherubs that sit in the corners of ceilings in churches all over that beautiful country. She makes notes in it while she waits for her room key.

"You keep a diary?" I ask her.

"I write down my dream." She says the word with a reverence, as if she hasn't made a mistake putting it in the singular, and means it to be not only what is in her mind when she is sleeping, but her goal in life. I cannot help wondering if maybe what she hopes for is more than a meal ticket. But that is only me being a romantic, something I put aside along with my academic career. The world no longer honors aspiration, which has a breathlessness in it, like the hope of love. It's all about ambition now. And that entails money. Not that I mean to rise that high in the hotel world, but I do intend to stay alive.

At this point a heavyset blonde woman of more than a certain age, (a polite description would be 'an uncertain age' but besides the years her face is weighty with disappointment and stored-up anger) blows in through the side entrance. "I need help with my luggage," she demands in an edgy voice.

"If you'll be kind enough to wait for a moment," I say.

"You have any idea who I am?"

She says it like I should.

"I'm Louise Felder," she proclaims, absent only a gong that signals 'Pay attention.'

"If you'll just wait for a moment," I say again, as calmly as I can in the face of her onslaught, which it really is. I know the name

of course. She was the most powerful agent in Hollywood when Hollywood was still really Hollywood, absent these breakable figurines that pass now for actresses. She all but stamps her foot to underline the show of impatience.

"I'm not used to waiting," she says. "My suite was supposed to be ready at nine."

"Would you check to see if Miss Felder's suite is ready?" I say to Naomi. Naomi riffles through the notes beside her computer, and checks the computer itself. Her cheeks redden as she searches.

"And so we don't waste any more time, have someone bring in my luggage." Felder hands me the key to her car. "I have calls to make."

Naomi shoots me a desperate look. She is a dark-haired, dark-complexioned young woman, but she blushes like a thin-skinned blonde at the first sign of pressure, which this obviously is.

I make my way around the desk and lean close to her, so she can tell me what is wrong, which something obviously is. She points to the computer screen. The hotel suites are all occupied, and there is no reservation for Felder.

"I'm sorry, Miss Felder," I say. "But there seems to be some mistake. We have no reservation for you."

Her shadowed eyes get very small, and I think I can see smoke coming from her nostrils. The fact that she had a reputation as a dragon seems to have become a part of her physiognomy. "You got to be kidding."

"I'm afraid not. I'd really like to accommodate you, but all the suites are occupied."

"I will kill that bitch," she says, opening her cell phone, clutched in her left hand, and punches the speed dial. 'Lemme talk to Dorothy ... What hospital? ... I'm supposed to give a fuck about her mother? Why wasn't my reservation taken care of ... I know

that's not your job, it's her job. Tell her she no longer has it." She shuts the phone.

"Look here, Mr ... "

"Riccioni," I say.

"They're termiting my house and my secretary fucked up. I need to stay here till the tenting comes off."

I picture what is probably her gated Bel-Air mansion with the big blue tent over it, covering it completely, poison fumes being pumped into it, and regret that she isn't inside. Power when it flexes its muscles has never impressed me, especially in a woman, which may sound sexist and probably is. But I see none of the rumored wit, the charm that has been attributed to this virago. Only the self-absorbed, self-important bully.

'We'll certainly do our best to accommodate you, but you'll have to wait your turn," I say.

She looks literally taken aback. Probably no one has made her stand in line since MGM had more stars than there were in Heaven, except now they are all in Heaven if there is a Heaven, and there is no more MGM.

I turn back to Rita, and hand her the room key. "Please make yourself at home," I say. "Se accomodo. The bellman will see you to your suite.'

"You give her a suite and you don't have one for me?"

"She has a confirmed reservation," I say evenly.

"Grazie," Rita says, and moves towards the elevator, a shimmy of fur and a clunk of very high heel.

Miss Felder looks after her contemptuously, all but snorting her annoyance. Annoyance isn't exactly the word. Contained rage would more likely nail it. "You must be used to working at Ellis Island," she says to me. "Maybe I should have come looking like I was just off the boat."

I understand that sarcasm is her weapon of choice, and am tempted to turn to it myself. But irony doesn't work in the hotel business. So I am silent and smiling, understanding that will probably irritate her more. It pleases me to be raising her blood pressure, as the tales about her are legion, and from her blustery, inconsiderate entrance, I believe them all. The story is also that she was once very funny, winning really. But as they say here, that was Then.

"So what are you going to do for me?" she says.

Vance Willson passes through the lobby. He has just been named Sexiest Man Alive by People Magazine, one of those slicks that has taken over in place of real information. To me he seems an Empty Suit. Except in LA he would have to be described as an Empty T-shirt. Pushed up at the sleeves to show the overworked muscles, loose around the armpits so we can see the hair, the assertive black patch of masculinity. He doesn't stay here but he likes the bar, and one of our bartenders, a sharp little hottie named Amber. Also I think he's hoping to meet one of the European moviemakers who pass through our hotel. He may be all over TMZ and the magazine stands, but he hasn't made a winning movie in a while, and his trail is cold.

"Little Lulu!" he says on seeing Louise.

"Oh, thank God, a sort-of leading man. Not a moment too soon!" Louise says, and gives him a Show Biz hug, kissing the air beside his well-defined cheeks, the ones on his face. "You have to tell this fellow who I am."

"I know who you are," I say, checking the computer. "It's a question of logistics. We can only do our best."

"What do you mean, 'a sort of *leading man'?" Vance says, not very successfully hiding the hurt on his generically handsome face. It is an aspect of his braggadocio that he doesn't use*

*underarm deodorant. But he has a sweetly cutting odor, as if he
has lavished himself with light cologne.*

*"Don't you have a guest room in your hillside mansion as
recently shown in Architectural Digest?" she asks him.*

"My mother's visiting me."

*"You actually have a mother?" Louise said. "I thought you
sprang full-grown from the forehead of Al Pacino."*

*"There's a single on the third floor, looking down on the
pool," I say.*

*"I prefer looking down on people. But I suppose I could do
that right here in the lobby."*

*"Of course I have a mother," Vance interjects. "She's very
proud of me."*

*"Would you like me to phone over to the Montage and see if
they have space?" I say. "It is Awards season." That means
everyone who has an interest in Hollywood is in town, so rooms of
any kind are at a premium.*

*"If I wanted to be in the center of things I would have booked
the Peninsula. Vance…" she whines, and suddenly her voice is that
of a little girl, the not-so-little girl who came and took Hollywood
when she was in her twenties and according to local legend gave
new resonance to the expression "Star Fucker," starting with
those who were already stars, expanding her horizons to those she
made into stars before fucking them. "Save me. I'm not having a
good time."*

"What did you mean, 'a sort of leading man?'"

"Do you want me to book the single?" I ask her.

*"Can you believe Lulu is being treated like this?" she appeals
to Vance, oblivious to the hurt she has caused, aware only of how
quick she is, how clever she seems, if you are not the object of her*

darts. That was, I would guess, her modus operandi throughout her career. "Obviously these people don't read Vanity Fair."

In fact, I do. But the piece on her was in a very old issue. I could probably strike her mute by saying that. But that is not my way. Besides, at some level I feel sorry for those whose greatest glory is behind them, even when they have the sensitivity of armadillos.

"Do you want the room?"

"Well, at this point I seem to have no choice," she says, and hands me her credit card. "Vance, you mustn't tell anybody where I'm staying unless Alec Baldwin decides he wants 'mature.'" She turns and looks at Rita, who is waiting for the elevator. "You think she advertises on Craig's List?"

"She happens to be royalty," I lie. "From the royal family of San Marino." I am so past irritated by this balloon of an ego, I'd like to take a little air out of her. The only thing that intimidates these people is family, since few of them actually have one. Or if they did, they left them behind, breaking off relations as soon as they were successful. And royal is always good, though not as good as it was when there was Diana.

Besides, I like Rita. And as with the tale of Andre Gide, it isn't likely anyone would know how to check it out. Especially as that country is important only to those people who live in it, and those who use it as a tax haven, and even they probably have trouble finding it.

"I didn't even know there was a San Marino," Felder says.

"It's a tiny country surrounded on all sides by Italy," I say, the truth, little known.

"What is she?" Vance says interestedly. "A princess?"

"She asks that we not give out any details," I say, lowering my eyes. "The paparazzi."

I see the twice-over Vance gives Rita who is waiting for the elevator. He seems disappointed she doesn't look back or appear interested in him, salt in the wound Felder has succeeded in inflicting. I give Rita a couple of points for ignoring him, as it is probable she has seen him in movies. He was very big worldwide, as they say in Variety, before he started making those clunkers. I don't mean to be judgmental but in a job like this you have to learn to appraise people pretty quickly or you might get stuck on a bill or find shit all over the room if they have a dog and no sense of common courtesy. I mean when Stewart was here, his pit bull had about the same amount of manners he did. You have to wonder about a man who travels with a pit bull.

"Hotel Royale, Good Morning," Naomi says into the phone. Like most of the young women in town, waitresses, secretaries, beauty salon managers, she is hoping to be discovered, using her salary for acting lessons, trying not to look like she is gazing out to sea waiting for her ship to come in. That worked for Meryl Streep as the French Lieutenant's Woman, but she was already the best actress in town, any town she was in. Besides, the sea is too far away from here to gaze out on. But everywhere there are palm trees, those lining the street right outside the hotel, the ones in the courtyard surrounding the pool. When there is a wind the fronds ripple like gentle fingertips across the imagination, and the place looks really idyllic, if you don't mind having your thought processes stultify.

About these trees: when they become lofty enough, a second growth emerges from the trunk, a tight cluster of hideous flowers like those sold at exorbitant prices at the florists, called Birds of Paradise. You can spot them by their slick, hard shells, ending in what looks like a beak, while from their crown spurt shafts of color. Sometimes I am moved to think of people who live here, especially those who work in movies, as birds of paradise, except that their shells are harder, and, in many cases, emptier.

Vance is barely able to contain his excitement. If he were a better actor he could maybe pull off seeming cool. But the dark hairs on his arm are moving visibly, showing he is aroused. "I'd like to get me a piece of a royal," he murmurs.

Rita gets into the elevator, and pulls the metal gate closed.

"I don't trust anybody who can walk in heels that high," says Felder. "Especially so young."

"You can't hate somebody for being young," Vance says.

"Maybe you can't." Louise turns back to me. "Well...?"

Her hands are not quite on her hips, in that posture that means "You want to tangle with me, buddy?" But then her hips are better concealed than her anger. She is wearing one of those Muu-Muus popularized by the late producer Allan Carr in-between the stomach by-passes that made him thinner from time to time, or Elizabeth Taylor when she was bingeing. There is little that I haven't taken note of during my stay in this village, which it really is. Not a city, but a tiny village. Kind of the vitriol version of 'Our Town.'

"You are more than welcome to the room we have," I say. "May I have a credit card?"

She pulls out a platinum American Express, and hands it to me.

"Thank you," I say, and give it to Naomi to record. "Is there anything special you will need?"

"I'd appreciate it if one of your maids could help me with unpacking," she says, almost civilly.

"I'll send someone up right away," I say, and do. Just because I don't take a particular shine to a guest doesn't mean I

*don't know how to do my job. She did, after all, say she would
appreciate it. That was probably a giant step for Hollywoodkind.*

*Just now comes a fuss that indicates the senator is back. Clever as
we may be as a rule in discouraging the paparazzi, he is beyond
high profile, having recently emerged as a champion villain,
humiliating his extraordinary wife by proving the whispers about
his screwing around behind her back were unfounded: he was
doing it right in front of her face.*

*He is safely inside by way of our secret rear entrance. Back
access to the Royale is copied from the Ritz Bar in Paris, where
Princess Diana made her final exit through a revolving door,
imagining, I would guess, that at that fateful moment she was
escaping the press. But there is no escaping Destiny, especially the
dark kind. Following Jon Bon Jovi out into the alley behind the
Paris Ritz, Diana went straight into the supposed security of her
waiting limousine. As the world learned at the time, to its universal
sadness, there is really no such thing as security. Or a clever way
out when the Fates or the cards are stacked against you. Still, we
harbor at the hotel the illusion that there is always an option for
those whose personal safety is at risk, with that secret exit.
Important, as we do have a high profile clientele. So protection is
all, after profit, and the policy is to coddle our guests.*

*Understanding that this is a country, a village, a world that
feeds on scandal, especially among those considered high, we have
all still been struck cross-eyed by the extent of the senator's
arrogance. Hubris, really. A conceit so blustery as to challenge the
gods, if they still exist. One wonders at moments like this, at least I
do, if there is anything like justice on this earth, where this
magnificent woman, in her own way genuinely royal (as opposed*

*to the alleged princess from San Marino) has been dishonored by
this oaf.*

*But we do not let opinion influence what guests are welcome
at the hotel. This is a capitalistic society. Bankers with platinum
and diamond-faced Rolex watches still roam the streets where lie
in the doorways homeless people there because they were deluded
and scammed by those bankers. But Christ, I think it was, said
'Judge not that ye be judged,' and irreligious as I might be, I hew
to his illuminated line, in view of who sits on the High Court now.
Who wants to tangle with those guys? Especially since they have
made it clear that the country is to be run by big business, giving
corporations the okay to be considered a person and buy their
candidates into office.*

*And we are in business here, too, after all. As noted, rock stars
and self-imploders notwithstanding, we do not bar anyone but
longtime offenders (Stewart.) The senator had checked in before
his situation hit the ravenous-for-scandal airwaves, and once he
was ensconced, there was no way to un-ensconce him legally,
though a few of the chambermaids refused to clean his room. We
had an actual meeting about it.*

"The man is a pig," said Consuelo, the head housekeeper.

*"All men are pigs," said Valiente, a maid who had learned
English the hard way, linking up with a car salesman so she could
get her Green Card, then finding herself responsible for his debts,
which she is still working off.*

*"Not peegs," said Mimea, her English at a learning level.
"Dogs."*

*I was tempted to ask the difference, but did not want the
meeting to extend any longer than absolutely necessary, as I had a
lot to do. Women, when given the opportunity, can rattle on
endlessly about perceived wrongs, especially to other women. I*

work out in my own mind that the difference between pigs and dogs is that pigs are always in search of food, whereas dogs constantly sniff out not just food but holes. That sounds about right for the senator. I promise them all extra privileges if they will overcome their justifiable distaste and change his dirty linen in spite of his flaunting it in public.

He has arrived the back way, the locked way, so the photographers who have attached themselves to his every movement are kept out, and haven't got the brain cells to figure out a better way to stalk him. Eventually they leave. In truth, the story is already old: there will be a new and better disgrace surfacing any moment, to feed the gaping maw of the public's boredom with their own lives. The next one will probably be coming from Washington, as we're edging close to election season, and those guys rut and steal and cheat better than Reality 'stars' and movie actors.

"My room key, please," the senator says.

Naomi blushes dark as she hands him his plastic card, her eyes averted.

I, personally, avert my soul, in case I actually have one. A magazine Samson did not live to collect, but I flipped through, had a story on the senator and his wife when they were courting. She was a radiantly plump young woman obviously in the grip of infatuation. How shyly pretty she looked, lightly freckled and rosy with excitement, her bright blue eyes alive with the enchantment that seemingly great love brings. Plump, I said. Actually she was a chub. How she must have suffered to pare down those pounds, will-power carving out those glorious familial cheekbones, so the betrayed, brave wife now facing the TV cameras with "no comment" could add to her description, besides philanthropist and spokesperson: gaunt.

Apparently unsettled by having lost my complete attention, Vance opened up his Blackberry, checking it or Twittering something inane in 140 characters or less. He has entered the Land of the Curse of the 21st century: people who can't be where they are. It made me sad in the beginning, couples walking down the street, texting. Handsome young couples, Love by their side, their attention someplace else. Now I just find it irritating.

"Hey," he says indignantly, looking at his screen. "Were you pulling my leg?"

"What do you mean?" I say.

"I Googled San Marino. It says 'the world's oldest existing republic, having never had a ruling royal family (like Monaco or Liechtenstein), looking back instead on nearly a thousand years of communal governance, and a democratic constitution written in 1601.'"

As impressive as it seems to be that anyone can find anything on the Internet, I am appalled that such a lout can have access to answers, without even a smattering of education, or, in his case, an actual thought. "I just didn't want to tell you the real story in front of _her_," *I say, in very hushed tones, as Felder closes the brass gate, pushes the button, and the creaking elevator ascends.*

"What is the real story?" Vance says. "How do I get the inside track? I mean, the whole world must be hitting on her."

"You have no idea," I say, because he doesn't. I am not a sadistic man, but the sight of this six-foot two poster-boy for Self made so sucky-uppy truly delights me. I usher him into the alcove by my office, and lower my voice even further, so we are truly conspirators together. "The real story is... Do I have your word it's just between us?"

"My hand to God," he says, holding up his hand, I presume, to God.

A whisper. "She is the grand-daughter of two of the greatest, best-looking movie stars of all time. The two most beautiful people ever to be in movies."

"Who?"

"No names. This is what the late great Hollywood columnist Army Archerd would have called a Blind Item." I capitalize it with my tongue as Army would have with his old typewriter. He was part of the lost glory of the recent past, a gentleman who never had an unkind word to say about anybody. Army, like Samson, my magazine benefactor, was deeply in love with the past of Hollywood, which, I guess, had actually been his present. He died not too long ago, but left a heritage of good will and the idea of a Blind Item, where you insinuate your ass off but nobody is named, thus avoiding a lawsuit.

"You have to tell me who."

"You need to vacuum your own memory and think who there was in the Fifties, breathtakingly beautiful, the man and the woman both, who had a forbidden romance."

"Why was it forbidden?"

"She was the longtime love of the man who made her famous," I say.

Samson loved nothing better than movies except gossip about movie stars, and schooled me in the history of the town, and the romances therein.

Now, understand that to be able to call something a romance here, once you're past Norma Shearer and Irving Thalberg, is close to a miracle, one Scott Fitzgerald picked up on for The Last Tycoon, big romantic that he was and a sucker for Hollywood, trying to make it into more than it was, so he did. If you are a great artist you can make a work of art out of a cockroach as Kafka showed us, and Fitzgerald did that with Hollywood, the harbor for the shipwreck of his young dream. But other than what he did with that book, it's a stretch to characterize most on-set relationships here as romances. They're more like erotic hysteria. All those good, hot bodies together on the set, waiting hours for the cameras to be ready, with nothing to eat up the boredom. What else could they do but fuck?

"They fell in love while they were making a movie in Spain," I say. "He was stylish. An enormous amount of class. Charm. Wit. All those things that hardly exist in movies today."

"So what happened?"

"You enjoy Googling. Google the big movies made in 1957. There's a video on You Tube of the woman dancing the flamenco, and you can witness how intensely he was watching her when they were making the movie, observe him falling. A veritable nosedive. He was truly in love with her."

"So what happened?" Vance is holding his breath, which I can tell from just a few feet away is lavender scented.

"As much of a gentleman as he was, she was a true lady. A great lady. She had been under the wing of this much older man since she was a teenager. So even though her co-star was crazy about her, she was loyal and went back to marry her protector.

I exhale a great breath. "But not for a while. And nobody knew about the little girl."

"What little girl?"

"The baby they had together. Midwifed by nuns in a convent." His mouth is literally agape. Deception, when aimed at someone pretentious, is its own reward, as virtue is supposed to be, but seldom is. "All of them, of course, were sworn to secrecy, which you can really count on with nuns,"

"But how could you possibly keep something like that a secret? Especially in this town."

"Are you kidding? Clark Gable, the biggest star of his day, had an illegitimate daughter with Loretta Young, the most prominent Catholic in the industry. It wasn't until their kid was old enough to write a book that anyone knew."

"So what happened to the baby of these other two?"

"As a child, she determined to live a life of celibacy, her only real mother figure being nuns. But sometime around her twenty-ninth year, the hot blood in her took over, she fell for some guy, and got pregnant. She died in childbirth, but the baby lived. And that's who you saw coming in the door of this hotel today. Their grand-daughter."

"Oh, come on. You expect anyone to believe that story?"

"Expect them to believe?" I look as incensed as a Jane Austen heroine. "I don't expect anyone to hear it! You gave me your word. Does your word mean nothing?"

He looks suitably mortified at this challenge to his integrity. "This is their grand-daughter? That's really true?"

"Truth is stranger than fiction. Especially in this town. I'm really trusting you."

"Your faith will not be misplaced," he says.

From behind the door I watch him go out into the garage and get into his car. He waits for what must be, oh... maybe as much as forty seconds before picking up his cell phone and calling someone.

CHAPTER TWO

"DO YOU UNDERSTAND English?" Louise asked the maid as she unpacked.

The maid shook her head. "Poquito," she said, putting her fingertips together with her thumb to indicate how little.

Louise lay back on the big double bed, the bolster under her head, her arms crossed behind her neck. "Well, at least the bed is comfortable," she said. "You say your name is Mimi?"

"Mimea," the maid said, unpacking.

"Well, Mimea, it's a little early in the day for me to be exhausted, but I am."

Mimea looked at her, uncomprehending.

Louise lay back against the mound of pillows, her hands behind her head. "It gets harder and harder to get up in the morning. You wonder if there is anything really to get up for. Everybody you loved, or at least the big stars you slept with, and the few men you cared about till they fucked you over, they're all dead. Except for a few behind-the-scenes veterans who are still breathing and loved Lulu, enjoyed how bright she was, remember all the great deals she made, nobody cares. I can give one of my fabled dinner parties and the new young celebs will come out of curiosity, because I <u>am</u> legendary. But nobody really cares about the actual me. Au contraire. I am a hated woman."

Mimea looked at her, held her palms beside her ears and shook her head.

"I understand you don't understand. That makes it easier to be truthful." Louise took a deep breath. "I never meant to be hated. I wanted to be feared."

She sat up a little, leaning on her elbow. "No. That isn't true. I wanted to be loved. But it was easier to make people afraid of me. People are more quick to fear than they are to love."

Mimea held up a plastic packet of toiletries and looked quizzical. "In the bathroom," Louise said, and pointed. "Bano."

The maid went inside.

"So here I am, the face that launched a thousand shits… And they were, really. Most of the people I gave a start to and helped build did absolutely nothing to make the world a better place. I suppose that sounds silly coming from me, at least it would if you understood English and knew my reputation. I mean it's not like I went out of my way to help the needy, although you'd be surprised how needy most of these stars are. And I was always there for them."

"But who's there for me, now? I can hardly get anybody on the phone."

"Perdoneme?" Mimea said, coming out of the bathroom.

"It's all right, querida, you're not supposed to understand. This is very liberating for me, really. Most of the shrinks I went to are dead now, too. Besides, they almost never said anything helpful. And the psychiatrists now are so worried they won't be reimbursed by the insurance companies, they don't even want to listen, they just hand out meds.

"I must admit I really like meds but I'm afraid they will slow down what's left of my brain. So it's great to be able to vent and know that you won't tell anyone. Because you couldn't understand a word I said."

Mimea just stood there.

"You're so lucky. At least you know what your purpose is. You probably have a couple of squalling babies you take care of. The first man I loved told me I would probably eat my young. He turned out to be a total cad—that's a word that's gone out of style, as he did—but I really loved him. Oh, but he was right. I would have been a terrible mother. So in a strange way, I envy you. Everything you do is for survival.

"But this town is all about being important. I'm not important anymore. I'd like to be important again. I want to be the biggest name in the room."

She swallowed a sigh. "I never told that to anyone. Well, actually, I may have told it to Bunyan Reis, but I'm sure he was drunk at the time, and didn't take it seriously. He thought I just wanted to be <u>with</u> the biggest name in the room."

"Senor Reis?" Mimea said, snapping suddenly to attention.

"Huh?" said Louise. "You know Bunyan Reis?"

"Eees aqui," Said Mimea. "Here. In hotel."

"Sometimes there's God so slowly," said Louise, and reached for the telephone.

"But my darling I thought you were in the south of France if you were living at all," Louise said as they met in the bar.

"Kumquat!" he said, and held his arms out to her. "Imagine your being in this hotel! Are you staying here so you can be the biggest name in the room?"

"Shit," said Louise. "I thought you were drunk."

I can see them on one of the security screens in my office, embracing with the phony enthusiasm of old friends who are aware the other one, too, has fallen out of favor. After all, this is Hollywood, and sincerity is not the order of the day, no matter how close you might have been to immortality while still alive, or how lauded, as no one was more than Bunyan Reis. Everyone knew his name, even those who did not know anything about art. And Louise had risen higher than a great many of those she represented, her power being indisputable among industry insiders who usually had disputes about everything.

Bunyan pinches her cheek with a stubby hand that sports several rings. They are oversized and silver, very much sidewalk craft show, one of those events everywhere on the planet where people who thought they had a future in museums now find themselves selling off carts beside the road where vendors are also offering waffles. The rings have the same cast as what is left of his hair, and different colored stones. One of them looks like a college ring. But when he first checked in and made it known he intended to stay a long time, I looked him up to know the full extent of his accomplishments, and he never went to college. Not that that makes him less in my eyes, certainly, as I didn't finish. Besides, I have seen some of the work he did when he was at his best, and it was quietly dazzling. If Samson were still alive they might have become lovers. Bunyan Reis had the same heft in the art world as Andre Gide did in his time as a literary figure, and is cut from the same epicene cloth.

That is to say, that even as he embraces Felder, his eyes are drawn to the glass doors siding the pool, where Lord Bunty is about to take his morning swim. He arrived last night from London. He is in pretty fine shape for an Englishman, ever so subtly fey as any number of Brits seem to be, but then the best of them were shunted off to boarding school when they were barely housebroken, so what could they have for their first experiences but other little boys.

There is a look on Reis' face that is halfway between longing and despair as he watches Bunty dive into the pool. I am a little sad for him, to have to be staying in a hotel, pleasant as it is here, considering he was once celebrated as the world's most sought-after perennial houseguest. Hostesses vied to have him at their tables, enhancing their lives by being associated with his talent and wit, if only for the duration of a dinner party, more often than not inviting him for the entire season. There were seasons then, in their society, times that were bookended by horse races and coming-out parties, or the wedding of someone from Old Money, the kind that gushed from oil wells, or steamed along railroad tracks. That way of life seems to be vanished forever. So Bunyan Reis, too, appears a bit lost.

My God—if he only knew who was in that room at the top of the hotel, it could bring him back to vitality. His step is halting, but I bet he would find the energy to fly up those stairs, if he guessed who was behind the door.

Tyler McKay was a very bright boy, but he didn't have a clue about Hollywood. Much as the self-styled power-brokers in entertainment had pursued him since he became a musical sensation, heart-throb though heart-throbs were no longer in style, he had no thought of becoming a movie star. That he had skipped out on his handlers in Los Angeles, the less glittering label for what the world considered 'Hollywood', was coincidence, and nothing more. His most trusted friend, who traveled with him practically everywhere, knew a private security service in that city, and he'd made all the arrangements for Tyler to slip away after his concert at the Staples Center.

Now, miraculously, for the first time in his consciously aware life, he was alone. It had been such an incredible struggle to be alone. Everywhere he went he was chased after, protected from screaming fans by security guards he couldn't get away from either. He had managed to trip out of their grasp at last, without alarming his mother. He had texted her immediately that he loved her to death, but needed time, desperately needed time to be by himself, that he was safe and perfectly fine and please not to let it out that he was gone, the last thing he wanted was even more of a drama than when he was present. Then he threw his cell phone into a sewer on Lasky Drive, after taking out the battery, so they wouldn't be able to track him even if they watched CSI.

He had come into the world with his own magical gift, manifest from the time he was two. He had started on guitar, then bass, then made his way to keyboard and piano, drums, and once his lips could pucker enough to blow, a sax, and clarinet, a French horn, and, when he grew and got enough strength to lift it, once, just for fun, a Sousaphone. He was, in his mother's eyes, and that of a legion of girls, his own brass band. And on top of all that he could sing.

"Like an angel," his mother said.

"Like Benny Goodman," said his grandfather.

"Benny Goodman couldn't sing," said his grandma.

"I'm talking about the clarinet."

"And what about the piano?" asked his father. "He's a regular infant Mozart."

Even outside his family circle, word of his talents grew. In spite of the prevalence of Reality Shows, and the vanishing of any kind of reverence for actual gifts, a few people still knew about Mozart. And in very short order, almost everybody knew about Tyler. Especially since he was not only gifted, but physically engaging. He was booked for back-to-back engagements throughout the United States. His next stop would have been London if he hadn't run away.

Nineteen years old and without a clue, except all he knew and felt and even dreamed about music, he was alone for the first time in his conscious life, thanks to the private cops who had spirited him away, and the tuned-in hotel manager who'd given him sanctuary. So he feasted on burgers and fries, normally denied to him. Everyone had struggled to keep him pure in the physical and spiritual sense as well as the sexual one, keeping his food organic and fresh and bland and boring, the girls he was introduced to the same. Safe at last in this small and unspectacular hotel, he downloaded on his room TV the movies he had wanted to see but hadn't had time to, and lived, for a few days at least, like a boy who was on top of the world except that he couldn't go out into it for fear of being mobbed.

Tyler couldn't enjoy the bright sunshine completely lest someone observe him by the pool. So he caught little rays of it on his balcony, trellised with wisteria, just now coming into bloom, soft clusters of lavender blossoms descending from the twisted wood like tissue-paper grapes. If he stepped too far out there was a chance that someone might see him. So he couldn't fully enjoy the spectacle—and it was a spectacle for him—of the curvaceous young woman on the level just below, spreading herself with suntan oil, lying naked on her chaise.

She was not particularly his taste, as roundly voluptuous and butterscotch-skinned as she was. Still, it excited him, the sight of a beautiful woman, stark naked and oiled. But having worked so hard and been on display from the time he was little more than a toddler, he was not quite sure what his taste was, really, except for burgers and fries.

A few doors away, hotel-room-wise, Louise Felder went to close her shades. Sunlight was much too bright for her now. In truth it had been too bright for her since her little-girl heart had been broken at the right time for hearts to be broken, in the beginning of her career in New York, when people still thought that Fire Island was the best place to go for summer weekends. She had found out then, as though it were a new and original insight, that men did not mean what they said, even when, or maybe especially when, they said they loved you. Before, that was, when a good girl said she wouldn't till 'after,' though she usually broke down and let him do it when it seemed he really cared.

She did not really let herself think back to those days, because it embarrassed her that she had ever been that naïve. Not too long afterwards she had begun her ascent in the entertainment world, and sealed over that foolish, vulnerable side of herself with the hot wax of callous wit, so no one would know what was underneath. People didn't respond to vulnerability. To them it felt like need, and nobody wanted anyone needy. So you had to seem like you needed nothing, and soon you didn't. It was very like the early days of her success when she had finally been able to afford everything she wanted, at which point people gave her things for free. Life was actually a shell game, and the smart thing to do was hide beneath a shell.

The hard shell she pretended to have fit her like a designer dress if she had been able to fit into and wear a designer dress. And on the few occasions when she attempted to shed it, and show the soft, sweet woman she really was inside, she found that as in some bizarre fairy tale, the mask she had put on had become her actual face, the shell had merged with her honey silk skin, and all that there was underneath was hard. The shell was no longer a shell: it was Louise.

But a woman had to survive. So she had adjusted to the personage she had become. Like the darkest veins of magic, that was who she truly was now: a gifted word flautist who could charm a snake, --lucky, really--since what many of the men she had had to deal with in Hollywood were snakes, especially those who, for a few moments at least, she thought she could really care for, before true caring fell off her agenda.

Still, she could lower her eyes as in the old, cute, flirtatious days.

Softened by the fan of her lashes—those, at least, had stayed the same, no matter how unkind the years had been to the rest of her—she could become absorbed in the ethnic wonder of her cheekbones. Her ancestors had been Slavic, with maybe a Mongol rape thrown in. So her cheekbones served as angular sentinels, guarding the gates of her feelings, once evident in her eyes, when she had been young and it was still possible to really mean the things she said.

It hurt to look down too much now. Her eyes were very dry, partly from the little lid-lifts she'd had—to be able to read better, she told those to whom she admitted having had the procedure— partly from a Lasik surgery that absolutely everyone in town had so they could read without glasses, --and partly from the word she would not speak aloud: A-G-E, spelled even when she said it to herself. Truly the ugliest word in the language. Carrying with it the prospect of dismissal. Assurance you didn't matter anymore. Dead you were more interesting than you were O-L-D.

She had learned to spell out words she couldn't bear hearing, even in her mind, a trick that made the whole process of growing O-L-D-E-R a little bit adorable, as she still was, in her way. Spelling it out helped soften the grating of reality, though it didn't decelerate anything.

But because her eyes were dry, it hurt her to look down. So she forced herself to look up towards the sky, as though she still felt hope. Even faith.

When what to her wondering eyes should appear but a beautiful boy on the balcony above and to the left, when she hadn't known a terrace was even there. The hotel, for all its fine design completely lacked the slick pretentiousness of the other Five Star hotels in Beverly Hills, free of crystal and curlicues. The one characteristic shared with the others was mirrors. You could not have a successful hotel in Beverly Hills unless people had a chance of glimpsing themselves everywhere. For all her disbelief in good things happening when you least expected them, even when you were sure nothing wonderful would ever come again, at a desiccated glance it looked like the boy was Tyler McKay.

All her professional life, from the time her career started to take off, when she'd stolen her boss's Rolodex so she'd have some important phone numbers, till the moment her career peaked, the Fates or Serendipity—she wasn't sure what she believed in, if Anything, but there were always mysterious things happening you couldn't explain-- had placed great talent in her path. And when it didn't, she would find out where it might be, and coincidentally elbow her way into that place, too. She would dazzle whatever Up- and-Comer or already Up-and-Came with her amazingly quick wit, her little pink rosebud mouth that was faster than most people's brains, as they tried to catch up with a sentence several sentences before. Soon, lo and behold, as in the fairy tales she didn't believe in though they seemed a part of her actual life, the talent would sign with her.

Tyler McKay. No hotter name in the entertainment world. And her on the balls of her influence.

Now if there was one thing Louise understood to the depths of what had once been her soul, it was adolescent feelings. Adolescence had been her most sensitive time, as it was in most girls who believed in love, but were so uncomfortable in their own skins they could not easily suppose it would ever come to them. The part of her that was still Little Girl, much as she'd tried to kill that off and mostly succeeded, absolutely tittered. Aloud. "Tee-Hee."

"I'd like to know who's in the room with the balcony above me," Louise said to Willie at the desk.

"There is no room above you," Willie said.

"To the left. Catty-cornered or however the fuck you say it."

"I'm sorry, Miss Felder," he said, obviously intimidated by her posture of authority combined with the easily spouted obscenity. Willie himself was not a particularly impressive person and knew it, practiced daily looking himself squarely in the eye when he shaved, but always lost the courage, and had to look away quickly, as though the mirror had caught him being a Peeping Tom. "There is no room upstairs from yours, cater-cornered or anywhere else."

"Cater-cornered, huh?" said Louise. "Your knowledge comes from on high even though there's no room?"

"I beg your pardon?"

"As well you might. Who's up there?"

"No one. The most we might have up there is some storage space."

As ungainly as she might have become in the world's view, when the time came to move, Louise could really move. With a physical dexterity that would have amazed those who had watched her sitting on couches for the frustrating years she had been out of favor, she slid out the emergency exit at the end of the hall, holding on to the bell that might have signaled 'alarm' and made her way up the metal stairway.

I can see from the security screen that marshals the front of the hotel that the paparazzi have gone away for the moment. But still hanging around is Buzzy, a camera-ready kid of a slightly older vintage who has a hard-on for movie stars the way they used to be. As a manager these days has to be part private detective, a career I never considered but admired in the prose of Raymond Chandler, all those crisp, spare sentences, not to mention the Bogart characters he and Dashiel Hammett gave rise to, I watched him shadow Karen Engel *this morning as she left the hotel. He always reports back to me what he has seen, trying to establish with me what passes in this town for intimacy. It is as good as having eyes in the back of your head, having them in front of someone else's. She didn't drive her car out of here after all, but got something out of the glove compartment, and then went on foot to the plastic surgery clinic across the street.*

As you can see from the front of the hotel, it's a plate glassy kind of building, dark mirrored windows, four stories high. There's a slight air of mystery to it, especially in the bouncy brilliance of the day, the best thing Southern California has to offer, along with the dream for those who don't know better. Karen Engel, I imagine, knows better than anyone. One of the magazines Samson left me is that issue of Photoplay bordered in black, with her movie star mother's picture on it, and the story inside of little Karen's finding her with her razor-slashed throat, the room so full of blood it dripped through the floor to the ceiling of the kitchen below. Even though she is in fantastic shape and should have recovered by now, after decades of therapy and a few marriages, you probably never get over something like that. Her most recent husband, a Dutchman, is wanted in several countries and a few offshore islands. He was involved in major financial folderol resulting in disaster which the global lack of a moral compass allows to spread more easily than E coli.

There seemed to be a slight sadness to the slope of Engel's shoulders as she crossed the street, and I could see her almost visibly reminding herself who she is, or at least who she was, and that she is supposed to be some kind of example for women. She straightened up and held her well-shaped head high, just in case someone was watching, which I was and also the little paparazzo.

Having set aside my education I still have these little bubble bursts in my head of how did this happen, when? so it was easy to get really interested in the history of Hollywood. If I had majored in anthropology, I could have maybe divided the citizenry into various groups and studied their foibles like Margaret Mead. Coming of Age in Encino, might have been the title of my thesis. Tinsel and glitter notwithstanding, this place has captured the attention of the world, so although intellectuals might dismiss it out of hand, there is something strangely important about it. Glamour is a Scottish word that means 'to cast a spell, so people see beauty where it doesn't exist.' You can't get much clearer than that.

I am filled with all kinds of that now useless information, having come, in my idealized fantasy life, from a family of academics, which is not the truth. As much as it pleasured me to spin a tale for Vince, it gives me equal joy from time to time to kid myself. So it is that I still pretend my marriage ended because my wife left me for another man when the truth is it was another woman.

There is a loud splashing from behind the glass doors that lead to the pool. Lord Bunty, checked in last night, has been in there for almost an hour, swimming laps, with the strong stroke of a committed swimmer, and the muscles that go along with that. I see Bunyan Reis pause by the exit from the dining room, looking. Rapt, I guess you could say his expression is, more remarkable for the fact that his pallor, combined with his pale eyes, seems to blank out real expression. There's a plastic surgeon who frequently makes mistakes that have to be repaired across the street, with a recording on his office phone that says "The eyes are the mirror of the soul." I love it when people who want to seem intelligent get a quote wrong. Correct, it's William Blake: "the eyes are the window of the soul." But in Bunyan's case, the misquote is accurate, as his silvery eyes look like mirrors, at once expressionless and sad.

Bunyan is more than a little unsteady on his feet. He was in the bar for a long while with the Felder woman, and I see where either the drink or her company has taken its toll. He half feels his way along the wall to the elevator.

I leave my office and go to offer my help, pretending as best I can that it isn't too obvious how much he needs help. "Good afternoon, Mr. Reis," *I say.*

"Is it afternoon already?" *he says, his curiously silver eyes with their albino lashes hardly blinking.* "I thought it was the shank of the morning."

"Well, we're both right. It's just coming up noon."

"We can't both be right. There is only one Truth. Absolute."

"As you say."

"Unless of course you prefer Ketel One." *He giggles. It is a girlish sound, as if he were at a children's party. His teeth have the same grayish pallor as his skin, so he looks like the monochromatic paintings that made him famous, except there is not the difference in textures that his art had. He stumbles.*

"Let me help you," *I say, and reach for his elbow, trying to steady him.*

"God helps those who help themselves," *he says angrily, and shakes off my hand.* "Do you believe in God?"

"Here," *I say, and pull open the metal gate of the elevator.*

"Are you avoiding a theological discussion? God is very strict, you know. She doesn't like cowards."

I press his floor. "Will you be all right?"

"I am fine. Even great, some have said. As if anybody cares anymore." *He makes an attempt to stand tall, as bitterness twists his mouth.* "Andy Warhol..." *he all but chokes on the name.* "... has his own museum... Of course it's in Pittsburgh...So one can't be too envious."

The elevator ascends, taking Reis with it.

When Karen Engel crossed the street and turned the corner into the plastic surgery center, she had not been aware of anyone's following her. That part of her antennae had long ago been put to rest, the skittish expectancy that she was of great interest to the press, or what had become of the press, the anxious little flies, as the Italians christened them in Fellini's 'La Dolce Vita.,' giving the world 'paparazzi.' She had retired from films twice before the last time, when she had been firmly convinced she meant it. The first time she had retired because she was exhausted from so much film work: there was no important role, tragic, dramatic or lightly comedic she had not been offered when she was in her twenties, her chameleon-like ability to transform herself into the personality called for as striking as her beauty. The ghost of her mother shone from azure eyes, so even those who did not remember that actress felt something multi-dimensional.

A spate of important movies, a number of flirtations, a divorce, a widowing and a few slight repairs to those eyes behind her, Karen entered the clinic. "I have an appointment with Dr. Bernard," she said to the woman behind the desk.

"Your name?"

"Karen Bos."

"There's someone waiting for you," said the receptionist.

"Excuse me?"

"A young lady." She indicated an alcove to the side where a woman in her thirties sat waiting. She was in a sweatshirt and jeans, overweight and looking angry about it.

"Olivia!" Karen said, hardly able to contain her surprise.

"Hello, Mother." The tone of her voice was as cool as her look was cold.

"How did you know I would be here?"

"It was on TMZ that you were back in town. I guess they ran out of today's stars to talk about. I figured if you were in LA, this-" She flapped her hands, indicating the clinic—"must be why you came. I knew it couldn't possibly be to see me."

"Oh, Olivia…"

"Is that why you named me that? So you could sigh with sorrow when you said my name? Oh, Olivia," she mocked. "Can't you ever do anything right?"

"Why are you here?" Karen asked, the heat of her daughter's resentment turning her steely.

"I needed to see you. So I called here pretending to be your secretary and asked what time you had your appointment. At least I'm clever about something."

"You're clever about a lot of things," Karen said.

"Except how to be the daughter you wanted."

"You've got that turned around, my darling. It's not so much that you weren't the daughter I wanted, as I wasn't the mother you wanted. So you're wrong."

"Accurate," Olivia said.

"Why do your very first words to me have to be confrontational? Is it any wonder I didn't call you right away?"

"No wonder at all," Olivia said.

"I had hoped your being married to a therapist would help you with your anger issues."

"He isn't a very good therapist. And, anyway…" Olivia's eyes, the same hue as her mother's, turned sad, started to tear. "He's left me."

"Oh, honey," Karen said, and moved to her, took her in her arms. She was a head taller than Olivia, so her hand touched the top of her daughter's head, soothing.

"Don't pet me like a dog," said Olivia, shrugging her off.

"Jesus Christ," said Karen, infuriated, backing off.

"I'm just sorry about all the money you spent on the wedding." She started to sob.

"It's okay," Karen said, and this time put her arms around her daughter solidly, with full intent not to be put off. "It's only money."

"I wish I had never been born," Olivia wept.

"You don't really mean that."

"Yes, I do."

She snuffled, the way she had when she was a baby, and hadn't known how to blow her own nose. Something deep within Karen shifted. She pulled a Kleenex from her purse and held it up to Olivia's nose. "Blow," she said. Olivia blew.

"When does it get easy?" Olivia asked, tears streaming freely now.

"It doesn't," said Karen. "Come. We'll go get you a hot chocolate."

"I'm too old for a hot chocolate."

"I'm not," said Karen, and telling the receptionist she would call back another time, left the clinic.

Just like in Alice in Wonderland, there was a door where no one would expect a door. Having reached the top of the metal stairway that no one expected would be there, either, Louise took an unusually deep breath. Halfway between a sigh and a gasp. It had been a long time since she had exerted herself in the least, and this had felt like the most.

So she stood on the landing just breathing until the strain was gone from her chest, and, she hoped, from her voice, before she opened the door to the hallway, and knocked on the door that no one would expect would be there. "Who is it?" came the uncertain voice from inside. He sounded uncertain not just of the identity of the caller, but the identity, in the truest sense, of the asker himself.

Louise had never actually heard the speaking voice of Tyler McKay, had paid precious little attention to how he sounded when he sang. But she'd had a hard time avoiding the barrage of song that seemed to come from everywhere, driving her car, clicking past the channel she didn't mean to watch on TV, as a young nation succumbed to their newest Lorelei, so enchanted they didn't see the rocks or even care if there were any.

"In-and-Out Burger," she said, imagining that her suspicions might be as clever as her instincts once had been, and that her answer would be acceptable to any teenager.

"But I didn't order..." said the young man as he opened the door a crack.

"It's a gift," said Louise.

"Who from?" he said. "Nobody knows I'm here."

"And I'm certainly not going to tell them," said Louise. "You can trust me."

He opened the door.

"Hi," said Louise. "Do you believe in Santa Claus?"

"No," said Tyler

"Well, neither did I," said Louise. "As it turns out we're both wrong."

All that was missing is Paul Revere's ride. One if by land and two if by sea might have sent a more traditional signal, but the phone and the Internet in modern Hollywood were a lot more quickly connected. Ever since the Hollywood Reporter had gone to once a week publication, and the benign Army Archerd had left the scene, scandal chat in Hollywood had accelerated to a whole new level. There were websites and TV channels devoted exclusively to everything slightly this side of slander, often crossing over, with a battery of well-paid attorneys at the ready, to make sure there were no heavy losses, as in the old days of Confidential. In that vanished era, the presence of that particular magazine, when found in thinking people's houses, was usually blamed on the maids. Homeowners claimed "the maid must have bought it, and left it in the bathroom." But in this new period of socially networked smut, the toilets, as it were, had been brought into the living room, so the worst magazines were on the best coffee tables.

Besides the unashamed dignifying of all that was whispered about, nothing much had really changed but the speed with which the lies or insinuations could be spread. So the true, alleged, or presumed identity of the young woman at the Royale previously known in Europe as 'Rita Favorita' whipped through the film colony like wildfires in a Santa Ana wind. By three o'clock that afternoon everyone with a cell phone or an Internet connection was aware of who, they were sort of sure, unless of course it was a lie, her forebears were. By seven that evening, when the televised gossip shows went on the air, 'DIVERSION TONIGHT,' leading the pack after the actual real news, whether or not there was truth to the suspicions was beside the point.

"An air of incredible excitement has settled on a small hotel in Beverly Hills, with the arrival of a glamour princess, not yet old enough to be a Queen," said the television commentator, old enough to be a queen, as was the actual queen who did the fashion reviews. The blue eyes of the 'reporter', as she referred to herself, glittered, their shine intensified by drops, her blonde locks glistened, oiled with gels and arranged by the show's hairdresser, her white teeth gleamed, their glow contributed to by caps, whitening, and an affair with a dentist that had ended as soon as her mouth was the way it should have been.

"All of Hollywood is atwitter, including Twitter itself, which is fast communicating the news that true Hollywood royalty is back," cooed Alana, pursing her lips for the camera. Then came the televised shot of Rita sunbathing on her deck, a nude photo obtained by an ambitious paparazzo who had climbed up to the roof of the hotel.

Out-of-focus, blurred according to the current mode of puritanizing exposed genitalia on disturbed young celebrities who stepped out of limos wearing no panties, were her nipples and mons veneris. But the rest of it was all gloriously tanned and gorgeous Rita, as the press had already begun calling her, there not having been a redheaded Rita for them to love since Hayworth, long enough ago for the name to seem fresh, as the new Rita did in the photo, even blurred. The stretch of her arms, the languid look on her face, the outreach of perfect legs all combined to make her first presentation to the public erotic, slightly pornographic and irresistible. Then of course there was the clouded story of her heritage, to which all commentators alluded but no one referred implicitly, since her not-quite-openly- alleged mother was still alive, and much revered in the film colony, which generally revered only the dead, who could no longer take work away from anyone else.

It was, the Royale manager Nino Riccioni could not help thinking, catching the broadcast on the TV set over the hotel's bar, His Finest Half- hour. Not since the nude calendar shot of Marilyn Monroe had there been such an exquisite stretch, of both the body and the truth. He considered himself a genuine benefactor to the consciousness, such as it was, of contemporary society. The world was richer for a little piece of news that did not involve disaster, murder, or politics, all of which seemed to be dovetailing into a single depressing category called How Things Are. That the story was not really 'news' made it all the richer in his mind, since it was proof of how ridiculous it had all become. The hunger for Infotainment, as the new mindless mix of information and entertainment was known, had raged completely out of control.

How ludicrous it was came second in his mind only to how clever he had been, how far seeing and newly powerful. In a world where, once, even a cat could look at a queen, now even a hotel manager could create a royal.

By eight-thirty that evening, Louise Felder, having thoroughly confused the young and more-than-impressionable Tyler McKay into thinking she was the head of a powerful entertainment complex that had unsuccessfully tried for months to reach his representatives, brought in the lawyer she'd used to sue the agency that had dumped her. He was holding out the contract.

"You just have to trust me," she told Tyler, as they sat in his secret suite.

"Why?" he said.

"Because I can see firsthand now what all the fuss is about, and what a complete innocent you are. No wonder you ran away from all the people who were supposedly protecting you."

"But they were," Tyler said.

"Then why did you run away?"

"It was all too much," he said. "I freaked. So many people. No time to be by myself. I mean, I like people, but there's a limit."

"With the right representation none of what you go through will make you uncomfortable. Sign this and you will be carried on a tray," Louise said. She was in her snake charmer mode now, hypnotic, a quality she had kept even while all else deserted her.

"Believe it," said the lawyer, extending the paper. He looked a great deal like an uncle of Tyler's, a dull man who spoke seldom.

"Why?"

"Because this contract is foolproof," said Louise.

"What does 'foolproof' mean exactly?" Tyler asked.

"That means even a fool couldn't fuck it up." Or, Louise thought but did not say, it was proof that anybody, if spun a good enough tale, could be made a fool. "Forgive me. Mess it up."

"I don't mind bad language," Tyler said. "Everybody's usually so careful around me. Hearing that kind of talk when you never get to hear it, when you know real people talk like that feels… almost…what's the word?" He batted the air with his long-fingered young hands.

"Refreshing?" Louise said.

"Yeah, right. Refreshing."

"Like you are," said Louise. "I understand now why everybody considers you so adorable. But with adorable comes vulnerable. That's what you have to guard against." Her mind was working so fast she did not even allow herself to allow in echoes of her own lost feelings, the truth that she had once been adorable, and believing that others actually saw that, allowed herself to be vulnerable, and that was when she had been deeply fucked over, and why she had learned to do the same to other people. But she wouldn't even think about that. "That's why you need real representation. Not this road company farmhand stuff."

"My uncle's not a farmhand. He's a notary and a CPA.."

"And that's who handles your bookings?"

"Him and Chester. My manager."

"Who comes from where, when, and how?"

"Yorba Linda. Where Richard Nixon came from."

"And that's supposed to make you trust him?'

"He went to law school there and studied entertainment law. So he knows."

"Maybe he knows Yorba Linda," said Louise. "He certainly doesn't know this town. Where the real deals are made. You haven't got a real deal, even though you ARE the real deal. Look in that mirror. Have you ever seen a cuter face? I certainly haven't, and obviously the world hasn't either, or there wouldn't be so much of a fuss that you are driven into hiding out in this hotel. Where's Chester when you really need him?"

"He'd be here if I wanted him here, if I told him where I was" said Tyler. "He's my next-to-best friend. He's the one who made me successful."

"You made yourself successful. Talent made you a success. And success is far more perilous than failure, Noel Coward said."

"I don't know him."

"Never mind," said Louise. "He never wrote anything you could play. But Shakespeare... that's where you should be headed. Romeo. You'd tear their hearts out."

"I saw Leo do that." Once a bunch of Hollywood stars had come in a limousine to his concert, and told him he should call them by their first names, and not be so respectful, --it made them feel old. So it had clicked in his brainpan that he should call everybody whose talent he admired by their first names, lest he age them. It thrilled him to be able to call Leonardo Leo, even though he couldn't really call him a friend. "I couldn't do it. I can't act."

"That's now," said Louise. "Imagine what you could do with the right acting coach. Leo's coach."

"He still studies acting?"

"Learning never stops."

"I'm really happy doing what I'm doing," Tyler said.

"Then why are you hiding out?" asked Louise.

"You should just sign," said the lawyer. "We'll make sure you're taken care of."

By nine o'clock the paparazzi knew exactly at what hotel the mystery girl was who wasn't exactly the mystery she'd been before all the TV gossip shows aired and the news went out on TMZ. But nobody said the story about her antecedents aloud, at least not on the air. The love that once dared not speak its name, was singing and dancing in the streets now, but you had to be careful about straight people with lawyers.

Where the girl was staying, though, was completely and openly spoken of. People knew, especially the paparazzi, that carefully cultivated—not in manners, but in having been taught—bunch whose livelihood depended on how well they spied. They gathered in camera-ready packs in front of the Royale.

Everyone in the hotel was now aware of what was going on, except Rita herself. In spite of how strong and young she was, and how used to being upside down, she had succumbed to jet lag, and was more than sound asleep.

So she wouldn't understand until the next morning how important she had become. In a different way, of course, from how she was famous/infamous at home.

When Elisa, now Rita, awoke the next day, brushed her teeth, her shiny copper hair, and put on her movie star sunglasses with the crystals on the frames, she was ready for whatever awaited her. Or

at least she thought she was. Even having grown accustomed in her
native land to press attention that bordered on hysteria, and endless
TV interviews, never having been through a cattle drive, she was
unprepared for the Hollywood paparazzi.

"Rita, Rita, Rita!" they shouted at her as she exited the front of
the hotel. For a moment she could hardly believe the name had
caught up with her, California had seemed so quiet, so calm. No
more.

"Is it true?" asked a reporter, and murmured the name of her
alleged antecedents.

"Perdoneme?" she said, totally baffled, genuinely innocent, of
this, at least.

"What's in the book?" a reporter asked her, pointing to the
brown leather diary she clutched in her left hand.

"My dream," said now and apparently forever Rita, being
familiar at least with that question, since the manager had asked it
of her the day before. He came out of the hotel, pushing his way
through the salivating multitudes surrounding her, a protector,
wearing a fine dark blue suit that made her feel accompanied to an
important meeting.

"You need to give her room to breathe," Riccioni said.

"What's your dream?"

"Che dice?" Rita asked the manager. He translated the
question.

"Voglio essere una'Movie Star,'" she said sincerely.

"She wants to be a movie star," Riccione said.

"You think you have some special qualification?" asked a
reporter, trolling for the direct answer they all thought would prove
the rumor. "You think it's in your genes?" asked another. "Your
DNA?" asked a third, hoping she would let it slip who her
forebears were.

"Non capisco," Rita said, turning to the manager.

"They want to know why you should be a movie star," he said, in Italian. "What makes you think you could do that?"

"Oprah," said Rita, definitively.

"Oprah?" asked the crowd, almost as one.

"Oprah dice si vuole abastanza, e posibile."

"Oprah said if you want something bad enough, you can get it," translated Riccioni, delighting in the reassigning of responsibility.

"You watched Oprah?" asked a woman from an entertainment show.

"Ogni giorno," said Rita.

"Every day," said Riccioni.

"But how awful that her show is off the air now, so she won't be able to help you," said a woman reporter.

Riccioni translated.

"I help myself," said Rita. "Questo e il messagio di Oprah."

"You really believe you can be a movie star?" asked a network videographer, collecting footage for that evening's show.

The manager translated.

"Non credo. Lo so. Se ci credi veramente, con bastanza forza, diventa la verita. Oprah dice."

"She doesn't believe. She knows. If you believe something strongly enough, then it becomes so. Oprah says."

Standing inside the doorway of the hotel, Louise Felder could not help being impressed. By then, she, too, had heard the supposed story of Rita's origins, and knew it to be absolute bullshit. But the young woman had balls. Maybe as big as Louise's own. It would do no harm to have two clients that would capture the attention of the industry. And from there America. And from there, the world.

And in no time at all Louise would be bigger than those sons of bitches who had taken away her power. And what she would do with that power back again would be devastating. In a positive way, of course.

CHAPTER THREE

WHAT DECENT NEWSPAPERS there are left in this world, at least the English speaking part of it, besides those owned by the scurrilous and moneymaking scandalmonger whose lackeys hack in on the dead, were slow to pick up on the outrageous story I invented. So there is, perhaps, still a degree of tasteful skepticism in the world, and caution. But those with discernment and fact checks will probably be the next papers to go out of business.

The Internet, however, and television, famished for a continuous flow of slime, considered the improbable tale of Rita's origins very High End, and could not get enough of it, though never naming exact names. They just continued with the spew of innuendo, and the flashy photo of Rita sunbathing naked, her snatch and nipples fogged out but not enough so you couldn't imagine, and delight in what these days is no longer considered obscenity, life itself, in its courtrooms and halls of government, having become obscene(see most politicians.)

The whole business of not naming names exactly, but making everything into a guessing game, is a semi-honorable tradition in Literature, whose days are also numbered, going back to the <u>roman a clef</u> (pronounced 'clay') meaning a book with a key, first *started in the 17ᵗʰ century by Madame de Scudery, so she could write about all the well-known people of her time, and get everyone guessing as to their true identities and not have anyone kill her. Proust did it, Hemingway used it in The Sun Also Rises, writing about his friends in Spain, the least likeable of whom wrote his own novel in self-defense but nobody cared, and in recent years Joe Klein did it in Primary Colors, which was really about Bill Clinton but by that time there was so much stuff about old Bill that it was jizzum under the bridge. Mostly the roman a clef provokes lawsuits from those who wish they were as well-known as the authors, and would like some of their money.*

But the Internet and TV, having no mind, and therefore no conscience, are apparently free to rampage without checks, so whether or not anyone could prove or disprove Rita was the descendant of those not exactly named was beside the point. She was gorgeous, she was flashy, she had an obvious appetite for notoriety, and now she had Louise Felder representing her. So in no time at all, Louise had arranged for a screen test through what was most likely her one remaining heavyweight connection in the film industry, Chet Sinclair. (She had put the call through the hotel switchboard, the old-fashioned one we have just for color, but it works, and accidentally, of course, I had kept a key open while she connected with him.)

Sinclair is notorious around town as having been so whacked out on coke for so many years he had no idea he was out of power. The studio itself where he once held impressive sway had put him out to pasture with plenty of hay (ie: a guarantee of a producer's fee for a two-picture deal, especially considering that his ghost attorney, that is, one not visible, was the most notorious and well-connected bad guy lawyer in Hollywood.)

The secret of bad guys who can get away with anything, especially if they're smart, is that they have something on everyone, so they don't even have to threaten: they just make a phone call and everybody and everything falls into place. That's who that lawyer was. The deals he made and the secret negotiations he came out on top with, representing just about every heavyweight that people were afraid of, as well as many organizations, some legitimate and many not so, were infinite. And nobody dared not to call him a hero. So much for him, whom I will not even bother to a clef. He is dead now, and the dead have no rights in court, but people are still afraid of him, which is probably smart as he might still have connections.

So now here out of the antique elevator in our lobby comes the dazzling, suddenly totally together Rita, with Louise Felder at her side. There have been moments in Hollywood history when people actually held their breath at the sight of someone, and this is one of them. I had heard from an old Hollywood producer who knew Sharon Tate in the pre-Roman Polanski/ Manson murders time, that when she walked on Fifth Avenue, traffic literally stopped. People couldn't believe it, and had to pull over, they were so joyfully stunned. There is a lot of traffic outside the hotel now, cop cars and security forces trying to deal with the paparazzi, the limousine that Chet Sinclair has sent to pick Rita up for her screen test, but if it was not already gridlocked, and the drivers could see into the lobby, traffic would stop.

Whatever Felder might have lost in the echelons of connection, they do not include hairdressers and make-up artists. Rita is certainly ready for her close-up. Her coppery/auburn hair is drawn up into a glistening topknot, one thick rope of it freed and dangling artfully down, arranged so it falls over the top of her gloriously tanned left breast. The dress she wears is a simple green sheath, a shade darker than her eyes, cut down just to the top of her magnificent breasts, the almost wasp-like tininess of her waist emphasizing their fullness and roundness. The back is cut low to show the somehow heartbreaking dimples above the full curve of her ass. Heartbreaking, I guess, because there is something so innocent about dimples, even in the place where they are now revealed. Her legs are very long, and look polished, their sheen from the sun. The heels her fairly large feet (but didn't Garbo have big feet?) are slipped into are not very high,-- she's a big girl already-- the same fabric as her dress, as though she were going to a prom for Goddesses. She wears no jewelry, except for her eyes.

Felder guides her by the arm, and as if the mere contact with that elbow had some restorative, rejuvenating power, she looks almost pretty, the phantom of the bright, plump, young honey-blonde she had once been, according to her personal legend, breaking visibly through the tough cookie. Victory seems to be back in her grasp, and in her eyes.

"Rita! Rita! Rita!" cry the bottom-feeders from outside the hotel, their swollen ranks held uneasily in check by the private security people and the cops, who are conspicuously trying to seem present, professional, and completely competent. The last, I cannot help thinking is a direct result of their having declared "closed" a recent disturbing case of drive-by murder, attributing the crime to an ex-felon who committed suicide. He supposedly shot the press agent victim five times in the chest from a bicycle he was on. Sure.

"Let me just make sure you can get through this," I say to Rita, as she and Felder head for the door.

I use my very strong arms—there is a gym in the basement and I take advantage of the rowing machine on breaks to work off some of my frustration—to clear a kind of Charlton Heston parting the Red Sea path for them through the people the cops can't manage.

The limo, an excessively long stretch, but then any stretch is excessively long, the factory having literally stretched the rear end of a perfectly fine car so it would look even more offensively expensive in these very difficult times, sort of the automobile version of what those annoying late-night ads call 'male enhancement,' is waiting at the curb. Everything around this seems to be a stretch: the story about Rita's origins, her posture on the lounge outside her room as she sunned captured by a photographer, the limo.

"Rita! Rita! Rita!" they are all screaming at her, trying to get her to look towards their lenses so they get the best shot, the one that will be heard around the world. Or at least seen, and sold for the highest price, like the first picture of the senator's illegitimate son, conceived in Liberty, as Abraham Lincoln might have said, that all men are created shitheels. Well, maybe not all of them, but the percentage is staggering.

The gorgeous creature and her old girl Pygmalion get into the limo, and the cops do the best they can to move the crowd out of the way so the car can proceed. I realize I am doing an injustice to call Felder Pygmalion, because she has not transformed what was cold stone, only acted on seeing what might have been obvious to anyone perceptive without an axe to grind. I realize that both these observations are pointless, since there are not too many people in this burg who celebrate being perceptive, since that implies sensitivity and sensitivity gets your feelings hurt, especially if you have them,-- and few are those without an axe to grind in a culture, as Marlon Brando said "whose most pressing moral imperative is that anything is acceptable if it makes money."

I lean over to close the door in the back of the limo, as they are seated comfortably inside. To my astonishment, Felder reaches over and puts a gentle hand on my wrist.

*"I want to thank you for all the help you've been," she says,
with what seems to be sincerity. "And are being," she adds,
investing me with future responsibility.*

*I look into her face. She seems actually peaceful. Winning
works for her.*

The great gates of Marathon Pictures had stood majestic and
imposing since 1912, when Samuel Goldwyn was still Samuel
Goldfish. Even now, as the limo approached them, Louise felt an
inner jolt of awe, the wide-eyed excitement that had characterized
her as a very young woman, even when she tried covering it with a
jade veneer. That she could have come so far and reigned so long
as a kind of entertainment icon, becoming as big a name as some
of those she represented, was still a source of wonder in the part of
her that had kept honest. Not that big a part, really, but it was there.
For as much as she had never doubted herself, she doubted herself,
and the crash into seeming oblivion, in Hollywood terms, had felt
pre-ordained, inevitable. Absolutely right, in a very wrong way.

Her rise had been phenomenal and almost mythic, though she
wasn't sure exactly which myth it was. Maybe Icarus. The one
who'd flown too close to the sun. But in many people's eyes she
had seemed to be the sun, blazing brighter that anyone, especially
around the tongue.

"Now, you're going to do great," she said to Rita. "Fabuloso."

"Lo so." Rita said. "Capisco."

"I think you capisco a whole lot," said Louise. "But then a
certain amount of seeming naivety will serve you well. It worked
for me when I was first starting out. They like us wide-eyed."

"Scusi?" Rita said.

The guard at the gate stopped them, clearly just a gesture, lasting only for the moment it took for the driver to give Louise's name.

They were waved onto the lot, and instructed where to park, what stage to go to.

"I feel like the mother of the Bride," said Louise. She smiled and reached over to pull the renegade coil of shiny rust hair from behind Rita's shoulder to the front, so it hung just over her breast, as Casey Anthony's hair had suddenly burst free and flirtatious, once the Not Guilty verdict in the death of her baby daughter had come in from the jury. "Although as Andre said, I probably would have eaten my young."

"Scusi? Andre?"

"Born Arnold. My first love. Amore."

"O. Amore. Capisco."

"Than you're smarter than I am," Louise said. "I never understood why we love the people we do. Though in your case, I get it. The yacht. The parties. Money. Bunga bunga."

"Bunga bunga?" Rita said.

"That's what they called it in the papers. All his orgies, fooling around with young girls. The newspapers. Giornale."

"Non legge giornale," Rita said, waving the offending newspapers away. "No like."

"I'm sorry I brought it up," Louise said, and patted her hand. "Don't trouble your perfectly coiffed head."

The screen test had been arranged so there was very little that had to be explained to Rita. But just in case, they had brought in a language coach from Beverly Hills, where crash courses in various tongues were given for elevated fees to those about to travel abroad, who didn't want to seem too American, mostly at the time when Americans had been most resented, when they still seemed ahead of the game. The director engaged for the screen test was a once storied, thoughtful craftsman, known for humanistic people tales, out-of-work for all the decades that movies had turned mechanical and violent.

Rita seemed comfortable with all of it, her peridot eyes wider than usual at the size of the set, the height of the cavernous ceiling, the lights shining in her direction. She turned her head different ways on command so the camera could catch all the angles of her face. The make-up woman, seemingly a bit annoyed that much of her skill had been made superfluous and unnecessary, came in to powder away the shine in-between shots.

"Her skin is a little too dark," the make-up woman complained.

"Looks good to me," the director said. "Now let's have a smile."

"Sorriso," said the language coach.

And there it was, like magic. A smile so glittering and transformative, made strangely touching by the slight overlap of front teeth, it seemed to warm the whole stage, vast as that stage with its 75 foot ceiling was.

"Eat your heart out, Julia Roberts," said Louise.

"But you wouldn't have believed it," Louise said excitedly to Bunyan Reis, back in the hotel, at a table in the bar. "She's absolutely pops."

"Pops?" Bunyan said, over the rim of his martini.

"Jumps off the screen. Comes out at you. Like 3D before it was actual 3D. It's fucking star quality. And she's genuinely talented. I mean, she played a comedy scene with some young actor and bounced off him like she'd been doing this all her life."

"Well, she <u>has</u> done a lot of bouncing," said Bunyan.

"You must do away with your cynicism, in this case at least. It's like a miracle. Like everything in her life, what we know of it, at least, has led up to this moment, preparing her for stardom. I mean genuine stardom."

"Is there any other kind?"

"Absolutely. The kind they've been trying to manufacture these past few years. It hasn't worked. All those thin-armed ingénues. This girl is going to be the biggest thing since Monroe."

"Or the supposed grandmother?" Bunyan said, and signaled Amber to refill his martini.

"No talk I started," Louise said. "I take no credit for that rumor. Or the blame either. It all happened without me."

"Hard to imagine anything could."

"She's the real thing. I mean it, Bunny. True natural talent. She seems like she can play anything. "

"A good quality for a hooker."

"We must stop even thinking of her like that. She's a born actress. Even the sad scene she did, where she was dying. I actually wept. Me. Weeping."

"Maybe it was the prospect of all that <u>soldi</u>."

"I don't know that word."

"Money," Bunyan said.

"I never cared about the money. I never focused on the money. It wasn't money I really wanted."

"I know. You wanted to be the biggest name in the room."

"You have to forget that, too. I never really meant it."

"Of course you did," he said.

"But I'm over it. That's not what I want anymore."

"What do you want? What's your idea of true success?"

She gritted her teeth. The jaw that had seemed to retreat into flesh squared, fixed, jutted. "Not to have to eat any more shit."

He smiled as Amber brought over the fresh martini, lifted the frosted glass, and held it up towards Louise. "I'm relieved to see you've never lost your soft side."

In truth, she hadn't. Of course, it was no longer a side. More accurately, it was a kind of cyst, a hard crust formed around the spongy inner blemish of hope and longing she had had as a girl, when she still believed that anything was possible. Her career had demonstrated that anything was, but not as she imagined it. Bigger in many ways, more impressive. Triumphant. But absent that bubble of absolute joy she had supposed would be there, like orgasm, when the moment came.

She had had more than a moment. She had had years, decades if she dared try to measure it. But the pain of what had come before when everybody disappointed her, from her first love to her first star crush to her first big name client, had never been completely eased by the balm of success. Especially as it had turned out to be an Indian gift: something she'd thought was actually hers to keep, taken away.

So the re-entry of hope, which in her case meant a return to power, was an aphrodisiac, dizzying, awakening a part of Louise she had thought was dead. Or, rather, that she had tried to anaesthetize, because it embarrassed her, that smart as she was, as abused as she had been by the system she had seemed to conquer, as abusive as she herself had seemed and (sigh… sorry) actually had been at the top of her game, she still harbored a kernel of innocence.

She was transferring that now, in her innermost being, which she thought might still be there, to Rita. Of course it was possible that it had all been a façade, the aimless little hooker, up and ready for Bunga Bungas. A girl had to do what a girl had to do, an agent who was even tougher than Louise became told her when she was just starting out. So there she had been, little Rita or Whatever Her Name Really Was, an orphan, probably, or certainly spiritually. On the sidewalks of Naples or Milan or Rome, one of those gorgeous tourist destinations where the wrong streets were piled high with uncollected garbage. And so she had reached out, like Alice in Wonderland, for the key that would make her the right size, big enough to get out of that hole.

A girl had to do what a girl had to do. And that held for Louise as well, as long ago as it had been since she was actually a girl. One of the shrinks she had been to when she still believed in Everything told her that she should picture her inner child, the little girl she had been once, and hold that inner child in a mental light, let her know she was loved. She had come to loathe him of course, as she loathed all those who acted as if they could fix things and didn't. But it was still a nice image. Little Louise, held in comforting arms, rocked gently to try and escape the unsettling rhythms of reality.

Closing her eyes now, she lay back on the bed in her hotel room and tried to visualize herself as a baby. But it was too long ago, and she couldn't really remember what she had looked like when she was little, as her mother had thrown away all her pictures because she wanted a child who was beautiful, not one who was fat. So instead Louise pictured Rita, little baby Rita, all golden brown with those riveting eyes, pale green with darts of gold, like a cat's, stunning limbs baby-fied, made chubby(not <u>too</u>,) and pinchable, a diaper clasped with a Tiffany pin, over a navel that, even on a baby, looked sexy. One of those smart little In-sies that only the lucky girls had, the ones who grew up to be effortlessly thin, long-waisted, desirable.

Louise held that baby in mental arms, and rocked her gently as the doctor had prescribed. And everything in her that had never really wanted a child, because Andre born Arnold had said she would eat her young, welled up in her. And she was washed over with something that felt a lot like love as she had imagined but never experienced it, filled with compassion and empathy and the wish to make everything better, as no one had ever really made it all better for her. "It's going to be all right," she whispered to the infant Rita, who now became also the squalling faceless infant Louise. "Everything's going to be all right. It's going to be better than all right. It's going to be wonderful."

The first person she called the next morning was Allegra de Sevigny.

Setting aside any memory of the deep feelings she had experienced the evening before, like a one-night stand that had turned out to be with someone unimportant when she checked his wallet, Louise moved on with her life. It would be straight ahead now, she could see that. She had surprised everyone at the studio with the actual, true luster of the talent she had brought them, combined with that face, not to mention the tits and ass. She had an even bigger surprise waiting for everyone in the room upstairs.

First she would hold a press reception inviting all the A players, who would come because Allegra would be co-hosting it, she was sure, introducing them to Rita, along with the announcement of whatever picture it was that the studio would slate for her debut. She would help them think of something perfect. The Beverly Hills Hotel, she thought, would be the right place for that proclamation, one of those cavernous round rooms where abandoned children honored their narcissistic movie star parents once they were gone though still managing to hurt their children's feelings. And just as the whole event drew to a close, not so it would steal any of Rita's thunder, she would hit them with her bolt of lightning: Tyler McKay. The most ebullient energy of the no-longer-so-new millennium, brought to the movie-going public for the first time, by none other than the Star Finder herself.

And they had thought she was finished.

But first she would tell Allegra. "Sweetheart," she said into the phone, being one of the few people in town to have Allegra's personal number. It had been given before Allegra had become Queen of the May and even June and July, and had been still borderline desperate, wondering if she should become political or social or just rich, and thought Louise was big time. She would not tell her all of it. Just enough so she would be assured of capturing a few front pages. Or gigabytes, or whatever the fuck they were called, on the Internet.

The letter that Karen Engel had been waiting for arrived with the morning mail. That the mail came at all was beginning to seem a kind of miracle, as various deep potholes emerged in cities where there wasn't enough money to fix them, and lifesaving services like police and fire fighters and teachers were being eliminated or, at least, drastically cut back. It was a less than joyful time for the country, and though neither rain nor snow nor gloom of night had kept those couriers from their appointed rounds in the old days, now post offices were closing along with libraries, and carriers were being forced into early retirement that eventually wouldn't provide them enough nourishment to fill in a pothole.

So the mails' arrival at the hotel signaled a moment of great relief for Naomi, sorting it out at the front desk of the Royale. Her mother was a big fan of Karen Engel's, an actual contemporary who looked at least twice Karen's age. The first time she had seemed glad about Naomi's being in Hollywood was when Naomi told her that Karen was staying in the hotel where she worked. Temporarily, of course, till something came through from her agent. Even a commercial.

"I have a letter for you," Naomi said now into the phone. "Would you like me to send it up?"

"No. I'll be right down," Karen said.

'Right down' at the Royale could only be accomplished on the stairs, as the elevator, for all its quaint, authentic antiquity was, as Louise Felder who had ridden up in it with Karen the night before commented, 'slower than shit.' Naomi had been in the elevator with them and noted that they hadn't spoken to each other, avoiding each other's eyes, making no attempt at even a polite smile, a frost having settled on the antique box that held them as it creaked slowly upwards. It was, as Naomi could not help observing to the manager, because that was part of her duties, she was sure, an absolutely Arctic moment.

"They have to know each other," she told him the next day. "After all, this is basically a small town, and they <u>are</u> in the same business. But it was a chill you could actually feel. Blood-curdling."

"Perhaps you haven't noticed," Riccioni said. "Our Miss Felder does have a way of antagonizing people."

"But this went both ways. I mean, they literally wouldn't look at each other. There was a pulpable freeze."

"I believe you mean 'palpable,'" said Riccioni, since if there was one thing he couldn't stand, it was a snitch trying to sound articulate, and not coming up with the right word.

Fortunately for Karen, she was in shape for stairs. Stairs helped to keep her in shape. Keep the heart beating that beat even faster at the prospect of the letter waiting for her at the front desk.

My beloved,

How I have wanted to call you, to hear your sweet voice . But they are looking for me everywhere, and I am afraid of the telephone. There has been all this hacking, a terrible word, an even more terrible practice, phone lines, cell phones, everything. No one is safe, including, I hear, the Queen of England. So I do not dare even try to call you, as those people would be the first to reveal my whereabouts, and our plans, if they had any clue to them. I must keep silence, much as I am longing to talk to you, to have your breath in my ear. And other places.

But it will not be much longer till we are together. I trust you have made the arrangements. I am traveling under a different name, one I am not telling even you, my Best Beloved. How I long for your touch. The feel of your skin. The cleverness of your tongue.

I will arrange from this end for a limousine to take me to your hotel, and will call you from the car. I will be in touch again closer to my departure date. I will get there in time to go through with the arrangements you have made. I know I can count on you as I have never been able to count on anyone, including myself.

Many are the people who would like to see me dead. It will be joyful for me to look into the eyes of one who is glad to see me alive. But I think it best you keep up the appearance of being done with me. Thank God, you're not.

My great love, always
HENDRIK

It was not as passionate as she had hoped, but it was better than nothing. For all of the husbands and lovers she had had, almost non-existent was the partner, seemingly permanent or temporary, who had ever written her love letters. As little as she felt envy, Karen did envy those who had lived in literary times, and were separated by distance or station, and so had poured their hearts and eventually their sexual juices onto paper. Only her second husband, Olivia's father, the one who had really loved her most deeply, but couldn't stay long, cancer rampaging through his healthy body, feasting on its energy and youth, had been sentimental enough to put anything in writing. And then, because he didn't feel he was as smart as she was, had kept it minimal. He had always teased her about being too effusive in her gratitude, as she always was, kindness was so unexpected in her experience. So the notes he left—and they were little more than notes that came with elaborate gifts, said things like: "Shut up. Just say thank you. I love you." She had gone over all of them, over and over again after he was dead, the now-ness of his handwriting underscoring the loss. Of everything, pictures, shirts, jackets that had kept the smell of him, the warm, clean, protective, manly smell that she clung to, going to his closet and inhaling deeply, as though she could still breathe him in, till she finally gave his wardrobe to charity, videos friends had made of them together,-- nothing spoke so achingly of his absence as the sight of his handwriting. It seemed so present, even though he was past.

But Hendrik was still alive. And he was coming to her. And together they would fool everyone, and make greatness out of the rest of their lives, whatever time was left. But quietly, of course, as the world was after him.

"Well, si, oui, seguro, of course. Senti, listen!" Allegra said on the phone. "I already heard she was a great surprise."

"And more beautiful on film than in the toasty flesh," Louise said. "The film editor called me. It's one of those things that happens so rarely, when the camera really loves you. Makes you seem to look better even than you do if you're beautiful. It happened with Sandra Bullock and Julia…"

"And Elizabeth," Allegra said, brandishing the name like a sword.

"Oh, no. Not Elizabeth. Elizabeth was exactly the same not on film. Breathtaking when you looked into her eyes, if you didn't see how short she was. And before she got fat, of course."

"And O-L-D," said Allegra, who had merrily picked up Louise's habit of spelling out words with a reality she couldn't bear.

Their friendship, or, telling herself the truth about Allegra, their seeming friendship was a source of great amusement to Louise. As clever as Allegra was, and warm, Louise understood that she used people like cutlery at a sit-down dinner: with great good manners but a voracious appetite. Her happiness manifested mainly when she was brandishing some important celebrity, increasing visibly when she became a 'name' herself.

They had met at the tail end of Louise's reign as the top agent in town, bonded, in the way that smart, showy women found each other when they weren't really looking for men anymore. Allegra was away lecturing on a cruise when the shit hit the trades. So she had missed that flurry of humiliation for Louise—more than a flurry-- more like a blizzard. Everyone who had nothing really to talk about in Hollywood that day had breakfasted and lunched and dined on Felder's downfall, as the cormorants descended with the rapidity of the greedy women in Zorba, who, even as a woman lay dying, riffled through her drawers for treasure. In Louise's case, everybody moved in to claim her clients, all of whom of course had sworn they would never leave Louise. Two of them actually stayed with her, but that was because they were getting older and had enough money so they didn't want to work that much anyway. Short of putting her on display in Salem-like stocks by the swan pond at the Hotel Bel-Air, there was little more the village could have done to show her she wasn't wanted anymore.

By the time Allegra returned, Louise had run away to the villa where Bunyan was a houseguest for the summer, offering her the sitting room of his suite as sanctuary. As unreliable a friend as he might have seemed at times that he himself was on the prowl, when the chips were down Bunyan always came through. So what Allegra had found out on coming back was that Louise had left the agency to go visit Bunyan Reis at the di Portanova's summer palazzo, and of that she could still be envious. So they had stayed friend-ish, as Louise had correctly branded most of her relationships, in the old days when she was still a little sincere. She did not include in that wary, arms-length category her lovers. But by then the feel of flesh was less important to Louise than the feel of victory.

By the time Allegra might have caught on to the dark truth of Louise's being ousted, she was tethered to her own ascent, which had genuinely started. The smarter part of television, that is, the part with a negligible audience, was burning up all the 'talking heads,' those people who seemed like they might really know something. Not only did Allegra know a few things, she could talk about them in several languages. She became more or less the unofficial greeter, the go-between, as it were, of Hollywood, for visiting foreign dignitaries, who, no matter how high they had risen or how deep their influence and concerns, still gaped at meeting movie stars. In addition to her unofficial role as a symbol of international savvy even though she lived in L.A.("Ze weather, les temps, darling," she said to the host of the TV talk show on which she was a frequent and reliable guest, when asked why she didn't live in Paris or London,) she became herself a noted writer of books on manners, which she might have actually written herself.

Louise had been a great help to her, connecting her with Harry Langdon, Junior, a photographer who had photographed everyone from Ann-Margret to Nancy Reagan, and whose lenses actually seemed to transform, so Allegra's hawkish good looks appeared less intimidating when smiling from the backs of her books. And generously, it seemed to Allegra, Louise had given her numbers of stylists and hairdressers so sought after their phones were unlisted. Soon nobody had her <u>éclat</u>, a word that she herself used on the air, explaining to the program's hostess it was sort of the word equivalent of a thunderclap, a brilliant success, except possibly Arianna Huffington. But of course she was Greek. Not that Allegra had anything against the Greeks, it was simply that their economy was in the loo, a word she used all the time even when not in England.

Her own nationality was a source of speculation, since the spate of languages that fell from her very thin lips was dazzling. Some said she was French, some said Spanish, though she was probably far too naturally blonde, almost platinum, to give much substance to that, and there was a rumor of Montenegro. Those who didn't like her very much suggested she was Romanian. She herself on being asked would only give the Giaconda smile she practiced often in front of her mirror to try and overcome seeming too frank. Pressed as to her origins, she would say in her multi-cultural way, "I just growed, comme Topsy."

But as much as such women could be, she and Louise were friends. She would be able to call in Allegra like a marching band, to beat the drums about Rita. Along with her other skills, Allegra had become the town's most notable hostess. She would be the chic majorette at the head of the parade, stepping elegantly up to the rostrum in the Crystal Ballroom of the Beverly Hills Hotel to introduce Rita. All Louise had to do was convince Allegra it would be better publicity for her than it would be even for Rita, who still needed the right last name.

"She's so young," said Louise on the phone to Allegra. "I can't understand why I like her so much. But she is truly darling. There's such a surprising freshness about her. I believe in the pit of my belly which I can still hold in on a good day, that she's going to be the biggest thing since Marilyn."

"Senti, listen," Allegra said. "We should give her a party."

"You really think so?" Maybe there was a God.

CHAPTER FOUR

THE LAST NAME they settled on was 'Adona.' Rita Adona had that European feeling, combined with the subtle idea she was a female Adonis, and a not so slight echo of Madonna who was pretty much over, much as she exercised.

Rita Adona, The Great Movie Star-to-be (Louise was sure now, especially since she would have the endorsement of Allegra, even without Louise's having to ask) was still a bit on her European schedule, so she took naps in the afternoon. It was a great temptation to look in on her and make sure she was fine. Louise had no idea where those impulses were coming from. In some way she didn't understand, it embarrassed her, the degree of concern. She had never accepted generalizations about women, knowing whatever the supposed generalization was it would not necessarily apply to her, maverick that she had always been, except in matters of love, when she'd been as stupid as anybody. But that was long ago and far away as Cole Porter had written in a song when you could still sing them because they had actual melodies and words you could understand.

But one generalization that she had heard from a genuinely big star had stuck with her, because when she heard it she'd held her tongue, and that was not like her. In her late middle youth, as she characterized it, she had gone to Agoura, a desolate region a trek from L.A., to the Renaissance Pleasure Faire, an elaborately medieval, Elizabethan celebration replete with costumes and psychics and 16th century food. She and a slew of the young celebrated had ridden in a double-decker London party bus, hosted by Jack Haley, Jr., or, as Louise thought of him, the son of the Tin Man. All of Young Hollywood of that era, had been on board: Goldie and Liza (whom she thought of as Judy Garland, Jr.) and coming up in the ranks, the young Jack Nicholson.

That gifted, explosive actor had, in a moment of vocal melancholy, nasally lamented aloud "Women have less mercy than men." Louise had been moved to dispute him. Given his personal history, which she was later to learn, but had not known at the time—the woman who'd raised him that he thought was his mother was really his grandmother, his actual mother the girl he had known as his sister, --she could understand his fuming, and accept what confusion and sense of betrayal he had experienced. But at the time all she knew was that it was a generalization she couldn't agree with.

She could line up mental arguments why women were more merciful. War. Discontinued if women were in charge, because it was such a waste, so pointless, so cruel, life lived being cruel enough, with its losses and disappointments and ultimate finale, which she didn't like to think about at all.

Once she had heard a really bright woman say the reason there wouldn't be war if women were in charge was that women wouldn't want to sacrifice their sons. Of course Louise couldn't relate to that, since Andre had said she would eat her children, so she accepted as truth that she had no maternal instinct. Nor was she conscious of particular pride in being a woman.

Still, she had the impulse to get in Jack Nicholson's face and tell him he was wrong. But she had yet to establish her place in Hollywood, having brought with her only a little of her New York caché, and the Rolodex with its unlisted numbers, stolen from her boss at the agency. She needed some unlisted numbers of her own, and one she really wanted to have was Jack Nicholson's. So if he was upset about what he considered women's lack of mercy, she could only imagine how riled he would be by a woman's seeming smarter, or trying to seem smarter. Not that she found fault with his male chauvinism. Had she been a man, she imagined she would herself have been a male chauvinist pig, the angry expression of the day.

All of these thoughts had gone through her head in the time it took to pass Woodland Hills, a small suburb of Los Angeles, which to Louise seemed itself one big suburb. So she opted not to open her mouth, a rare discretion on her part, and one she never regretted. Because whenever Jack Nicholson saw her at parties after that jolly, carefree excursion, he would smile at her, as though they had shared a pleasant experience though he probably wasn't sure exactly which one. In any case, he seemed friendly enough, though he never signed with her.

All those who had never signed—and their numbers were impressive but not as impressive as those who <u>had</u> signed, every major actor or actress she had really wanted to represent, including the one she thought the biggest star of all, who had dumped her over a personal issue, best friends though they were, Ha!—would be sorry once she sailed forth with Rita.

Rita Adona. It was absolutely perfect. She could almost sing it, if only she'd had a real voice, and not just one of those reedy things that sounded like Anna Maria Alberghetti with a head cold. My God, there was a name from the past. A name like that, and

she'd made it anyway. Imagine what could happen with Rita
Adona.

The Crystal Ballroom of the Beverly Hills Hotel cost $25,000 to
rent just to the bare walls. Of course, it being the Beverly Hills
Hotel, the walls were not exactly bare, but striped, or rather, leafed
with great painted green rubber plants, as though Beverly Hills
itself was a jungle. The observation to be made about that
metaphor seemed obvious even to Allegra, still working on her
English-language skills, so she waited for Louise to say something,
and when she didn't, was relieved that she, herself, hadn't said
anything either, because she realized it might not be that clever.
Bare walls costing $25,000 meant that everything else, starting
with glasses and plates and what would fill them, was extra, and,
as befitted the setting, very expensive.

As much money as Louise had made during the flush years of
her career, and as impressive as was the amount they had slagged
on her when throwing her out of the agency she had helped build
up, as though burying her under wet cement, like Jimmy Hoffa,
spending money capriciously still made her anxious. There was
always the scary possibility she would live to be truly O-L-D, in
which case there would be no one to take responsibility or care for
her, as her family was gone, and nobody really loved her anymore
except maybe Bunyan, and he would surely pre-decease her,
especially if he kept up the drinking. So Allegra's coming up not
only with the party idea, but an apparent willingness to hostess it in
every sense, was past generous. Munificent, really. If they made a
movie about her she would have to be played by Greer Garson or
Paul Muni, someone of true seeming humanitarian stature even
though they were dead.

No one was quite sure exactly where her money had come from. But as she not only gave to the blind and those who read to them in libraries, and never said no to chairing a fund raiser, it was one area of investigative journalism that no one pursued. It was as though the film community, if it could be called that, had its own Lady Bountiful. Nobody had been that elegant and effective since Dorothy Chandler, and she, of course, had had a newspaper empire behind her, when newspaper empires were in the hands of decent people.

So it was that on a Monday evening, the slowest social night in Los Angeles, when almost nobody could say they had something else they had to attend, which, under the circumstances – Allegra hosting and all of the industry abuzz with rumors— nobody would have anyway, TOUT HAUTE HOLLYWOOD, as Allegra referred to them in her multilingual way, gathered in the Crystal Ballroom. Included as a courtesy, even though he didn't really matter was the manager of the Royale.

Not since the funeral of Harry Bell, the diminutive show business giant that had launched her, had Louise seen such an impressive array of the Great, the Near-Great, and the Would-be-Great. Allegra had pulled out all the stops, calling in friends and colleagues from all her worlds, the political, the Arts, and the just plain money. A private jet carrying contributors to spiritual charities and educators who had spent the weekend at the Southampton estate of George Soros had arrived at LAX in time to avoid the freeway jam.

"It isn't <u>tout haute Hollywood</u>,' Louise actually gasped. "It's <u>toute haute Everybody</u>."

Chet Sinclair, the once head of the studio where Rita had had her screen test, sat towards the front of the gathering, looking happily present, the rush of something actually going on in his life

superceding his need for cocaine. Those who had engineered
Louise's downfall had been too curious to send regrets, and sat
now eating hors d'oeuvres and what had been called in the old
days, when most of those in Hollywood understood Yiddish,
gedarem, which, freely translated, meant their own insides.
Congressmen and two senators who had flown in from
Washington, suspecting, as did almost everyone in Washington,
that Allegra had her finger on the pulse… of what or whom exactly
they could not be sure, … but were not confident enough to take a
chance of missing whatever it might be.

There were dowager doyennes from the fashion world, and a
very thin young man who claimed to have been the last lover of
Alexander McQueen, the real reason he had committed suicide,
rather than having felt there was nowhere left to go creatively, or
that he had been completely fulfilled by the show assembled of his
largely sado-masochistic but undeniably brilliant designs for the
Metropolitan Museum in New York. There were those who had
seen the exhibition who expressed the illuminated thought that
McQueen had had no fear of death, that death and life were the
same for him, and that was the source of his genius and certainly
his fearlessness. Many of those present who had pictures in pre-
production said he had agreed to do their costuming, because now
that he was gone it was easier to act like you had always admired
him. There was also a spike-haired redhead who'd come forward
claiming to have given Amy Winehouse a fatal dose, saying they'd
meant to make it a double suicide, but she'd fallen asleep.

It was, as Louise was to exclaim silently to herself over and
over again, an 'A' Vernaissage, a word she'd learned with some
difficulty from Allegra. They had them all the time in Paris,
Allegra had explained, saying it mean 'a launch,' of a perfume, a
car, a jewelry exhibition. In this case, the jewel was Rita.

"I am so happy to welcome you all here today for zis occasion magnifique," Allegra said from the podium. She was dressed in lavender chiffon, tight around her waist, flowing loose through the skirt so it blew softly around her, subtly orchestrated by a duo of fans. Orchids had been placed on either side of the microphone, lending an air of high-priced exotica to Allegra, which Louise could not help thinking might have been redundant. Gilding the lily, she silently said to herself, in this case gilding the orchid.

"Senti, listen!" charmingly commanded Allegra. "This is a very special day. We live in this ville where everyzing is chit-chat about ze greatest zing to come down the pike. I have always wondered where ze pike was."

A faint titter.

"I have to imagine it is somewhere between Paris Hilton and the Kardashians."

"Who?" Louise could not keep from exclaiming quite loudly, the habit of being a wise-ass too ingrained in her now to be set aside just because it was such an upscale occasion, one specifically engineered to be good for her.

"Exactamente," said Allegra. "Ze era of ze fake celebrity. Ze people famous for being famous, and personne understands why. But today I have ze privilege to present you what my friend Louise calls ze 'Real Deal.' A young woman of great beauty, mystery,,,and,,, here is ze kicker: true talent."

A gust of air from the well-placed fans blew at her skirt, so it floated around her like subtlety, giving Allegra an unaccustomedly soft look, balancing the severity of her angular cheekbones, emphasized by her hair style, pale platinum strands tightly braided in tiny rows on either side of her impressive skull. The design of her hairdo accentuated the height of her forehead, which seemed to indicate a formidable intelligence, just in case those present were unaware of what it was she had to offer besides grace, charm, and a lot of money. Her skin glowed pale pink, heavy lids with their long lashes tinted a glittering lavender to echo the color of her dress.

Looking up at her from a strategic place in the second row of the well-arranged bridge chairs, leather softened with woven threads of gold, (an additional $7.50 per chair,) Louise could not help wondering how she had had the luck to have such an impressive friend, no matter that the friendship didn't really go that deep. Never in her life, once the good part of it had started with the lie about Harry Bell, that she had been his last love, together with him the night before his death, and therefore knew how he wanted his wealth distributed, had she permitted herself to doubt herself, even though she often did. It had been that attitude, one of daring that surpassed Himalayan chutzpah, that had gotten her everywhere she wanted to be, and with everyone. Her fall from grace had come with such surprising force that she had been literally crestfallen, never imagining that once one had reached the crest she could be undone by morons, which her adversaries were, at least in her opinion. And the truth was her opinion was smarter than most people's, in her opinion.

Long ago she had paraded to prominence on the shoulders of a lie. Now she was ready for a last act that was based on the truth. Rita Adona was perfect from every angle, film-wise. Whatever she had been or done, and who her grandparents might or might not have been, was beside the point. It was what she was now and what she could be that mattered. Gorgeous. Gifted. An original, as Louise had been in her way, the way an original should be. Not like anyone seen before or likely to be seen again.

And Rita's new about-to-explode fame was not based on a lie. It was simply innuendo. Or as Sam Goldwyn might have said, Louise thought, innuendo, out the other.

"Mesdames et Monsieurs" Allegra was saying into the microphone, "I wish to present you ze plus grande vedette of tomorrow, ze belle—and en plus, she can act,-- Rita Adona."

From behind the pillar to the left of the stage, Rita appeared, clad in a low-cut Grecian style dress, draped in soft silk jersey folds across her improbably beautiful breasts, deep butterscotch skin warm against the soft white fabric, fretted with infinitesimal sparkles, so she appeared to literally shimmer, an absolute feminine deity. The whole room, larded as it was with those not easily impressed, seemed thunderstruck.

'Venus,' somebody murmured, but as with all murmurs in a society where whispers were the local currency, everybody heard.

"Bravo!" shouted an opera fan, leaping to his feet, applauding.

"ALL RIGHT!" cried a young actor, starting a wave of approving shouts and whistles and yelps and what sounded to Louise curiously like caterwauling. But all of it tumultuous, unmistakably approving.

And as though she truly had been born to the purple, Rita moved to the center of the stage and did a deep, royal curtsey, one perfect dimpled knee behind the other, dipping gracefully to the ground. Maybe, Louise could not help thinking, the circulated falsehood was true, even if it had started out a rumor. Maybe Rita was genuine Hollywood royalty. If she hadn't come by her alleged heritage honestly, she was surely going to come by it through beauty, grace, and talent. Her grandparents would have been proud of her, even if they weren't really her grandparents.

"Per favore." Rita extended a beautifully manicured, deeply tanned hand, towards Louise, fingernails silver against her skin, the same iridescent white glow as her dress. She signaled Louise up onto the dais, moved over to the short flight of steps and helped her up onto the stage.

"Mi patron," she said, a beatific smile on her face, as though she had been transformed not simply to movie actress but a Botticelli. "Mi mecenate."

"Is that what I am?" Louise said, suddenly feeling almost shy. My patron, the young woman had said. My benefactor. My friend at court. My good fairy who believes in me.

Nobody had ever looked at her with that particular combination of gratitude and affection before, not even the stars she had made into stars. Certainly not the stars who had deigned to fuck her in spite of how chubby she was because she had that smart little mouth and a lot of energy not to mention passion for the stars who deigned to fuck her, because in spite of how sophisticated she might have seemed to become, she was still a pushover, or even more accurately, a pushunder for stars.

She stepped to the microphone. "Unaccustomed as I am to public adulation," she began, "especially after I have been…" She started to say, then hesitated. "Fucked over," she thought, but stopped short of saying. Irony and bitterness didn't work in a situation where you seemed victorious. "Raised like Lazarus," she considered, but it was a little too Biblical for the room. Well, there was never anything better than Shakespeare, a reason he was still the Master, even though she had never been even vaguely tempted to go after Kenneth Branagh, who seemed to her fuller of himself than she had been at her worst.

"As Lady MacBeth might have said in her sleepwalking scene," she began, as she mimed washing her hands: "Who would have thought the old bitch had so much blood in her?" Laughs from the few not intimidated by the classics, and those who actually got the paraphrase.

"First, I want to thank you all for coming, and my incredibly tasteful and brilliant friend Allegra de Sevigny for throwing together this overpriced occasion." She paused for the applause and the wave of mild laughter that was forthcoming.

"Then I would like to thank Chet Sinclair and his studio-" she phrased it like that, deliberately, so he was practically the head of it once again, in his own mind, certainly, "for making it possible for all of us to see once again that there's no real substitute for talent." It had to seem she was talking about him as well as Rita, a confusion that could only ensure his supporting what was to come next.

She had planned it so carefully in her own mind once she had been present for the triumph of Rita's screen test that she wondered if it hadn't been designed by the universe, that the idea itself might have existed all along in the mind of the movie gods. "As you must have heard by now, the reverberations having wakened even those interred at Forest Lawn, my new client Rita Adona..." a bow of the head, a pause for applause, "has knocked the socks off everybody, with her beauty and talent."

"So Chet has come up with the inspired idea of starring her in a new remake of Eugene O'Neill's 'Desire Under the Elms.'" Applause, applause. Chet looked absolutely delighted at having had such a bright idea as well as a little astonished.

"As I'm sure you all remember, being such fans of classic American tragedy..." Pause for titters. "the play is about an older man, a New England farmer... We haven't cast him yet, but as we know most of our greatest talent in spite of all the plastic surgeons in Southern California is getting older, from Di Niro to Al... a widower who has left his farm to go off to find a new bride. In our version, she will be a mail-order bride, from another country. In this case, Italy. She is to be played by the lustrous Rita Adona.

"The tragedy occurs when the bride falls in love with the man's son. And who will be playing him is my other new client... "Wait for it."

"Tyler McKay."

Now gasps. Chokes from those at the agency that had dumped her. Many purple faces. But, to Louise's regret, no actual heart attacks as the curtain opened to show the beautiful boy she had shanghaied from inside the recesses of the Hotel Royale.

Holy shit, Batman! I had heard that she was conniving, and it was obvious that she was clever. But talk about a coup!

CHAPTER FIVE

F. Scott Fitzgerald was one of Hendrik Bos's favorite writers. Hendrik could read in several languages and was fluent not just in comprehension but enjoyment. Still, the favorite Fitzgerald quote for Hendrik was not one the young romantic had written himself, but one he said, to Hemingway: "The rich are different from you and me," to which tough Ernest had replied: "Yes, they have more money."

Hendrik didn't think so. He considered the difference to be that the rich were so admired by those who wanted to be rich, they were above suspicion, at least to those who admired them. That was what made them different from you and me, though not so different from Hendrik, who so enjoyed the idea of being above suspicion it made him want to do something that in ordinary people would have excited suspicion. So it was that he had been able to skim many millions in Guilders and Deutschmarks when there were still Guilders and Deutschmarks and Euros once they were Euros, from the great pile that belonged to the company for which he was CFO. That he didn't really need the money was beside the point. It was being able to take it with no consequences,

and no one's being smart enough to see what he was up to, that he
found so amusing.

He was not a cruel man, but he had great contempt for
stupidity. People were so eager to accrue wealth they latched on to
anyone who made it appear easy, showed off, and seemed not that
impressive except with the amount of money they threw around.
So it was that Ponzi artists(schemers they were, more accurately,
but there was a certain artistry to how they triumphed) like Bernie
Madoff reeled in their fish.

Hendrik was a lot more subtle. He had risen quite honestly and
naturally within the orthodox walls of his banking firm, becoming
at a decent age—his early forties—the Chief Financial Officer.

When he'd first met Karen, she was in Paris, suffering from
depression. As he was a businessman, a banker, he had always
considered depression a financial term, as he thought there was
little that could not be fixed if you had enough money. That she
was famous, still beautiful, and not in economic distress, but
seemed sad, a listlessness to her noted carriage, was fascinating to
him. He had had experience with American movie actors only
once, when he was a teenager, and an uncle in finance, noting his
cleverness and winning looks, marking his potential, had
bankrolled him to a season in Hong Kong, so he could study
capitalism at its exotic peak. Literally. The Peak was the place atop
Hong Kong where the very richest of bankers, merchants,
entrepreneurs, ex- pats and exploiters lived.

While Hendrik was there, Mike Todd had been in flamboyant
residence, making 'Around the World in 80 Days.' Hendrik had
carefully observed him, the most colorful of the high-risk players
in the motion picture business, a man who lived beyond his means
but still managed to be supported by everyone who knew he was
living beyond his means. Even more impressive, he had captured

the heart and apparently the inner thighs and what lay between of the dazzling young Elizabeth Taylor.

"He had to give her a jewel before she would go out with him," said a young actress working on the movie, at the bar of the Peninsula, where foreign bankers, mostly Brits, gathered as a rule when the sun went down, which they could hardly wait for. "Shirley MacLaine told me he asked her to arrange for him to have a date with Elizabeth, but first she told Shirley he had to send a jewel. I mean, I guess you can get away with that if you look like Elizabeth Taylor."

"You're as beautiful as she is," Hendrik said, being eighteen and wanting desperately to lose his virginity, knowing better than to risk it in the brothels of Hong Kong, which were everywhere, and where disease was undoubtedly rampant. It was still a time, and certainly an area, where men went mad from syphilis, improperly treated. Hendrik wanted nothing so much as never to go mad. Not even sex.

"You're just saying that," said the young actress, who, when asked what she did, always said she was a starlet, the term not yet having fallen into ridicule. When the movie business was just getting started in Hollywood early in the 20th century, every call girl picked up by the police gave her occupation as 'actress.' So it was that a legitimate talent like Mabel Normand, the first great screen comedienne, when called to give testimony in the investigation of the murder of director William Desmond Taylor, asked her occupation, rather than have people think she was a whore, had answered "Motion Pictures."

'Starlet' had evolved through the likes of Mari Blanchard, the sloe-eyed blonde temptress/inamorata of Turhan Bey in 'Son of Sinbad,' in real life as well as reel life till he lost his hair at an early age, and with it his career and Mari Blanchard. So it was a while before 'starlet' as a term became something of which a young woman could be proud, as it was now with her sitting on a barstool, her very fine legs showing all the way to her silk underpants, and driving young Hendrik crazy.

"I am sincere," said Hendrik. "You are as beautiful as she. It is my only regret that I cannot yet afford to give you a jewel."

"But you're in banking, right?"

"Ja."

"So one day you'll be able to buy all the jewels you want, I'm sure."

"I hope so."

"We'll have to keep in touch," she said.

At any rate, they did that evening.

He had been married in his late twenties, to a high-born Austrian, daughter of an officer of Deutsche Bank, whose motto was 'Passion to Perform.' That certainly did not seem to carry over for her into their bedroom. But Hendrik did not imagine his great romance would be about anything but money.

So late in life, with his young sons grown, and his wife, who had skied in Gstaad with the American author Irwin Shaw, much admired by Hendrik, an avid reader, and also with Leon Uris, not so high on his preferred list, in Verbier, gone off with a ski instructor a little younger than his sons, he met Karen. He was astounded by the depth of his feeling for her. She was, in spite of her age, quite open, childlike, very much the little girl he had never had, and, as it turned out, really wanted. His wife had had an assertive independence, a strength of resolve about even unimportant matters. So to meet this seemingly sophisticated woman, who'd had the attention of the world, and find in her a patent innocence, a naivete, a heart that was so obviously seeking, shook him to his stodgy foundations. She needed him so much, he was almost sorry he had pocketed so much of other people's cash, because he would have liked to be as artless as she was, as candid. But of course he could not go back and undo the wrong of what he had done, particularly since he'd never been caught.

They'd married in France, at the home of Anne D'Ornano, the elegant Mairie of Deauville, a close friend, who'd performed the ceremony. Their life together was what he thought he would be able to characterize as 'one long honeymoon,' except there was the unfortunate business of the auditor. Before Hendrik could be formally charged, he'd left the country, for places unknown, even to Karen, who'd pledged that she would love him regardless. And she had.

Now she waited at the Hotel Royale for the call, the letter, whatever it would be that would inform her that he was on his way back to her. When the phone rang, she could actually feel her heart racing.

"Hello?" she said into the receiver, with an ingenue's breathlessness. That about her had never changed, her voice. It was throaty and low, filled with hints of adventures she'd had that in anyone else would have made them jaded, but somehow had never transformed her from the candid, easily moved woman she was, open to anything, still hoping for most of it.

"It's only me, oh, Olivia," Olivia said.

"How are you?" Karen said, resisting the temptation to retaliate with the annoyance her daughter always managed to incite in her, and seemed intent on continuing.

"Well, how could I be?" she said.

"A drag," Karen was moved to say, but stopped herself, swallowing the unspoken words. All the world still accepting the Freudian myth that it was Oedipal, that girls were in love with their fathers, when the truth, as she had perceived it, was that they really adored their mothers, and were so angry about it they spent most of their lives confronting them. Trying to prove they weren't mired in competition, aching to show they were a better man than their mom. Caught in anger issues, fearing abandonment, and so, in Olivia's case, bringing it about. Wanting Karen to love her so badly she drove her away. "What's going on?" she managed, trying to work up interest in this abrasive little girl who by now should have been a woman.

"We have to meet with the lawyers," she said. "I'm using Daddy's."

"Your father didn't have that sharp an attorney," Karen said. "I'd be glad to give you mine."

"Nothing Daddy ever did was good enough for you."

"Please, Olivia. I'm trying to be helpful. Your father was not a great businessman. He was a fine human being, but he was too trusting."

"I miss him," Olivia said, and started to cry.

"I miss him, too. But it's been a really long time."

"Well, you couldn't have missed him that much or you wouldn't have married that crooked Dutchman."

"I have to go now," Karen said, bristling.

"I have to go now," Olivia mocked. "That's all you've said to me my whole life long. You could have made a recording."

"I had a career. I had a family to support."

"Daddy would have supported us."

"Daddy couldn't support us. He wanted to, but he couldn't." Those had been difficult years, much as she'd loved him. Hollywood as an idea, not simply a place, did not forgive a couple where the woman was more successful than the man. It was before the time it was all right for the woman to be the bigger earner. Karen wondered if it was really all right now, if that much had really changed. Doors had been closed to him, rather than opened because of his connection to her. There was a palpable contempt for him at his being married to someone doing better than he was, a star. He was always "her husband."

"He did the best he could," said Olivia.

"As we all do," Karen said, her emotional rope fraying. "I'm doing the best I can right now. I'm doing all I can not to hang up on you."

"I'll save you the trouble," said Olivia, and hung up.

Karen stared at the phone, exhausted. Where did it come from, this struggle of mother and daughter? She had loved her own mother almost to distraction, so focused on that languid, strangely silent woman she had moved around and behind her like a literal shadow, straining for her light. She truly believed her mother had loved her in return. And she <u>had</u> loved Karen, Karen was sure of it. But not enough to keep the razor away from her throat.

The phone rang again. It was unlike Olivia to apologize. But she had to feel frightened, isolated, no one on her side except that dolt of an attorney. Forgiveness washed over Karen, and she picked up the phone.

"I'm sorry, too," she said, into the receiver.

"But for what, Liefde?" said Hendrik.

"My darling," said Karen. "Where are you?"

"Dubai."

Just as Louise said that everything in Rita's life seemed to have led up to this moment that was about to be hers in Hollywood, Louise could not help thinking her whole life, long as it was and filled with its seeming triumphs and disappointments, had been leading up to this, too. Everything appeared to have been preparation. If you lived long enough, your moment came, even if you thought you had had it already.

Much as she thought, and other people considered, that she had had a full plate, career and connection-wise, she could now review all the pitfalls and heartbreaks and see them as groundwork for this day. Signals and signs she had never realized were there were lining up like sentinels, leading to what would be her greatest victory. She was absolutely convinced of it. If what Rita believed about what Oprah said was even a little bit true, that if you believed something strongly enough, you could make it happen, and that all these things were happening with so little effort from her, made her ultimate victory inevitable.

And she had thought so much of her life was a waste of time. You just never knew. Even now as she reviewed the part of it that had been totally ignored by Vanity Fair as not fascinating enough for their readership, she realized that much of it was simply the scaffolding, the structure that would help her get to the ceiling of the Sistine Chapel, like Michaelangelo, so she could lie on her back (for reasons other than the usual one) and create her masterpiece.

To begin with, there had been love, as there had to be with every woman no matter how tough she might have wanted to be, and had ultimately become. Her first great passion—and he was— had been Andre, with his affected ways and his air of cosmopolitan nonchalance, complete with statuary and gilded portraits of Napoleon, whom he resembled, certainly in attitude even if he was a little taller. She had bought completely into his fantasy about himself and accepted everything, his self-absorption, his grandiosity, until he had brought another woman into their bed, and made her feel like a whore. It was after that she had moved to Hollywood, her Harry Bell fiction paving the way.

At her first big Hollywood party, she had met the young Anthony Perkins, first in line, everybody said, to replace the recently, tragically lost James Dean. Tony was gangling in a beautifully boyish way, his chocolate eyes with a slight cast to them. A sexually knowledgeable friend of hers said that meant a man would be a great lover. Louise didn't want to be pushy as well as plump.

So she didn't try to get too close to him too quickly. But she was very drawn to his playfulness. She had never had a boyfriend in high school, ("Because you're fat," her mother had said. "Youth is beauty. Fat is old. What would a young boy want with someone old?") Though she had let Andre hurt her heart in her first foray into what she'd thought was the real world, she was up for becoming younger again, playing the beginner, seeming actually inexperienced, because the truth was, except for that unfortunate alliance with Andre, and the exaggerated fantasy one with Harry Bell, she was.

Tony had a bizarre air of innocence, like an actual little boy. Skittish he seemed, even as the party stirred around him, conscious of his being a potential big name in the absence of any of the promised attendees who were already arrived, in the Photoplay magazine sense.

"Rice pudding," Tony said, his eyes not looking directly at her, but the only pair at the party not looking for Marlon Brando, either, the rumor having buzzed around town that that hot young, lean, powerfully animal actor would be coming. It was the heyday of the Actor's Studio, and Brando was their hood ornament, a new beginning in the way leading men in movies were to be perceived. "In Egypt you cannot tell if they are flies or raisins."

"Huh?" Louise asked into the garden darkness.

"What movie is that from?" asked Tony.

"I haven't any idea."

"Well, you're smart. I can see that at a veritable glance. Find out and I'll take you to dinner. Tell me who said it, you'll even get dessert."

He spoke to the leftover adolescent in her, the one who was experiencing sexual feelings, but wasn't yet ready to act them out, and wanted to feel safe with the boy of her dreams. Which he was, no doubt about it, as he was soon to become the boy of many adolescent dreams, his picture scotch-taped to the inside of thousands of high school lockers.

She was back in that mental place where a "good girl" didn't do it till "after." It was a mindset that was soon to vanish from the vicinity and the culture, but it played out very well on Horn Avenue, the little street where she found out he lived, actually following his car one day up Sunset, turning right when he did, seeing where he'd pulled in, and driving very quickly by, ducking her head like a character in a Raymond Chandler story, but not one of the sexy ones.

"Rice pudding," she repeated to everyone she knew to try and find the answer. It was the pre-Google era, when in order to get information you had to know at least a little something. Nobody knew. So when the telephone had rung in her tiny studio at the Park Sunset in Hollywood, where Harry Bell's attorney was staking her to rent money till she connected, prior to their settling the estate, she felt giddy with apprehension, guessing it was Tony.

"Did you find out?"

"No. But I really tried." For a moment she held her breath, literally held it, fearful that her failure would make him lose interest. He was really interested, wasn't he?

"'Five Graves to Cairo,'" Tony said. "How can you imagine you could make a career in Hollywood when you don't know things like that? It was Erich von Stroheim who said it."

"I'm sorry I didn't know."

"How sorry are you?"

"Really sorry."

"Really and truly sorry?"

"With whipped cream and cherries on top."

"Well in that case, I'll take you to breakfast. Meet me at Googie's," he instructed, citing the place where the young hopefuls met, newly arrived in Hollywood to carpe if not the diem, to seize the dream. It was a cheesy Deco coffee shop on the Sunset Strip, with starry sprinkles embedded in the marbleized counters, and red leatherette booths, where everybody went, because Jimmy Dean had liked it and his ghost might still be hanging around. Maila Nurmi, who played Vampira on television, introducing old horror movies for a local network, had contacted Jimmy on the other side, she told her intimates, almost everybody weird in town who needed a place to hang out that wasn't Schwab's Drugstore. According to her, Jimmy had reported he wasn't quite prepared to leave the planet so quickly. It had all happened so fast, his spirit still needed someplace to go on the earth plane and try and figure out what had happened to him, so he was regularly visiting Googie's. Maila also told Louise that Tony Perkins had been at her house when a picture of Jimmy she had on the wall came way from its nail and fluttered down on Tony. It turned out to have left the wall at the exact moment of the fatal car crash, she narrated eerily, her kohl painted eyes narrowing to even further obscure the opalescent blue that had made producer Hal Wallis proclaim when she was twenty that she was meant to be in movies, until he spent a little more time with her. So it was past being simply a sign: it was metaphysical fact that Tony was meant to inherit the kingdom Jimmy had left unattended, along with some unintelligible dialogue for the soundtrack of 'Giant' which there hadn't been time for him to re-dub before his death.

Of course Louise didn't buy into any of that West Coast spiritual crap, but it was still fascinating, as Tony was. His attractiveness increased exponentially as he began to be announced for a major role in almost every important picture his studio was making, they put so much stock in him, were that convinced he was going to become a big name. And there was an original audacity even in that: 'Perkins.' It was such an unlikely moniker for a movie star, in a land that had belonged to the Gables and the Powers, and even, for a darkly brilliantined moment, Matures.

Now she had seen Tony on the screen, genuinely touching in his debut in Friendly Persuasion. In a <u>movie</u>, everything became more impressive than it really might have been. Still, even without that overlay of celluloid wizardry, he was appealing. So appealing, Louise felt privileged to be holding his hand, which was the most they did, and that but rarely. Still, it had been the beginning of what she was simple and starstruck enough to consider their romance.

After the pseudo-sophistication and the pain of Andre, it was fun to play with Tony like a child, which she seemed to be doing. They went up to hilltops and flew model airplanes he had made from the backs of cereal boxes, and put adversaries in them when they crashed, columnists who had knocked him, people who had been unkind about her, made fun of their relationship, which she was convinced they were having. It was all very teenager-y, a period she hadn't really experienced fully, she had been so self-conscious, so sure nobody would ever love her. And now he seemed to, at least in the way she tried to view him: the Boy Next

Door, Tom Drake to her not really that talented but yearning Judy Garland.

Once she had moved into her own apartment—not that far from his-- he would call her every morning at four A.M. and say "What's for breakfast?" She would jump out of bed and make him popovers that were better than his mothers', he told her all the time, and strawberry jam from scratch. Her kitchen ceiling was splattered with red from the morning the fruit had exploded. It seemed to her like remembered attention from him, souvenirs of visits with him, so it warmed her rather than irritated, looking up and seeing the comical trail of her culinary disaster, proof, in a way, that he really cared. At least she hoped so.

Every day he would leave for the studio after breakfast, and say he would call her at ten. She would wait all day for the call that never came, not even going to the bathroom, for fear she wouldn't hear the phone, and her extension cord didn't stretch that far. But he did, on occasion, take her to the movies, and once, even to a premiere.

"Well, he's obviously crazy about you," her mother said on the phone. "I read in Sidney Skolsky that he took you to an opening." Skolsky had called them 'the odd couple' in print, and now, standing beside Tony, so long and lean and lank, with her so short and round, she could understand what he meant, as hurtful as it felt.

"But he's never even kissed me," Louise said.

"That's because you're fat," said her mother. "He obviously enjoys your company. Imagine what would happen if you became more and more beautiful before his very eyes. You would be irresistible."

So she went on another of what had been a lifetime's worth of crash diets, and checked his very eyes to note if the expression in them had changed into one of longing. It hadn't. But one day he held his hands in front of those eyes, and made them into circles so he could peer at her as though through a lens. "You ought to be in pictures," he said.

"I never wanted to be an actress."

"You can just be yourself. Sharp. Colorful. They're making Marjorie Morningstar at Warner's. You can play Marjorie's friend Marcia Zelenko. A smart New York Jewish girl. It's veritable type casting. I'll call Tab and ask him to set up the audition.'

Tab was Tab Hunter, the teenage blond heart-throb and Tony's good friend. She had met him a number of times with Tony and thought him pleasant but a little slow, and wondered what someone as bright as Tony found in him as a friend.

"You think he's a little slow?" said Kranko, an acerbic set designer who hung out at Googie's. "What about you?"

"I don't understand," Louise said.

"I'll say," said Kranko.

It was the end of the Fifties, when the biggest male stars were those with the least plausible names, Rock and Tab and for a few moments, Troy. All of them in the stable of agent Henry Willson. He was sitting at the next table at Ciro's when Louise went there with Jolie Gabor, Zsa Zsa's mother, who thought Louise might make her a star, since Louise was planning on becoming an agent.

"I'll have a Screwdriver," Jolie told the waiter at the top of her quavery Hungarian voice. "And a truck driver for Mr. Willson."

It was also the time when 'gay' was enough to abort a man's career, particularly if he was a romantic lead. So everyone with male image to preserve was in the closet. Louise would wait for Tony to come at the end of the day to visit her as he'd promised her that morning at breakfast he would, and went to sleep without having heard from him, deeply disappointed, angrily frustrated, borderline enraged. Then the phone would ring, waking her. She'd wakened from a restless sleep, hoping it was Tony.

"He's at the beach with Tab," Kranko said.

"Shut up, shut up, shut up!" she would scream, and hang up the phone.

She refused to believe it. All the same, one night when he called with that disturbing alert, she got out of bed, dressed, and went to Tony's apartment. She felt around his garage in the darkness. It was empty. She could feel the heat on her face, rage reddening her cheeks, as she vowed never to speak to him again, went home and anaesthetized herself with Miltown, the tranquilizer of choice of the day.

When he called the next morning at four, saying "What's for breakfast?"--she picked up the phone but did not speak, sticking to her oath.

"You know... sometimes," he said, hearing her breathing, "I park my T-bird on the street, just to confuse you." It was as though he had been spying on her, tracking her tracking him, watching her fumbling for him in the darkness. That's how canny he was. And how desperate she was. Having returned to the time of life that hadn't worked at all for her—"Nobody knows what it means to be unhappy unless they weighed 182 pounds in high school," the great actress Maureen Stapleton had told her—and although Louise wasn't quite that heavy, there was no doubt she had been fat, as her mother kept reminding her.

"I need to know," she said to Tony when he came to breakfast that morning, having found out from a family friend of his that the popovers that he said were better than his mother's was a particularly interesting observation since his mother had never cooked. The widow of the once honored actor Osgood Perkins, who'd played a gangster in the 1932 Howard Hawks' production

of 'Scarface,' she was apparently a very cold, distant woman.
"How do you feel about me?"

'I care for you as much as I have ever cared for any woman,'
Tony said, with what she later realized was great honesty that she
didn't quite comprehend at the time. "We will drink from the same
cup. We will be like Katherine Cornell and Guthrie McClintock."

She didn't know that much about backstage Broadway gossip
either.

So they became what Skolsky wrote in his column with
perceptible rancor, "like the Trylon and Perisphere," symbols of
the 1939 World's Fair. Skolsky had his own axe to grind, since he
had written a movie script he wanted Tony to do and Tony turned
it down. The columnist also had an actress daughter Louise's age
who should have been dating Tony and getting all the publicity.
Together they put Sidney Skolsky in one of the model airplanes
Tony had cut from a cereal box, and rejoiced as it crashed.

By this time she had taken her Rolodex to a friend from New
York who had just started his own talent agency, and joined him.
And Tony became her client.

It was obviously not really what she wanted from him. But she
had begun to understand and accept that what she wanted from him
would never be forthcoming.

They never really spoke about his secret reality. Except once
she commented on his obvious morality, and he said, almost
angrily, "I am about as moral as Ilse Koch." She never asked him
what that meant, because she was afraid that, for once, he might
actually tell her.

But it all became beside the point. Around that time she
started being invited to important parties where the big stars were,
and she would go up to one of them and say quite audibly, so
everyone around could hear how liberated she was, "Lulu wants to

fuck." They would be at once so shocked and so charmed that they would usually accede to the request/demand, because nobody talked like that except seventeen-year-old Dennis Hopper, and everybody knew what trouble he was and that his career would probably go nowhere.

So she represented Tony, took pride in his becoming a star, along with a percentage. And she watched from a less anguished place as he publicly courted his co-stars, arranged publicity by his studio. Knowing better, at last, than to be jealous of the women he acted with, she still had a hard time when he made <u>Desire Under the Elms</u> with Sophia Loren. Even if Louise lost all the weight and had her ribs removed, she would never look that good. It was hard not to be envious of her out of principle.

"It isn't just her beautiful breasts, and that incredible face," said Dorothy Jeakins, the costume designer on the movie. "It's the unexpected delicacy of her rib cage."

Louise suspected that Dorothy was infatuated with Tony, too. But of course, neither of them had to worry about losing him to Sophia.

She watched with a faint sense of personal loss his leaving behind the romantic young leading man he'd been to become the eccentric caricature that was Norman Bates in <u>Psycho</u>, the role that was unfortunately to define the rest of his acting life. He'd morphed himself from handsome young leading man into gangly weirdo, having decided that his very broad shoulders, which she'd always considered magnificent, were too big for his head. So he'd dieted into what he imagined was correct proportion, losing what had been in him, at their first early encounter, great male beauty. And she'd watched with a kind of happiness his marrying the gifted photographer Berry Berenson, and his pride in their two sons. Her heart had ached for all of them when he died of AIDS.

Three years later, on the anniversary of his death, as if there were some improbable, terrible curse, Berry had been in the first plane to crash into the World Trade Center, on September 11.

But now, in a happy way, it seemed all to be coming full circle. Tyler McKay reminded Louise to no small degree of the young, just beginning, deeply appealing young Tony, with so many talents that had in Tony remained mostly unexpressed. Musical gifts, latent in Tony, who had only noodled on the piano, were explosive in young McKay. He had the matching ability to engage, to completely charm. Golden curls that hugged his skull like a sculptor's embrace. The same dark brown eyes, except that Tyler's didn't dart about as Tony's had, since he had nothing to hide. At least as far as Louise could tell.

She felt absolutely joyful at the prospect of a re-beginning. The Buddhists, (a few of whom she'd actually represented for films, in between their spiritual conversions) said 'You couldn't step into the same water of a river twice." But maybe you could if you really knew how to keep swimming.

Full circle. At least as full as a circle could get, it seemed to Louise now as she waited for Rita in the lobby of the Royale. The Fates. History. Imagination. Lies. Everything that went into making things work in this most improbable town, and this most improbable business that had caught the heartbeat of the world.

"They've finished termiting my house," she said now to the manager of the Royale. "They're just waiting for the fumes to clear, and then we'll be moving back in."

"We?" asked Riccioni.

"I'm taking Rita and Tyler home with me."

"Of course you are," he said.

"I mean, what's the point of having a house in Bel-Air if you can't offer hospitality to your friends. Especially when they're the great superstars of tomorrow."

"No point at all that I can see," Riccioni said.

"But it's been surprisingly pleasant staying with you. I shall recommend the place to all my friends in future."

"All of them?" he said.

"Well, the ones who aren't dead," said Louise. "And the ones I haven't made yet, but will now in the blink of an elephant's eye. Nothing succeeds like success."

"I'd heard that," he said. "I'd also heard that nothing exceeds like excess."

"I suppose you're talking about Bunyan," said Louise. "Keep an eye on him for me, won't you?"

I shall be genuinely sorry to see them go. In the annals of opportunism and manipulation, the lifeblood of this vampirical village, I have never seen anyone that heavy so fast on her feet, which somehow she manages to keep out of her mouth. Of course I shall be sorry not to see how this plays out, though I suspect fiendishly clever as Felder is, she will have most of it on the airwaves 'ere the cock crows thrice. So we will all get to see what happens, although from a distance, or TMZ, or the less than nuanced words of Annie Charm, that most un-aptly named of all the TV commentators who command a large audience by being more obnoxious than the people they are dissing. Felder understands it all, that much is clear. The Bullshit, the 'authenticity,' the latest buzzword of a hypocritical society struggling to pretend it is sincere.

Sad am I, as Jerome wrote when doing his own lyrics for 'Yesterdays', that Samson is not here to watch any and all of this. What a good time he would be having. Though glad am I (second line) that I am not so low as to put a bug in Felder's phone as You Know Who would be doing to hack in on the coming events, before they go on Diversion Tonight. But oh, to be a fly on her wall.

CHAPTER SIX

ANNIE CHARM AWOKE ready to put her teeth in. She did not have false teeth, but sometimes when she first opened her eyes in the morning with a feeling of unexpected happiness at just being alive, she had to fight the impulse to be benign. It was her bite, her refusal to let anyone get away with anything, even those that thought they were loved, that had made Annie the much watched and often revered harridan she was. People in her native land just loved her. She'd been born in Texas, though fact checkers at a rival network tried to find out if she wasn't really a foreigner, a verbal terrorist from a government hostile to the U.S., simply affecting a Texas accent. But much as they struggled, they could find no trace of anything alien. She was truly American. Corn-fed, and oozing oil from every pore.

What would have seemed antagonistic and moronic in a man who had strong opinions without much education or insight to pin them on, in a woman to many seemed brave and almost true. With the hard times that had come, the country seemed now to be living for bad news about those they considered lucky. And if there was one thing Annie Charm could provide, it was bad news.

She had a staff of sixteen armed with the mental equivalent of trowels, ready to march like an Army of Crusaders for the Christian cause, or, in her case, the un-Christian one, absent pity, absent mercy, and totally absent forgiveness. They could go back, if necessary, like archeologists of the unacceptable, and find out what were becoming known as 'factoids,' little pieces of information designed if not to kill, certainly to maim, from someone's early life. The earlier, the better. If she had been able to ascertain that Tyler McKay had had a hidden secret, like a Mongoloid baby brother, she would have oh, so reluctantly brought it to the surface. The surface of the surface was her favorite place, somewhere scaly without softness, preferably with pimples that could be coaxed or irritated into a boil. It was she who had first put film on the airwaves of the hapless baby Trig, the "challenged," as people tried to soften it, son of Sarah Palin, carried everywhere during the previous presidential campaign like a small sack of laundry.

But oh, Heavens be praised, Annie could find out not a single bad thing about Tyler. She had spent time on the phone with his mother, Belinda, a gentle woman of seemingly endless patience and kindness, about whom she couldn't unearth anything terrible either. That woman, according to Annie's fact-finding team, was exactly what she seemed: small-town, religious, with an openly expressed love of God. Her only liability was that she actually watched commentators like Annie Charm, though she was quick to tell Annie there wasn't anyone really like her, and that she was thrilled to get her call. Nor would she explain or defend her decision to let Tyler be handled—though Annie suggested strongly, as a matter of fact came right out and said, which was her way, that the boy would instead be manhandled—by Louise Felder.

"She's a predator," said Annie. "A true gentlewoman like yourself has no experience with someone like that." She stopped herself from adding the words on her tongue, that Louise would eat him for breakfast. It would be a little too vivid for a prairie flower like Belinda.

"You're wrong," said Mrs. McKay. "She's a lovely woman. She won't be a bad influence at all. And Tyler is a very strong young man. He may seem like the baby he was only a few years ago, but his spine has grown along with him."

"As for Miss Felder, she flew up here especially to see me, in Mr. Chet Sinclair's private jet. They served me lunch on the plane. One of Wolfgang Puck—don't you just love that name?—one of his personal protégées cooked the meal right there on board. It was as fine a meal as I've ever had. Not that I've eaten in that many fancy places, certainly none as fancy as that plane. Foie gras, if you can imagine. I never knew liver could taste that smooth! With a star fruit sauce! Star fruit! All the way from Bali, Indonesia, but Chef said that was the only thing right for me, because my son is such a star."

The words were pouring out of her so fast with such enthusiasm it was all Annie could do to take them all in, which she really hated to do, controlling her impulse to interrupt, which was her way when she had a point to make. But she understood that before you burst someone's balloon you had to let them blow it all the way up.

"Louise, which she ast me right off to call her, answered absolutely every single one of my questions. Where he would be living, right in her house, so she personally could make sure everything was fine all the time. Gave me the number and address of her personal Blackberry so I could reach her night or day. Night or day, that's what she said."

"You let yourself be seduced by a private plane and Wolfgang Puck?" Annie's disbelief, bordering on outrage, both at Louise's having been that clever and obvious, and Belinda's being that easy, temporarily trumped what little she had in her of subtlety.

"Oh, don't say that," Belinda said. "Don't even think it. I never been seduced. Tyler's daddy and me were sweethearts since we were ten, and we were married by our minister in the family church. The one where Tyler sang in the choir."

"I didn't mean it like that," Annie said. "I know your whole family is above reproach." Of course her investigators were still checking on an uncle said to have gone to jail. "But aren't you the least bit worried?"

"My Tyler is a good boy. God is watching over him. And cousin Chester is going down there to stay. In the same house. Louise invited him."

"Why don't you go?"

"Tyler gets a little nervous when I… what's the word? Hover. He says sometimes I'm like a helicopter. He's clever like that. It isn't just the music. He's got the words, too. Songs come out of him like little angels sliding off his tongue."

"Well, if I were you, I'd get down there and hover," Annie said. "Don't you remember what happened to River Phoenix?"

"Who?" said Mrs. McKay.

"The beautiful boy who O.D'ed at the Viper Room, on the Strip?"

"O.Ded?" Belinda repeated.

"Overdosed."

"And what's that Viper Room?"

"It's a nightclub."

"Where they do striptease?"

"No. I'm sorry. Excuse me. It's <u>on</u> the Sunset <u>Strip</u>. Sunset Boulevard. It used to be owned by Johnny Depp."

"We don't know those people. And Tyler won't use drugs, you can be sure."

"Well, even though you may not remember River, he was almost as beautiful a boy as Tyler, though nobody is really, and certainly not as gifted. But River said, and I quote, " And here Annie paused to read a quote from Wikipedia, one of her best sources, "I've kept my ego and my happiness completely separate from my work. in fact, if I see my face on the cover of a magazine I go into remission. I shut myself out and freak." And then he died from snorting heroin."

"My son doesn't 'snort,'" said Belinda. "My son understands that his gifts are from God. He's a young gentleman."

Her minister had counseled Belinda not to talk to the press. But in her mind Annie Charm was not the press, but almost a personal friend, an absolute presence in her life, one that riveted Belinda every weekday afternoon. Whenever there was a missing child, or God forbid, a dead one, Annie was right there on the spot, like a good-looking bloodhound, never resting till, as she put it, she "nailed the perp."

It was her firm conviction, based on what she'd been able to uncover about Louise's past, that Louise was as guilty as anyone who'd ever committed an actual crime. The whole story of Louise's involvement with that old man Harry Bell when she was just a young woman herself was disgusting, and showed what she was willing to do even at an early age to get ahead. That such sweet innocence as Tyler McKay should fall into such tough and sophisticated hands made Annie sick to her very soul, which in spite of what her many enemies said, she knew she had.

But not so Louise Felder. There was a soul-less woman if ever God created one, though obviously God had nothing to do with it. The Devil Incarnate, she was sure. What she would have to do is get something concrete on the woman. That's what her industrious little staff was for. Nobody was completely without sin, except maybe herself and Michelle Bachman.

The whole idea of a movie of making a movie of 'Desire Under the Elms' seemed a flash of class in 1957, when the studio was busily trying to make a romantic leading man out of Anthony Perkins. To put him onto celluloid against the palpable sexuality of Sophia Loren had seemed the solution to his failure to emerge onscreen with any chemistry as a young lover.

That he instead was all but devoured by her lush femininity was unfortunate to say the least. Louise was determined to make sure the same thing would not happen to Tyler, in the shapely arms of Rita Adona. It could turn out to be even trickier, as Perkins had been twenty-five, at least the right age to play Eben, the resentful son of Ephraim Cabot, the old farmer who brings home a young wife, with whom Eben, against his will, falls passionately in love.

At the time, they had changed the name of the character of Abbie, the wife, into 'Anna,' so it would make more sense her being played by a luscious Italian. That part of the script would also work in the update for Rita. Young as she was, her potent sexuality, visible in the screen test, made her ageless in the best possible way: simply a hot young woman in full blossom.

The original screenwriter, Irwin Shaw, had to some degree rid the screenplay of the "A-yehs" and 'purty's and 'mebbe's. So even though it was still New England it hadn't seemed that heavy-handed that Anna had come to America and married the old widower, hoping to make her own home.

In a very strong way, Louise considered it past poignant that what was in the script was a carry-over into life, as far as her new client was concerned. "A home's got to have a woman," O'Neill had had the old widower say in his play, bringing home his new young wife. But "a woman's got to have a home," the wife had observed. It was clear to Louise that even more than wanting to be a movie star, Rita wanted to belong somewhere.

Everyone needed to belong somewhere. It riled Louise that in a corner of her famously important being, even when the entire Hollywood 'A' list had dined at her table, she had never felt completely at home. Her success was such fulfillment of a fantasy, quite literally beyond her wildest dreams, that she sometimes had the eerie feeling she was on a stage set that at any moment might be struck. When she read the script and Abbie, now Anna, spoke of wanting a 'hum', it resonated with Louise more than she would have thought possible. All the houses she had been able to buy and gut and restore and improve, adding screening rooms and picnic areas by pools she never had real interest in swimming in, complete with terraced levels and tiny waterfalls churning over designer rocks, all the master suites in which she had bedded those she had once gasped to see onscreen, having to restrain herself from exclaiming their names aloud when she opened her eyes and saw who was pumping away at her, none of that had served to make her feel truly connected to where or what she was. Or safe.

She had imagined that success would bring about a genuine sense of security, emotional relaxation. But show business had turned out to be a dangerous frontier where you couldn't ever let yourself fall comfortably asleep. And she had. Smart as she was, clever as everyone acknowledged her to be, she had still let the

Apaches or the Cherokees or whoever the Fuck they were, creep into her tent and scalp her. To her recollected horror, she had actually <u>invited</u> them in, peppering the agency with bright young people who then got together to move her out. Scalped by her own petard.

But now she was ready to put the top of her head back on. The only problem—she couldn't see one coming with Rita-- would be to make sure Tyler had better luck than Tony, with the way he came across onscreen up against Rita's visible carnality. All the harder, because he was only nineteen, and to the best of her knowledge, had never had a real romance in life. For all the girls that screamed and reached for him during his performances, between the security guards and his own highly principled, religious persona, he appeared never to have been touched. Inarguably handsome as he was, with the fine jaw, tall frame, and broad shoulders that sang to Louise of Tony before he'd sabotaged himself by getting too thin, she worried about what could be perceived in Tyler as a lack of sensuality. He seemed so... what? Clean, that was it. American youth before it wandered into seedy, sexy alleyways.

Still, the acting coach she'd gotten to work with him, a bear of a man named Nick Papaduros told Louise she had nothing to worry about. "He can be anything. He's a natural," Nick said when she went to see him at his studio, which, for the sake of being 'authentic' he continued to keep in the Valley. In spite of all the heavyweights he'd coached, all the stars he'd helped make seem 'real,' he was himself a modest man, or that, at least, was the air he projected in-between quiet bursts of ego. Keeping it all together on Ventura Boulevard as his studio was, he could be sure those who came to study with him had a genuine wish to learn, not just hang out someplace glitzy.

The studio was upstairs from a Greek restaurant, near the Laurel Canyon exit, where Louise hadn't been since her first pool party, when she'd determined, as when she had taking the subway in New York, never to have to do that again. Her life at some junctures seemed to resemble nothing so much as Scarlett O'Hara's most poignant moment, when, close to starvation she had picked a root out of the ground, famished, eaten it and vomited, at which point she cried to the skies and God "I'll never be hungry again!"

Louise had actually had that same determined, passionate epiphany in her early days in New York City, when, hot and pressed by unloving bodies on the subway, she'd actually screamed aloud, "I'll never take the subway again!" That earliest affirmation and ambition, fulfilled, meant nothing but taxicabs. Except of course when Harry Bell, that famous showbiz producer, had picked her up in his limousine, and said "Put your hand on my cock." The vinegared 'romance' of that moment was surpassed only by his taking her, once again in his limo, to a dinner, which turned out to be at the Carnegie Delicatessen. The one time it had actually seemed he would squire her to a place where she could move to the forefront of a potentially admiring public, he had ripped her only good faux designer dress before the event, mauling her clumsily, so she couldn't attend.

The Carnegie Deli. God, the man had known how to live. But more important, he had known how to die, which was without leaving a will. So in the scuffle over his estate, she had stepped cleverly forward and said, sotto voce of course—there were moments when she was clever enough to be subtle—that she had been with him the night before he died. After all, it wasn't as if anyone could check with him.

That harmless—it was! it was!---falsehood had led to her rise, which it actually had been, as she began a veritable whirlwind of activity. Dead, Harry Bell was almost a bigger name than he had been alive, what with all the wrangling over his estate. She had been invited everywhere, by everyone, achieving the kind of celebrity that would have been hers anyway if that dirty little man had taken her the places he should have instead of just hiding her in his limousine and asking her to (ugh, the thought of it!) touch his shriveled thing.

Then, once she had come to California, at her first pool party, she had looked around and seen, dispiritedly, that the biggest name there was Rafael Campos, who'd been in Blackboard Jungle and gone on to marry, briefly, Dinah Washington. Louise shouted, though this time only in her mind, lest she seem anti-Hispanic, "I'll never go to the Valley again!' After that, once her West Coast ascent had begun, when top executives scheduled lunch meetings at La Serre, the 'in' place in the Valley for studio biggies at Warner's and Universal, she ("Oh, pretty pretty please, be kind to Louise") had them switch to the Bistro in Beverly Hills, or, when it was still where Orson Welles lunched with John Cassavetes, Ma Maison in West Hollywood. Her excuse for changing venues was always that she wasn't a good enough driver to manipulate the canyons, ("Lulu's afraid!") The truth was she had a genuine fear not of driving, but of the Valley itself, for the same reason she had never been able to return to the neighborhood she'd come from: that a skeletal hand would reach up to claim her and drag her down into the local sod, as in 'Carrie.' Stephen King had no idea what real horror was, as he'd never failed in show business.

"The kid has all of it," Nick said to her now as she met with him in his office. "Just like with the music. You don't have a clue where it comes from, it's just there. Part of his nature that he can tap into effortlessly. There's this intense heat just below Tyler's sweet, boyish surface. Like he's been through everything before, he just doesn't want to talk about it. But he remembers. Smoulders. And he's not afraid to open it, like a sluice in a dam. And then it just flows. Gushes. Remarkable."

"Have you read the script?" Louise said.

"I got my MFA from the Yale School of Drama," Nick said, not too subtly masking a slight underlay of superiority. "They have all O'Neill's papers. We had to read his complete works before we went to our first seminar."

He stood very erect, his great furry beard like an embroidered curtain around the pageantry of his words. "Eugene O'Neill is the greatest writer of American tragedy," he proclaimed. Then, dropping his voice: "And that's the tragedy of American drama."

"You don't think he's good?" she said, surprised.

"What does it matter what I think? What matters is the kid can play it. He even seems to buff up physically when it comes to his first scene with Anna. Like the onset of lust has been a workout at the gym. And he's been working with a trainer so his body is changing.

"I never saw anything like it, except maybe once. I had a friend who was a psychologist at Attica when I was doing a prison movie, let me come and observe. He counseled Mark David Chapman, the nut who killed John Lennon. Chapman had gotten married to one of those repressed flakes who writes to jailed murderers. It was the day she was coming for her conjugal visit, and he was absolutely pumped. Spindly before she got there, a regular Sylvester Stallone when she arrived."

"The same thing happens in the scene with Tyler, when he first sets eyes on Anna. You can see the physical transformation from boy to man. First the hating her, because his unloving father has come back with a bride who poses a threat to his inheritance. Then the undeniable sexual pull, that both characters feel even through the wall that separates them. O'Neill put it right in the stage directions, that's how on target he was about mother love."

"You think it's about mother love?"

"I don't believe there's a boy alive who wasn't a little bit in love with his mother, no matter how much he thinks he hates her, or what trouble he gives her. There's the breast, you know."

"I'd heard," said Louise.

There were photos on the wall of students that Nick had coached on their way to fame, a standard décor that was everywhere in Hollywood, both sides of the hill, in restaurants and drugstores and dry cleaners and places where actors copied vocal recordings, any locale a performer, arrived or yet to be seen, could have gone and left a glossy, autographed to whoever was running whatever establishment it was, whether manager, or, in the case of Nick, mentor. A few of those smiling out from the knotty pine were well-known Scientologists, but Louise was smart enough not to get into any of that as she didn't want to find a snake in her mailbox.

"So can I see Tyler do a scene?" she asked.

"You're better off being surprised. And you will be surprised. There hasn't been a raw talent like this since Montgomery Clift. As curiously sensitive and sexy and interesting and beautiful as Clift was in the beginning, before he smashed his face. Like in 'A Place in the Sun'."

"Really?" she asked sincerely, an actual thrill in her voice. For all the hot air she knew how to blow, and had blown, along with smoke, over the years about her clients, the idea of actually being able to bring forward a new talent—and he would be new to the film world, no matter how high he already was on the Billboard charts—excited her.

"Like he's been doing this all his life," Nick said. "And since his life hasn't been all that long, you have to maybe factor in previous lives."

"Oh, right," Louise said sardonically. "This is California."

"You don't believe in any of that?"

"I'm from the real world," Louise said.

"As far as you know," said Nick. "Maybe you haven't gone deep enough."

When she went to sleep that night, fitfully as always—she thought she could detect the odor of the termiting clinging to the duvet on her bed—with Tyler and his yokel cousin Chester safely tucked in down the hall, and Rita in her sunbed, which she all but slept in, wanting to keep up her golden glow for the actual filming, Louise dreamed that Tyler was actually Tony. Of course there hadn't been time enough for Tony to reincarnate, had there? The soul needed to rest on the other side according to a Tarot reader she hadn't really paid that deep attention to at the time of her reading, at a party where Shirley MacLaine had invited her, predicting Louise's future in her gossamer weave of what she saw in the cards. All Louise had been genuinely interested in was whether or not she would be a big success in Hollywood.

"Women want to know about romance," the reader had said. "Unless they're actresses. Then they want to know about their careers."

"Well I'm not an actress," said Louise. "But that's what I'm really interested in."

"And you don't care about love?"

"I had love," Louise said. "It fucked me over." At that time there had been only Andre, if you didn't count shtupps, which she didn't, as in some corner of her self she was ashamed that that was all they had been. A woman who didn't involve her feelings when she was having sex was no better than a man. "What I need to know is how I'm going to do in this town."

"You're going to cut a very wide swath," the reader said.

And so she had. And so she would again. Now she dreamed that Tyler was all of them, the legends of yesterday, Valentino, Monty, (she allowed herself to call him that as if they had been intimates, since she was dreaming,) maybe even John Garfield, except he was a little dark, and Jewish—did you change religions in the afterlife?—and Tony if he'd only buffed up and hadn't starved his shoulders away--- and yes... there he was... Jimmy Dean. Oh, she could hardly wait to get up in the morning to admire Tyler, and check him out for traits of long gone leading men.

It was okay for her to be crazy when she was dreaming. As a matter of fact, it felt almost relaxing, allowing herself to be lunatic. After all, it was California, and maybe for the first time, at too long last, she really belonged.

I suppose I shouldn't be surprised that he's run out of money. The sad thing about artists, even those who have their moment, is that their moment is usually over, and my luck, it has to happen in my hotel. What Bunyan Reis doesn't understand is that none of this is really up to me. I have no autonomy here. Most of us 'hoteliers',-- and I give us that most glittering of labels, being in French, which always glitters, -- are really just managers, and unless we can buy into and own a piece which you could maybe do in the beginning with Four Seasons or some of the other 5 Star groups, there are always owners or banks who control everything, and don't even promise retirement benefits.

"But I have another credit card," Reis says in a muscular voice, as though to speak as himself, with that soft, borderline whine, would undercut his credibility. As if the real world, with its limited attention span, had not already undercut him enough. "I shall have to give what for to that damned business manager of mine," Reis continues. "You'd think that all their planning to run off to Argentina with their clients' money would keep them more alert. Try it again, please."

Naomi does, running the Amex card through the machine. There is a fearsome buzz. Her cheeks redden. She looks up dolefully, and barely whispers "Declined."

"I shall have him hanged," Bunyan declares.

"Do you want some time to find your other card?" I ask him.

"I have a better idea," he says. "Have you ever been to Colombe d'Or in St. Paul de Vence?"

"Of course," I say. One of the first things you do as a student if you have any money at all, or even if you don't, is try and visit the south of France. Even if you have to sleep in hostels, and backpack, which I did. That I couldn't afford anything in that unbelievable locale, looking over the side of the terrace onto a multi-leveled, planted hill, which makes you hear in your head Streisand singing 'On a Clear Day you can see Forever' does not cause the experience or the memory of it to be any less vivid. Simone Signoret summered there with Yves Montand at the height of their passionate relationship, and it makes you wish they had stayed there for the rest of their lives, instead of his fucking around on her when she got older, like it was the real-life version of 'Room at the Top,' which she had been so moving and magnificent in, and their not being fully together again until Le Cimitiere de

PereLachaise in Paris where they are buried side by side. Oh, the time people waste when they are alive!

"Well, you've seen how all the walls of that charming inn are absolutely ALIVE with the best of the Impressionists..." he continues, selling. *"Matisse, Modigliani, Chagall. They all went there for lunch, or to stay for the season."*

"You're forgetting Picasso," I say.

"Would that everyone would. Completely over-rated, except for the Blue period and his sex life."

"But your point is....?"

"Let me give you one of my paintings. That's what that bunch did when they stayed at the Colombe d'Or and couldn't handle the bill. You can have it for yourself personally or put it in the lobby of the hotel."

"Our owners are from Saudi Arabia," I say with weighty significance. *Not that that means they don't have any taste or sensitivity, but they <u>are</u> from Saudi Arabia.*

"Well, as Billy Wilder said, 'Nobody's perfect.'"

"I wish I could help you out, Mr. Reis. But the rules are the rules. I've already stretched your stay past what you covered. And I'm only the manager." My heart really aches for him. All that talent. All that prestige. Vanished, along with an era. Not to mention the fortunes once paid for his paintings, which, life being how it is, probably went to the galleries that sold them.

There is a dark visitor hanging around the bar. By dark, I do not mean skin tone or hair color, or jacket or suit since they don't often wear those in Beverly Hills unless they are on their way to a funeral or a business meeting. I am talking personal shadows, which I am pretty astute at spotting. He is looking over at us interestedly. I know he has been here for breakfast a couple of times, and twice at the cocktail hour, trying to friendly up to

Amber, or the busboy, who is actually (Surprise!) a would-be actor.

According to Naomi, who for all her hope of becoming a successful actress, would probably do better as a Narc, he asked a lot of questions about Louise Felder. But the only one on the staff who really seemed to have had her confidence was Mimea, who confessed to me in her Spanglish she understood almost nothing of what Felder said. Not that she's available as an informant anyway, since Felder snatched her up and took her home, as if being able to change a sheet and tuck it tight were as rare a quality in LA as genuine talent.

So I see him now, this shadowy guy, straining to overhear what's going on with Reis. "I'd be glad to store your luggage while you re-locate," I say. Hotel-ese for 'How soon can you get out of your room?'

"No. No. It's all right. I wouldn't want you to trouble yourself."

"No trouble," I say, seeing the absolute panic in his silvery eyes, as he searches the inside of his brain for options.

"May I use your phone?" he says, holding the fingers of his right hand with the other to control their shaking. "I'm afraid I misplaced my cell."

"The one over by the bar." I point to it and tell Naomi to give him a line. Clearly A T&T has caught up with him, and they don't take paintings either.

"Louise!" he says with audible relief, when he is connected. "My tomatillo! How goes it with tomorrow's leading hunk, and she whom he will hunker down into?"

You can see the dark presence light up, in a shadowy way. He strains to listen to what Reis says, and, apparently satisfied by the results of his eaves-dropping, smiles. The thing about evil is it often comes with a palpable smugness. I don't like to think that is because it prevails, but this is not a world where the good guys mostly win.

Visibly relieved, Bunyan wipes his brow with a linen handkerchief when he hangs up the phone. The dark one approaches him, grinning, and puts a long-fingered hand on Reis' shoulder. I cannot hear what he is saying, but Bunyan looks shocked and shakes his head vehemently. Then the man cozies up to him, whispers, soothing, visibly beguiling. It is very like that moment in Pinocchio, one of my all-time favorite movies, when the little newly awakened –to-life puppet is off for his first day in school, and is waylaid by the fox, who promises him adventure and fortune. I would not be surprised to learn that Bunyan Reis is on his way to Pleasure Island, making an ass of himself.

"You should have called me right away," Louise said as the great iron gates guarding her estate swung open, and the taxi pulled in. She had come down the driveway to let him in herself, he had sounded so unlike Bunyan. His voice was actually flat, absent judgment, scorn, all the things that made Bunyan so dear to her, a fit companion in contempt.

"Well, who ever dreamed he would go to Brazil, don't you know?" Bunyan said through the rolled-down window. "I never thought he had that much imagination. After all, the man is an accountant."

"And he took everything?" She opened the car door for him, and saw, for the first time, how genuinely frail he looked, absent his usual hauteur.

"Apparently. My bank account is totally wiped out. I haven't been able to get his office on the phone, and you know I don't text." Bunyan shuddered as his sandaled foot touched the polished round pebbles of the driveway. "The very sound of the word!"

He shivered again, exaggeratedly. At least Louise hoped it was exaggerated.

"Would you please put his luggage on the porch," she said to the driver, more politely than she would have usually, genuinely thrown by Bunyan's descent into humility. If a man like Bunyan, for all his wit, his accomplishment, his once great fame, and, not least, his talent, could be brought so low—what would happen to what he once referred to as "the little people?" Of course, he was always quick to add that he didn't know any.

"OMG as those little bitches say today," said Bunyan, looking up at the façade of her mansion. "It's Tara!"

"Haven't you been here?"

"The last house of yours I visited was in your Japanese teahouse period." He looked away as Louise paid the driver. "I think Marlon Brando was still alive."

"I can't give you any of the big rooms," she said, as he followed her into the house. "Rita and Tyler and Chester the yokel are already very much in residence. But I can give you the Dame May Whitty room. It's got a lot of lace."

"Oh, she'd like that. So would I."

Louise signaled to the houseman to take the bags. "The lavender room," she said.

"Oh, praise God if She exists! Lavender. My absolute favorite. Elizabeth Taylor's eyes! I can't thank you enough."

"Of course you can. Just be your usual cunty self so I can restore my sense of disdain. I'm being lavished with so much love I can hardly get my bearings. Rita is all over me, awash with gratitude. And Tyler is a genuine sweetheart, so I have to guard my words. He says he doesn't mind foul language, but the very fact that he calls it foul language inhibits me. And Chester is such a dork I feel like I'm in the middle of the Andy Griffith show. It'll be a dismal joy to have you here, hating everything and everybody."

"I have a painting I want to give you," Bunyan said, looking up at the entry hall staircase, wide and high with carved banisters. "Do you think Rhett will mind?"

"Frankly my dear, I don't give a damn," Louise said.

"You never let me down," said Bunyan.

There was such sincerity in his voice Louise felt confused. She had just been being glib, of course, giving him the line from the movie, and thought for a minute that was what he meant, that she was always on target, being clever. But as she turned to tell her houseman where to put the luggage, she caught a glimpse of Bunyan, moved away slightly, wiping his eyes. And it looked to her, as unlikely as it was, that there were tears in them.

I remember a line from one of the great comedies made before I was born—a classic that used to be revived in little theaters before too many of them closed, because people preferred sitting on their asses at home—'Kind Hearts and Coronets.' It starred Alec Guinness at his most versatile and surprising, when they still made truly witty flicks, especially the Brits. The line was "Revenge is a dish which is best eaten cold." I do not think that would pertain to my recently departed guest, Louise Felder, as the heat emanating from her, the combination of internalized rage and the boiling cauldron of potential victory, all but gave off waves you could see, as she spirited off her luscious Italian and the Boy Wonder.

Revenge is clearly a dish she wants to eat hot. I have been on the periphery of the entertainment business since I was a kid, my mother working as a dialogue coach, kind of a down-market elocution (and also foreign accents) teacher for one of the studios, my father having gone back to Italy to make his fortune and send for us, neither of which he ever did. The studio gave me errands to run after school, because my mother was very sweet and obliging and obviously needy, so even people without any hearts were moved by her, and wanted to help. My runner duties got me enough money to pay for school lunches and buy some clothes, and give her the occasional gift. She used to take the trade papers from the garbage can of the actor next door, and read them as if she had an actual future in the town, a disease a lot of the people here have long after their time is over or in many cases not even begun. I bought her a subscription to Daily Variety and the Hollywood Reporter for her birthday so she wouldn't feel even more desperate than she already seemed to, scavenging for news of the profession that everyone in town and in many parts of the world want, though it be out of a garbage can. The trades are particularly popular because of the local attention span, which in the case of studio executives is about one and a half minutes, why any 'pitches,' that is to say, ideas for movies have to be 'high concept', spit out as quickly as possible. For example, a guy has inner rage which when triggered turns him muscular and green. Doesn't always work, but it does get it made.

If I hadn't become a semi-serious student, which I did while I was at UCLA, I can see where I would really have gotten caught up in all this. Even when you think you have perspective, it is hard not to get sucked in by the dream, despite seeing how un-dreamlike it may on a day-to-day basis. Remembering that 'Glamour' is a Scottish word that means a spell being cast so you see beauty where it doesn't exist, you can still understand, or at least I do, that seeing beauty where it <u>*does*</u> *exist—eg: Charlize Theron walking down Rodeo Drive in Beverly Hills, all olive-skinned and pale golden hair and that body, you forget things like her mother killing her father, and just go 'Wow,' or at least you would if you still used words like that. Nobody cares or they are even more interested than they would have been that your mother went insane if you are Marilyn Monroe, for as long as you are here and afterwards they can go on dissecting you psychologically, speculating about what really happened, if it was suicide or the FBI, giving material to writers on the level of Norman Mailer, and one more mawkish hit to Elton John, with magazines selling better if you're on the cover and people trying to make musicals based on your mishaps even when you've been dead for fifty years. I mean, that isn't casting a spell so you see beauty where it doesn't exist, that's creating an arena for beauty where it does exist and if you're in that arena it begins to drive you crazier than you would have been just goaded by vanity.*

How can you not fall in love with your own reflection when adoration is in the eyes of everyone around you, and everyone who would like to be around you? The trick is not to fall so deeply that you don't also topple into the water and drown, or, as in many cases in this burg, into a vat of booze or crystal meth.

Which brings me to my AA meeting.

I went there for the first time because my partner—love, I thought, not business,-- was convinced it would intensify our bond if we shared not only our strengths, but our weaknesses. His, the main one anyway, is fear of running out of money, along with most Americans, especially now. He is as bright a fellow as breathes this smoggy air. In spite of the propaganda about the local intellectual level, there are a number of really sharp people here, their greatest frailty being they enjoy feeling physically comfortable, and have had enough of frost-bitten noses and the cruel rejections that come without a swimming pool to heal your bruised souls, which they also have here. Souls I mean, as well as swimming pools. So Wilton came from whatever provincial background he admits to when stoned to capitalize on his comic genius, which I believe he has, because even when high he is quicker than anyone, though often forgetful of where he left his joint. The one he smokes.

He had an actual career writing sitcoms, the really clever ones with snappy dialogue, before TV became a rash of fat people and 'Reality' shows. I put quotation marks around that because if that is reality, I would like to climb my own hair, what's left of it, to the tower and be Rapunzel with no hope of rescue.

But as if the world didn't present enough problems, in Hollywood every so often there is a Writer's strike. One of the great stories about Samuel Goldwyn, a true one, is his striding through his company's lot, and listening, hearing silence. So he roared at the top of his voice: "Writers! WRITE!", which was immediately followed by the loud clacking of typewriters behind the open windows of every building.

I believe that to be not only the truth, but very astute. Because that's what's writers should be doing. Happily, and unhappily at the same time, they have a Guild. A really good guild, because writers need protection as much or more than anybody, what with their penchant for believing the world is basically benign. But what most writers like to do probably more than write is talk. So whenever they are treated unfairly, which happens often, since they are low man/woman on the Hollywood totem pole, they have a strike, and then all their members, even those who haven't worked for a long time, have something to do: picket and palaver. That I can attest to, because to intensify our relationship he took me with him to a guild meeting, and I mean to say they <u>do</u> go on. So I was

moved to imitate Goldwyn and cry aloud "Writers! WRITE!" But
that is easy to say when you are a hotel manager and know that
you have a steady income unless or until your company is bought
by Brunei.

Anyway, it was during one of those strikes that Wilton got
terrified he wouldn't be able to pay his rent, so started dealing
grass. Nothing lethal, you understand, just good old-fashioned
marijuana which makes the days pass even more gently than they
do out of inertia in southern Cal.

That is how we connected. After all, I lived in Los Angeles:
one must have controllable weaknesses. A friend of a friend gave
me his number, and I drove over to his place one torpid afternoon
and ended up on the floor literally rolling with laughter, and after
a while rolling with Wilton. Back then, his greatest fear, after
running out of money, was the law. But the law having changed in
California, with varying degrees of flexibility, starting first with
medical marijuana, his panic was that grass would become
completely legal, in which case he would lose his customers.
Meanwhile, to give the darling boy credit, he writes all the time he
isn't answering his doorbell, or going down to Abbott Kinney to
pick up that week's supply. So he has great seriousness of purpose
along with a fine quality of weed.

But somewhere during our third or fourth year he heard a
voice or something very Joan of Arc-y, and went to an AA Meeting.
Continued selling, you understand, but not to any of those
attending, many who had been his star clients, which he really had.
I mean, it was a first-rate double bill, sometimes, the guys who
were standing on his front step waiting for him to answer the bell,
two above-the-title names who arrived at the same time and were
startled to see the other one there. For example, Dennis Hopper
when he was downsizing from heavier stuff and Tony Curtis before

he switched to crack and had his pipe prepared and lit by his butler so he wouldn't burn himself. Anyway, Wilton asked me to stop smoking so we could see if we really cared for each other sober, and took me to a Meeting. As it turned out, we stayed loving friends but lost the passion, except in his case, the one for going to Meetings. I don't blame that on sobriety, but the hard truth that passion is only passion because it lasts for just a little while, so Romeo and Juliet were probably lucky. Imagine if they had made it into late middle age and seen each other in daylight.

Naturally I cannot say who was in attendance because it is 'Anonymous.' But if "Diversion Tonight" could have set up their cameras on the lawn fronting that church and videoed those in attendance, they would have had their highest rating since Farrah Fawcett died, with her intimates ready to give teary interviews except they were bumped at the last minute because of the sudden, untimely and much more glittering death of Michael Jackson.

Anyway, I still have the occasional toke, but in general have stayed off it, though like many I am still sort of addicted to the meetings. They are heavy with those who have become my friends in the coffee and occasional cinnamon buns that follow confessions and tears and material that would give several fraudulent books attributed to his own experience by James Frey. I am fond of those I know from Meeting, though both they and I keep up a mask when they come to the hotel, careful not to drink at the bar because they see me watching. It would be awkward were it not basically endearing, as I am very like the maiden aunt they all probably wish they had had. Still, with all the distance I manage to keep, I cannot help being occasionally stunned, as when I saw that dark character who'd sidled up to Bunyan Reis just before he was leaving the hotel, first at my Meeting, and then, later, at the hotel. For a terrible moment, I wondered if he was following me.

He was back at the hotel talking very intensely to Naomi, the receptionist/ would-be actress/Narc. I did not have to sidle up and try to eavesdrop as is my wont, since I knew she would report back to me every single word. Besides ambition and a questionable character she has a brilliant memory. She kept shaking her head as Bunyan Reis had done when this man approached him, but did not experience the apparent change of mind that had altered Bunyan, and set him off, like Pinocchio, on some potentially disastrous course.

When Willie took over at reception, I signaled Naomi into my office. "What did that man want?" I ask her quite directly. She is not necessarily a narc due to her nature but because she imagines, I think, that betrayal will get her ahead, as it often does, especially in this town.

"He asked me if I kept a record of the calls Louise Felder made while she was staying here," she says. "He told me if I would give it to him he would pay me 'a pretty penny,' he actually said. Imagine that. How quaint. A pretty penny."

"And you replied...?"

"Not even for all the ugly ones."

"Clever girl," I said. "Who would *you give it to?"*

"You, of course," she says, knowing that her future career as an actress is more than iffy, and she would be wise to go for a back-up in the hospitality business.

"And is there such a record?"

She goes with a minimum of wasted steps to a filing cabinet between reception and my office, and comes back with a folder with print-outs on it of extra charges, which include the numbers called and the cost to the guest. "Of course she did have a cell phone," she says.

Still, I visualize Miss Louise lying chubby and languid against her many pillows, kind of an updated Mae West, preferring a real phone against her shell-like ear (those don't change, except for the lobes) to the possibility of brain cancer. So I figure this is a fairly accurate rendering of how she spent her time on the phone. I have Naomi check the numbers from the phone at reception, and see who answers. If they are private ones of course she will know how to cover.

She is back in a slow twinkling of an eye. "A couple of them are to her old agency," she says, knowingly, having also kept up with the trades. "A lot of them are to Allegra de Sevigny. She sounded really pissed that I had her private number. I told her I misdialed, but I did recognize her voice."

"Hard to miss with that accent."

"The one to Australia I can check through A T & T."

As it turned out, it was to the summer home, it being winter in the US, for Baz Luhrmann, the occasionally Fab director (see 'Strictly Ballroom' 'Romeo & Juliet,' the young di Caprio version, 'Moulin Rouge') and sometime incredibly Boring (see 'Australia,' or, better yet, don't see it.) As far as I can figure, since I was at Louise's spectacular at the Beverly Hills Hotel Crystal Room (she didn't invite me at first, but I wouldn't have missed it. I already knew about it, as the assistant manager, Steven, is a buddy of mine and had alerted me to the booking. At the last minute Miss Felder, seeing I was out of my managerial dark blue got that I was on my way somewhere a bit more natty, invited me just in case I was going there, as the buzz about the event was big time.) So I knew even before it was reported in the trades(BIG HEADLINE) that the project for Rita and Tyler was to be 'Desire Under the Elms.' I guessed from the numbers called, she was foraging on the highest possible level for the right director. Nothing has been announced yet, so I assume they're still looking.

There is very little you can't find out in this town, or indeed most places if you are industrious and bright and ask good questions. Of course it does help when you've got an old-fashioned switchboard and some really clever spies. But I still want to know what that sinister guy was doing at my AA meeting.

I try to stop him as he is leaving the hotel, work at being charming, which I can be, really. But there is an acrid smell around him like an old meal left on a tray on the floor outside a room from that hasn't been taken away by Room Service, so I can't be who I really am at my best. He has one of those big, mottled, fat noses, repellent on the pockmarked face of it, and I am not enough of a phony to fake enchantment around sleazes. Still, "Would you like to have a drink?" I say, introducing myself as the manager, trying to be hospitable

"Yes, I really would," he says. "But I'm on the program."

Was that it, then? Is he genuinely a reforming alcoholic? Or was there someone else there he's trying to get the goods on?

CHAPTER SEVEN

KAREN AWOKE WISHING she had been a better mother. She had forgiven herself many things in the course of counseling, in the days when counseling was less hands-on, or at least less like the Interferon they gave cancer patients, and was generally about just letting it all out, with your doctor giving you the occasional word. Freudians, trotting silently through the rubble, nodding. They had helped, she was sure. But there was still, for all the smart guidance she had had, a lot of pain around the death of her own mother, which she considered to be ridiculous—not the death, but still having a problem dealing with it, since her mother's life had ended so long before. But she couldn't get over the feeling it was the worst kind of rejection, her not finding her daughter interesting enough to stick around.

She supposed that Olivia's feelings were more complex, since Karen had not even died but had still not been present enough in her daughter's life to make her feel sufficiently loved. In truth, she had adored her baby girl, but financial pressures had forced her to keep working. No. That wasn't completely true. It was her own pressure on herself to keep being who she was onscreen, where she seemed more real to herself than she did in her own skin. Even holding her satin-soft-and-shiny baby on her lap for the photo shoots her publicist thought were necessary, since her roles onscreen were so diverse, nobody knew what she was really like, and he wanted her shown to the public as the warm-hearted, loving woman she was, she did not know for sure if she was really that warm-hearted, loving woman.

Olivia had looked at her even then with child-wise eyes, as if she were not sure, either. As if Karen's leaving home to go to the studio, putting her child in the hands of what seemed loving nannies—she was fastidious about interviewing them, checking references, watching their behavior with the little girl with great attention before she took them on, but they were, always, nannies—meant to Olivia that she was no more engaged than Karen's her own mother had been, albeit alive. A child wanted to be the center of her mother's universe, that was so painfully clear. And to be truthful with herself, as Karen struggled to be, the center of her life had been career.

Louise Felder, who had briefly represented Karen,--- it ended badly, so even when caught in the same hotel elevator they didn't greet each other, -- had said once when the two were still close friends that she herself would have probably have eaten her young. Karen had covered her child with kisses, nothing ravenous behind it. But her failed first marriage to a pretty boy who turned out more hustler than husband had set her back to a lack of trust. The husband who followed, after a number of vignettes that had turned out empty, was Olivia's father. Darling as he seemed, and faithful, he disappointed her by needing her even more than she needed him. They lived in a cruel and unforgiving town, and the fact that her career went better than his, had made her work even harder, so she would be so caught up she could pretend she didn't notice. But she did. In some area of her being, even though she was what most people considered a feminist, she herself still believed that the man should be the head of the household, the one who kept it afloat.

And then he had died. Eleven weeks from diagnosis to death, just enough time, said a thick-skinned psychiatrist, for her to get used to the idea. She had watched Charley wasting away as through a slowed down, speeded-up motion picture camera. Showing a movie she didn't want to be involved in, much less see. She had been there for him, completely there, neither of them really able to take in the hard reality of mortality. It was all so fast and un-Hollywood.

What truly close friends they had, those who cared for both of them, not just Karen and 'her husband,' or those who genuinely loved her husband better, though most of them were hoping he could make a deal for something starring Karen, backed away, disappeared. He was only forty-one years old, the first one in their still-young circle to be suddenly, fatally ill, so everyone acted as if it might be catching. Or, as Karen's dearest friend from boarding school said on the phone when Karen called her, sobbing with pain and loneliness, "Death gives some people gas."

As though it had all been Karen's fault, Olivia moved even more bitterly away. "So what did you miss?" Olivia, then a teenager, said, once the tears were over. "Growing old together?"

Lying in her hotel bed now after a restless night, Karen could not help but think, 'Well, yes.' Old was what she was growing, and she wondered how Charley would have handled it, the husband who had loved her so as a still young woman. Probably not carried it as well as Hendrik, who had met her past what could be reasonably called her 'maturity.' Hendrik, to whom she had never even introduced her daughter in conversation their first few months together, so fearful was she of Olivia's behavior. Hendrik, who'd luckily been enmeshed in one of his very important negotiations when Olivia got married, so couldn't attend the beautiful and extremely pricey wedding in the garden of the Hotel Bel-Air. Not that Karen wouldn't have welcomed his support, his arm under hers, his impressive presence beside her at the dinner. But she already had more than an inkling that Olivia's union wouldn't work out, so wouldn't let him help her pay for it, lest it end up one of his few losing investments.

There was a scratching at the door, a light tapping. The Hotel Royale was a surprisingly quiet place, for all the centrality of its locale, and the restrained bustle in its bar. One could walk through the halls and never run into anyone, except if the Fates were working against you and Louise was in the same elevator. Karen had played the part of a tough, acid-tongued agent in a movie: everyone thought her performance was based movement by movement, gesture by gesture, intonation after pissed intonation on Louise, as Louise herself did, too, correctly. She had never spoken to Karen again, except to telephone her when Charley died, when all she said, very quickly, not giving Karen space to insert a word, was how sorry she was that such a sweet man had had such a short run, how good Karen was in her latest movie for which she'd almost won an Academy Award, and that most of all-- Louise had taken a deep, audible breath, ---- "I remember how much he loved you," she said, hanging up before Karen could even say 'Thank you,' or 'How are you?' or 'I've missed you,' which she genuinely had. Louise had been her fastest, cleverest friend, who, underneath the toughness was every bit as tough or tougher, but still sharper and better company than anybody. It was abrupt and unsettling, as Louise always knew how to be when she didn't want to give anyone breathing space, or the chance to make things better.

The scratching on the door now was even more unsettling, in view of how quiet the hotel was. Warily, Karen got out of bed. "Who is it?"

No answer. There was a peephole so you could see who was on the other side, but there was no one there. Yet the scratching continued. She opened the door a crack, and the little white dog belonging to the old Marquesa stuck her nose in.

"Well, what are you doing here?" Karen asked, opening the door a little more. The dog skittered inside and jumped up on the bed. "Off!" she said, but half-heartedly, as the truth was the dog was genuinely enchanting, as black-eyed little white dogs usually were, as long as you didn't have to walk them.

"Off!" she said again, and then moved to the phone. "I've got that little dog that belongs to the old lady down the hall here." She caught a glimpse of herself in the mirror, not yet made up, her hair uncombed, sleep still webbing her eyes, and wondered how she dared call anybody else old.

"Oh, I'm terribly sorry," Naomi said. "I'll send someone up right away."

Several moments passed, then several more. The little dog moved closer on the bed, cuddling against her leg, looking up at her with eyes so filled with longing for attention, she found it hard not to be touched. "What do you want from me?" she asked. The dog licked her leg, kissed her toes.

Impatiently she reached for the phone. "What's happening about the dog?" she asked Naomi when she answered.

"I'm so very sorry, Madame Engel. But the Marquesa had a stroke and they've taken her to Cedars."

"And…?"

"Would you mind just keeping her there for a few minutes till we get it sorted out? We're trying to get hold of her groomer."

"Okay," Karen said edgily, and hung up the phone. The last thing she needed in her life at this point, even for "a few minutes," was a creature that depended on her. It had taken Karen her whole life to get to the point where she felt really independent—not in the sense that she needed no one, but that no one needed her, so she had no further obligations. People wanted her, yes, that was different. That was enriching. But the specters that had pursued her were finally put to rest. At least she thought they were.

She was still lying on the bed, lightly stroking the soft white fur when the maid opened her door. Behind her stood Olivia. "I hope is all right," the maid said. "She said she was your daughter."

"The funny thing is they believed me," said Olivia, as the maid closed the door behind her.

"Why shouldn't they?"

"I'm not beautiful. I'm not gifted. I'm not any of the things a daughter of yours would be expected to be. Especially by you." She flounced to the chair by the window, stopping briefly to kiss Karen's cheek, flooding Karen's nostrils with perfume.

Like it was part of an emotionless but necessary ritual, Karen could not help thinking, curtseying before the Queen. Every time she parted from her daughter, if there had been no heated words between them, she imagined it would be all right the next time, and always she was wrong. It was very like the years after her mother's suicide, when every time she woke up she would think she would see her mother, and then after a few minutes remember she was dead, and could feel her heart almost literally drop inside her, coming to rest in her stomach. "Did you come here to fight with me?"

"I don't think so. I just really wanted to see you for some reason."

"For some reason? I'm your mother."

"That's right. And I'm your daughter. Hard as it is to believe." She sat up straight-backed in the chair, cushioned and comfortable though it was meant to be, ready for combat. "That should be enough for you."

"Well, it is."

"No it isn't. You want me to be more." Her face went through a range of expressions, the pugnacious set of lower jaw retreating into almost a quiver, as her eyes, the mirror image of Karen's own, started visibly to fill. She looked away. "I can't. I'm doing the best I can. And please don't say 'Oh, Olivia.' Even my name makes it sound like you're disappointed."

"But I'm not."

"Of course you are. I am, too." They brimmed over, tears starting to drip down the over-made up cheeks.

It was at that moment that Karen noted how heavy her daughter's make-up was. Olivia was in full make-up, and too much of it at that, at nine-thirty in the morning, just as the smell of her perfume was overwhelming. Biting back the observation that she had on too much make-up and was wearing too heavy perfume, Karen started to get off the bed to hold her. But remembering Olivia's angry sally, "Don't pet me like a dog," comforted the dog instead.

Where would it go, with no Marquesa? Where would Olivia go without the (Karen was not surprised) abandoning husband, and the lawyer who wasn't good enough to get her out of anything so it would be to her benefit. "You mustn't feel that way about yourself."

"How am I supposed to feel? I'm such a fucking loser."

"Don't say that!"

"But it's true. You want me to be exceptional. But there's nothing exceptional about me except that I have a movie star for a mother."

"I'm not a movie star anymore." She got up from the bed and opened the window next to Olivia so the drench of perfume would be somewhat dissipated. "I haven't been one for years."

"But you <u>were</u>. I've never been anything. The most I've ever been is a bride and I couldn't even keep that one going."

"You can't blame that on yourself. He was just not the right guy."

"You didn't even know him. You barely got back in time for the rehearsal dinner."

"Where his mother was drunk. That should have told you everything you needed to know," Karen said.

"It's easy for you to be smart now that's it over," said Olivia. "You were unavailable for years."

"I was here for you all the time you were growing up."

"But emotionally unavailable."

"Who gave you that phrase? Your husband?"

"You think I'm not smart enough to come up with these things myself? You were at the studio. You were doing a publicity junket. You had to take a call on the other line. You were never really <u>there</u>.'

"At least I hadn't committed suicide," Karen said, and to her surprise, felt her own eyes filling.

The little white dog moved closer to her, and licked her face. "Stop," she said to the dog, and reached for the phone, barely able to see it through the watery veil. "What are you going to do about the dog?" she said into the receiver, trying not to sound angry. To her surprise, she didn't actually feel angry. The tongue felt warm and sweet against her cheek. She reached for a tissue and blew her nose.

"Someone will be up for her right away," Naomi said.

"I didn't mean to upset you," Olivia said.

"Of course you did. That's what we do, is upset each other. I don't understand it."

"Well, Andy did."

"You call him Andy? That big lunk of a so-called therapist? That's a very affectionate name for someone who let you down."

"Andrew," she said carefully, "Andrew noted that it was the way I could be sure you would pay attention to me, to really get you to focus on me, was to fight with you."

"Is that what Andrew said?"

"I think he was right on."

"Did you love him?"

"I thought so," said Olivia.

"You'll find somebody better. You'll get more involved in your painting. You're very talented."

"I'm ordinary. Nothing I do is exceptional. You need to accept that about me."

"You underestimate yourself."

"No, I don't," said Olivia.

"What do you want?" She heard the way she asked the question, and realized it was exactly the same tone she had used to the dog. She had finally come to the point where all she herself wanted was for no one to demand anything of her. She was tapped out.

"I want you to love who I am. Not who I could be. Because I will never be that person."

"You don't know that."

"No. You don't know that," said Olivia. "And it's the truth."

"You're a lovely young woman," said Karen, and bit her tongue almost literally so she wouldn't add how much prettier Olivia would be without so much make-up. And if she only sat up straight. But she wouldn't mention that because she'd read an article that said young women who were round-shouldered had had mothers who were hyper-critical, so it was more an indictment of her than Olivia. So "I love you," she said instead.

"How could you get involved with that..." She was clearly raging, trying to come up with some killer epithet. "Hans Brinker," she spit out finally.

"Don't call him that!"

"...When you had a man like Dad?"

"He's dead. As Elizabeth Taylor said when Mike Todd's plane crashed, and she got involved with Eddie Fisher, '"I'm alive!"'"

"But now she's dead, too," said Olivia.

"That's right. And one day in the not too distant future, so will I be. I hope before that time, you and I can have a peaceful conversation, without upsetting each other."

"I hope so, too," said Olivia.

"But why are you wearing so much make-up?" she couldn't help saying.

The man who had seemed so dark to the Royale's manager, was indeed, dark. Men who had started the business of movies, those short little gonifs who had come from the Hollywood outside of Chicago and named their new setting after the home base where they really weren't that welcome either, were first and foremost impressed with the light in Southern California. So much sunshine, so good for filming. It actually made it possible to put behind them the dark truth that they had stolen the process.

But as in life, in film there could be no light without shadow. So it was that this business with so much money to be made by the most unlikely people, spawned a black underbelly: those who might profit by knowing things that, if spoken of, could diminish the luster of those in the light. And so it was, for example, --or so went what was not yet known as 'the buzz', --that Louella Parsons got her lifetime column in the powerful Hearst papers by catching William Randolph Hearst shooting Thomas Ince on his yacht by mistake, his real target being Charlie Chaplin, with whom Hearst's mistress, Marion Davies, was supposedly having an affair.

Now with the advent of twenty-four hour media, the gaping maw of a public hungry for information, but not the kind that would upset them, like facts, had come into being a whole new breed of professional snoops. All the elements that kept the tabloids going, lust, envy, greed, and, under the very happiest of circumstances for Annie Charm, murder, were everywhere in the entertainment industry, whose players offered a far more interesting canvas to the observers than their own lives. So it was that Annie had, along with her band of staff 'archeologists,' hired to dig up celebrities' pasts, employed a number of people who could forage through the present. The paparazzi operated in a pushy, mindless way, with cameras. Annie's people were more subtle, diggers of personal dirt using tiny invisible shovels of investigation and seemingly coincidental contacts, and words.

The list of well-known names in attendance at AA meetings was strictly off-limits, even though her #1 stalking dog, Nelson, had given Annie all of them. A recovering alcoholic was finding his own road to salvation, and salvation was what Annie sincerely believed herself to be about. Saving children from known predators who might be living on their block or in their town. Or, if the predators were not known, giving the public enough hints of their

whereabouts to ensure they would either have to move or, God
forbid, commit suicide, a sin against their own souls, but better that
than violating a child. The list of known felons who had made their
way into the cemetery with gentle prodding from Annie was long,
and in its shadowy way, shiny. She thought of herself as a savior of
children, which would have pleased the Lord Himself, her minister
had assured her. So it was that she had set out to save the very
young and beautiful boy-man who was Tyler McKay, from the
Fate worse than death that surely awaited him in the grip of Louise
Felder.

No longer of interest to her was the presence in the Hotel
Royale of the scabrous senator who had so defiled his family: that
was old news, as he was, along with old. It was youth that needed
to be defended, and saved.

So it was that Nelson's salary had been newly augmented to
include an expense account. He could go everywhere that Louise
Felder went that involved Tyler, and spy on the progress of his
corruption. Meanwhile Annie's 'archeologists' were digging up
everything about Louise's past. It included a lot of good reading,
as she had been the subject of countless magazine articles and was
in almost every book about the "new" show business, or at least
the show business that had still been new when her star started to
rise, propelled by her engagement to Harry Bell, never officially
announced, but very much a part of the theatrical and legal
landscape in the period following his death, when there had been
all the public wrangling over his assets by his next of kin and those
who were not really that close but still laid claim to what he had
left, which was plenty.

The estate finally had been settled as a result of Louise's
secret testimony, never officially made public, although the
resulting disposition of funds according to her rendition of his

wishes had been designated a "farce," by his relatives, ex-wives, and a few adopted children who had come by way of the women he had married, and called "bullshit" by all the unrewarded survivors, although they could not print that word even in The New York Post. In the end Harry's enormous wealth had gone, in large part, to the memorial Louise had testified (in chambers, but these things always leaked out according to his lawyer, Ron Abbate, who'd put in months of billable hours to settle the thing, and wished not to be quoted, but was) was what Harry told her the night before he died were his final wishes.

According to leaked testimony, they dined together that night—the servants were off-- on food she said she'd brought in from his favorite deli. They'd eaten in his house, the famous one on Fifth Avenue that had belonged to the heiress he'd been married to who sold it to him at a huge profit after their divorce. "I should never have married a woman who had more money than I did," was one of the things Louise quoted Harry saying that evening. A very Harry-like thing that no one would have said but Harry, helping to substantiate the truth of their relationship.

There could, of course, be no corroboration of Louise's presence there: the staff had been off, and there were no other guests. Because his secretary had been on vacation, (it was summer, with record heat) his body had not been found for a few days, the air-conditioning was not turned on, and there was exigency about his burial because of the smell. So it was that his Afterlife, not the one that might have been in the Hereafter if there was one, but on earth where they'd had to put his remains in a cooler till the arguments were settled, turned out to be as big a circus as anything he'd brought as spectacle to the stage in his lifetime.

The task of Annie Charm's non-production staff, those who didn't work on her TV show, was to uncover what might be hidden in the past. In the present though, it was Nelson's unaccustomed privilege to go to most of the new places that were considered 'Happening,' or at least he assumed they were or Louise wouldn't have been planning on going to them, with Tyler and Rita in tow, places like the Tower on Sunset Boulevard which stipulated online, where Nelson checked it out, that it had "a strictly enforced dress code."

Nelson had bought new clothes that he read in GQ were what the Hollywood stars were wearing for their night life, something he'd never really had before. He had gone to the John Jay College of Criminal Justice in New York, where he studied forensics, fascinating to him after having watched a season of CSI, which, because of his resemblance to David Caruso, red hair, pale, bad skin, and freckles, he thought might be just the ticket to the right career. He was a slow talker, and converted that into a low-key, low-voiced persona like Caruso's, but without the underlying hint of sexuality, and that, along with his diploma, impressed and relieved Annie, who could really do without sex unless it moved the story along.

In his college days at CUNY Nelson had not had the money to party, and in spite of his red hair nobody invited him. So this was a whole new world, the shadowing of Louise, as she moved Tyler and Rita into the light, which meant, in the current Hollywood, places to see and be seen.

Nelson had put a tap on Felder's home phone, as old-fashioned and freshman-year-like as that had started to seem in the very sophisticated ways there were now of intercepting people's personal communications. So he knew most of what she was planning, what places she was targeting as she brainstormed about how to construct Tyler's public image. As well known and adored and screamed over as the boy singer had been, it was the growing public face of the young male movie star she was obviously—well, maybe not obviously if you weren't tapping her phone—working on building. Nelson had not quite succeeded in putting a tap on her head, but he was getting to know her, and saw how she was constructing an almost military campaign. Patton, he thought of her as, having spent much of his only child childhood watching old movies on TV. Geoge C. Scott he thought could have played Louise very well: the crazed, stubborn set of jaw, the flashing eyes, when dealing with someone not as smart as he/she was, which was probably everybody. The ghosts of old Roman legions that Patton had seen in his visions, Nelson imagined Louise saw in her dreams, except her future conquests were audiences, the bodies of the dead the executives who had, as she put it in conversations he'd recorded, "fucked her over."

As old-fashioned a method of intrusion as it was, Nelson still found it helpful to be inside her phone, which he considered just a step behind being implanted in her brain. The man he had most admired a few Hollywood scandals before, had been Anthony Pellicano, who'd characterized himself as 'P.I. to the Stars,' or, as he tried to put it to clients, 'problem solver.' Unfortunately he'd been sentenced to fifteen years in federal prison for a few of the problems he'd solved, but Nelson still admired what had been his successes, some of which were saving stars from losing paternity suits by bringing in DNA results that proved the fetus half-belonged to someone else. How the DNA was obtained had never been revealed, but the assumption was the procedure had been more or less the same. That is to say, Pellicano must have gotten into the medical records of the obstetrician, if not the accuser's uterus. At any rate, Nelson still looked up to him in a behind-the-bars kind of way. It was a little like masturbating, secretly admiring something he had learned at John Jay was very much against the law, which really gave him pleasure.

Even now, as he listened in to Louise's call to Chet Sinclair, he felt an almost sexual thrill. "I don't think the Tower Bar," she was saying. "He doesn't drink. And I have bad memories from when it was the old Sunset Tower, and George Raft was living there. Harry actually said to me if I moved to the West Coast, I should look up George Raft, that he had the biggest schlong in Hollywood. What a prince."

"You can't still have bad feelings about him," Chet said.

"Maybe you can't," said Louise.

"Have you asked the kid where he'd like to go?"

"He knows nothing about this town."

"You could ask him," said Chet, having once been the new hot young man in Hollywood himself, and though remembering little else, remembered that.

Breakfast at Louise's was served in the manner of old British movies she'd admired, where people all from the same well-born family came down to 'table'—they never said 'the table'—dressed for the day, sat, nodded to the butler as he looked at them inquiringly and filled their coffee cups in answer to the nod. Then they got up and went to the sideboard, where there were silver-lidded chafing dishes, filled with eggs, scrambled and fried, sausages, scalloped potatoes, and, in honor of Evelyn Waugh, about whom she'd heard a funny story when she was visiting Gore Vidal in Ravello, and so felt a kind of connection, kippers. No one at 'table' ate kippers, and if left too long they did give off an offensive odor. But one never knew when William and Kate might show up on yet another extended tour of Movieland, she explained to Tyler and Rita.

"In Italy we don't eat often big breakfast," Rita said, her accent thick as ever but her English improving daily, thanks to her dialogue coach, who worked with her every evening as she lay in her sunbed.

"We don't eat a big breakfast <u>often</u>," Tyler corrected gently. A genuine camaraderie seemed to have sprung up between the two of them, and it pleased Louise as she had never imagined such a thing would, having her two young protégés in amiable synch.

"Certo, not... fish," said Rita, suppressing a shudder of distaste.

"That's so you could leave room for all that pasta," said Tyler.

"I've eaten pasta," Chester said.

"Have you really?" said Louise. "Perhaps you'd like to tell us about it."

"It wasn't all that exciting," Chester said.

"Hard to believe," said Louise. Then she turned to Tyler, smiling. "I spoke to Mr. Sinclair this morning and he sends his fondest regards."

"Nice guy," said Tyler, wolfing his egg.

"He'd like to take us all to dinner tonight. Where would you like to go."

"I hear B.J.'s is very heat," said Rita.

"Hot," said Tyler.

"Hot," she said. "Like me."

"You got it," said Tyler.

"He thought maybe you might have a preference, Tyler." She expected silence.

"I'd like to go to the Chateau," he said, without a moment's hesitation. "I love the thought of seeing Lindsey Lohan, fresh out of rehab, or jail. That's my idea of Hollywood."

Louise looked up, startled, checked him for serious. He had a wry smile on his very full lips. Was it possible? Could this young man also have wit? Along with the music and the stuff that Nick Papadourus said he had, the smoldering passion, the ability to buff up for a love scene, that she saw now was staying with him even outside preparation for the film, unmistakable male beauty. She had seen Harry Bell's statue of Michaelangelo's David in his front hall just before he tore her dress off, and Tyler genuinely reminded her of that most awe-inspiring work of art—hard to believe a man could be that beautiful. And the statue, probably a copy, but still... in somebody's front hall? She remembered Harry's watching her look up at it, as she stood wordless, overwhelmed, and his saying "I know what you're thinking." And her waiting for his (AT LAST!) sensitive reaction to how impressed she was with his art collection. "You're thinking you'd like to ball him, right?" What a prince, she had noted then, too.

But truly there was more of the young David statue than seemed possible about Tyler. Now that he was working out daily and the exercise had really taken hold, his body was starting to be as striking as his talent. She remembered something Tony Perkins had told her about a nineteen-year-old who had worked on one of his movies. "He would have given a hard-on to a statue." Somehow that sentence had worked its way into her long-term memory, and she couldn't help thinking of Tyler giving a hard-on to the statue of David.

He had been in her house for a couple of weeks now. Mostly he had been very quiet, hurrying through his meals so he could go back upstairs and study his lines, or go into the basement. Hers was one of the few houses in LA that had a basement. Rich owners in the era when people feared an atomic attack had built a bomb shelter in the earth below the house, like that would save them, as "Duck and cover," the ludicrous film that had been shown to school children after the war, actually suggested that hiding under the desk would get you through a nuclear holocaust. She'd had set up a studio down there so he could work on his music. Soundproofed, so he could drum.

But they'd had very few if any relaxed exchanges, so she had little idea of how or what or whether he thought. Mostly he'd behaved towards her like an elderly (she realized she was, hard as it still was for her to believe) relative he respected. There had been so much to do, with the accelerated tempo of the roll towards actual production of the picture, there'd been very little time for socializing. Especially as Louise wanted to avoid the paparazzi, who'd stationed themselves outside her gate from the day Tyler had moved in. Not all the private security guards she'd hired, or the Bel-Air police could get them to disperse.

The presence of Rita, which Louise had so feared might cause an explosion of ugly media stories, especially in view of the continued slide of Italy and the problems of the EU, seemed to have fallen completely off the prattle radar, so fixed was the press on Tyler. Even Annie Charm, whose dogs Louise could feel sniffing at her heels, seemed to have abandoned any discussion of the brouhaha across the sea, to concentrate on Tyler. But all she said, in the Tyler update that she regularly bulletined on her program, as once she had reported daily on the disappearance of Natalie Holloway and what happened to the man who had probably done her in, was that Tyler was behind locked gates in Bel-Air, California, where no harm could come to him except perhaps from his hostess. Louise's lawyer, who had stayed loyal to her all through her personal downslide, called several times to ask if she wanted to sue. But she told him that would only dignify the silly attack, draw more attention to it, and she really didn't want to get into a wrangle. Not yet, anyway.

The great carved walnut double-doors to the dining room opened, and Bunyan came in. His eyes were still heavy with sleep, almost closed. He wore a black and red embroidered silk-satin robe with black satin lapels, like a smoking jacket gone long, that barely covered his knobby knees. "Am I too late?" he said. "Or am I too early?"

"Just in time," Louise said.

"A wonderful tune by Julie Styne," he said, as he moved towards the sideboard, humming it, and doing a little two-step, his leather slippers flapping against the floor. "Adorable man. Did you ever sleep with him, Lulu?"

"We were friends," she said, "and he was on dialysis."

"That never stopped you before."

"Enough," she said. "The children."

He looked over at them and nodded. "It is a lot like that, isn't it? The beautiful, gifted progeny you always wanted."

"Not me," said Louise. "Andre said…"

"I know. That you would eat your young. Maybe he didn't know everything." He lifted a lid. "Kippers! As I do live and breathe, but not too deeply, lest I smell them. What are we doing, Brideshead Revisited?"

"I'm not sure," said Louise. "Who are you being? Henry James in that robe?"

"Oscar Wilde," said Bunyan, and put some eggs on his plate. "Actually he gave it to me."

"He died before you were born," Louise said.

"An unfortunate error on the part of Destiny. We would have been great friends. He said 'America is the only country that went from barbarism to decadence without civilization in-between.' And he hadn't even <u>been</u> to Hollywood! How I would have loved him. And vice-versa. Of course his vice was completely versa."

"Enough," said Louise. "The children."

"Wasn't Oscar Wilde a ho-mo-sexual?" asked Chester.

"Actually," said Bunyan, sitting down with his plate, "he was a screaming Queen."

"I don't think so," said Tyler. "His feelings for Lord Douglas were painful for him. Have you read 'The Ballad of Reading Gaol.'?"

"Huh?" said Louise.

"Huh?" said Bunyan.

"Huh?" said Chester.

"You have a lot of time on the road to read. I like poetry."

"Fetch me my lamp!" said Bunyan. "A sensitive teenager."

"Maybe you underestimate us," said Tyler.

"Isn't he gorgeous," said Rita. "Voglio... I wish I could understand la meta of what he says. Half," she said, with some difficulty.

"You're a whole lot smarter than you think," said Tyler.

"Really?" she asked sincerely, suddenly an ingénue. All eagerness and willingness to believe.

"Of course. You need to see yourself as you really are, and not as other people see you."

"O, what a gift the goddies gie us," said Bunyan. "To see ourselves as others see us."

"Robert Burns," said Tyler.

Louise dropped her fork.

"I don't think that would be the gift," said Tyler. "The gift would be to see ourselves free of wanting what anybody else wanted to see in us. Not looking for our parents or an audience to approve us. Knowing in ourselves, all we could be."

"I think I have to go lie down," said Bunyan.

"So what do you think, Bunny?" Louise asked him as they walked through the grounds of her estate. She had never really meant to have 'grounds', or asked the realtor to find her someplace with 'grounds;' it was enough to have four bedrooms, the master suite hers. But once she had seen the front of the house, and it did, it did look like Tara, with the great white columns, she had pretty much accepted that this was her place. That there were acres where she could actually stroll and have conversations, like a fucking peripatetic student of philosophy, which she had actually studied for a semester at Queens College, had done nothing but make her uncomfortable. There weren't that many people she could really talk to, and her friendships, except for a couple of them, mostly didn't last. So it was an unexpected joy, not a dismal one at all as she had said to Bunyan, that he was there now, listening to her. "You think it's possible? Besides everything else, that he's got intellect?"

"Well, why not? When genius comes, it hurtles in with the whole package. My God, you should have seen Brando when he was young, and thin, and heartbreakingly handsome. He was brilliant in every way. I was there the summer he directed and starred in 'Arms and the Man,' at the Falmouth Playhouse right after he turned the movie world upside down. It was the last time he did a play, and he only did it so all his friends could have the work, and a summer out of New York.

"I was a fan of Janice Mars, a bellicose, gifted girl singer he'd punked when they were all starting out in New York, sharing apartments, him and Wally Cox and Maureen Stapleton and Janice. Whenever he finished with a woman, which was often, he'd pay for her analysis so she could get over him, and got her some kind of employment. That summer took care of the actresses. And the actors, too.

I went to visit Janice and was at the back of the theatre before rehearsal. She was standing beside me and said in her adorably bellicose, bitter way, "There's only one thing wrong with this production: the whole fucking company is in love with the star!

"Then Marlon came in and looked at the set the designer had built, and said 'This is Shaw, for Christ's sake, not Gorki. It looks like 'The Lower Depths.' If I hadn't been in love with him already, that would have done it. Intellect is like electricity. It finds a conductor."

"But the people Tyler comes from..." Louise started to say.

"Don't argue with me," Bunyan said. "When I'm right, I'm right."

"How was Brando in the play?"

"Terrible. He played Sergio, the comic hero. It doesn't matter how much of a genius you are, comedy is hard." He looked at Louise. "Don't you worry at all about the two of them, Tyler and Rita?"

"Of course. I worry all the time. But they're going to be wonderful."

"I'm not talking about that," said Bunyan. "I mean about their being together. The former whore and that beautiful innocent. They are both young and gorgeous and full of juice."

"I really think she's too respectful of him," said Louise. "She's genuinely awed by his talent. And obviously by how smart he is. She's left her Bunga-bungaing behind her."

"But not her hormones. He is to eat. Barbecued, I think, would be the most delicious."

"I trust you'll stay away from him."

"I'm too old and ugly," said Bunyan, sorrowfully. "He wouldn't be interested."

To return to the Chateau Marmont was, for Louise, quite literally a trip. It had been the place where Anthony Perkins had lived when he first came to Hollywood, up a steep drive, with limited parking that had not been improved with all the modifications and improvements made at the hotel, and all the attention it had received as first one, then three generations of movie stars and film makers made it fashionable again, most recently Sofia Coppola, who'd used it as a setting in her last feature.

There was an outside terrace where you could have drinks, and that was where Tyler stationed himself, paying no attention to the hushed whispers, elbowing, and rolling eyeballs indicating others noted his presence, and were alerting their companions, in the low key local manner of those used to seeing celebrities and not wanting to seem like tourists. Still, it <u>was</u> Tyler McKay. A perceptible stir went through the place at his presence.

Rita, all glowingly bronzed, outfitted for a night on the town, in a silvery beige that clung to her perfect body, setting off her tan, picking up the pale glints in her peridot eyes, looked radiant in the not-quite dusk. Louise could not help feeling proud, even as she struggled not to. This was, after all, less than her creation. Tyler had become Tyler on his own. Rita had emerged herself, sort of

Venus on the half-shell, rising from a lathering sea of scandal, as the beautiful, --and who would have thunk it?—talented young woman she was. It was as though her unexpected emergence as one who might have something to offer had wiped her clean of the soil of her past. Bunga-bungaing no more, she sat erect, perfect posture for a young lady indicative of who she was becoming.

Louise was finding it difficult to think of her in terms of the turmoil that had spawned her. Even as Louise ordered her drink she marshaled in her mind the publicity campaign they might be able to go for. Maybe they could bypass the rag press, and hold her up as an example to every young woman with longings. To come out of the rubble, in a city where garbage wasn't collected, not as a piece of coal, but a diamond. Maybe they could even go for 60 minutes on a key Sunday, rather than Diversion Tonight. Inspiring women everywhere. All any woman would need was motivation-- oh, and maybe a gorgeous face and a perfect body, and the nerve of a... what? She could not think offhand of a metaphor that was apt enough. Maybe the nerve of a Louise Felder.

Just then there was a whisk of air, as though the wind itself had a flounce in it. She looked up in time to mark the huge, unseeing, pale blue eyes of the tall, pretty young woman with the fixed stare, passing their table.

'That was her," said Tyler. "Yip-pee. I am in Hollywood!"

"You want to sit out here?" asked Chet Sinclair, just arrived. He was wearing khaki slacks, a dark blue sports jacket, unbuttoned, with a white and blue striped shirt underneath, a print ascot around his neck, blond hair newly highlighted, looking like he was ready to be discovered by Norma Shearer if she didn't mind his being a little old. "I've booked a table inside, but if you think you'd be happier here ..."

"Oh, I am happy enough!" exclaimed Tyler, and getting to his feet, extended his hand. "Thank you so much for inviting us, Mr. Sinclair. It's really good to see you."

"Manners," said Chet, beaming. "Is there no end to this young man's assets?"

"You have <u>no</u> idea," said Louise.

The search for a director to helm the remake of 'Desire' had not gone easily. Oliver Stone was on a spiritual retreat in Koh Samui, Thailand, and Sydney Pollack, who had long been Louise's favorite, was dead. D-E-A-D she supposed she should start saying to herself, as the word, with its fearsome reality, pained her almost, though not quite as much as O-L-D. They had wanted someone who was good with actors, but also had a sense of movement, as the trouble with O'Neill was that most of the action came from inside the characters. Except for the love scenes, and the scene where Ephraim, the old man, went a little crazy and started dancing a jig to show he was still young and virile, almost everything was words. Words of course had fallen out of favor with the new generation, unless they were abbreviations. So wanting an ally to put the movie over the top when it was actually finished shooting and being edited, and was ready for marketing, Louise had called her BFT(Best Friend Temporarily) for input, making her a part of it all.

Allegra de Sevigny knew very little about film making, except for the gossip and power play parts. But like everyone in town she read the trades, and thought she knew as much as the next person, if the next person had been one of the most important movers and shakers in the land. Her influence had spread far beyond the borders of Southern California, Hollywood being like the kite to which Benjamin Franklin had attached the key that attracted lightning. The initial bolt might have struck there, but wires now carried the electricity everywhere, what with the 24 hour news cycle, and the truth that television and the Internet had made information available throughout the world. There was now even a TV show called <u>Indonesian Idol</u>.

Allegra came up with some names, as might have been expected, of European directors, starting with Roberto Benigni, his being Italian meaning he would put Rita at ease. But in the end she agreed with Louise that his touch might be too light. She then suggested a few Frenchmen, since they were much more grave, among them Louis Leterrier. The name sounded good, but Louise remembered that he'd directed <u>The Incredible Hulk </u>and <u>Clash of the Titans</u>. She did not actually laugh aloud at Allegra's ideas, though she did hold in a snigger. She explained, rather patiently, she thought, that O'Neill wrote mostly emotional things, that there would be no special effects, and that the best French director because he had a great sense of story and was wonderful with actors, would have been Louis Malle, but he was D-E-A-D. But she did listen patiently to the rest of the list, because she understood that Allegra was genuinely trying to help.

Everybody wanted to seem smart. Most people, probably across the land and seas and into the air would have loved to have some connection with movie-making, with the historic exception of J.D. Salinger who'd said "I don't like plays and I don't like movies, I just like books." But he, too, was D-E-A-D.

In the end, the director chosen, with the surprisingly clarified thinking of Chet Sinclair, was Nick Papadourus. He had made only one successful film, and that some years before, since he had said, right after the quite successful release of the picture, in a very Salingerish interview with The New York Times, that he preferred working with actors in his studio rather than on celluloid, which quote had come back, as they said in Century City, "to bite him in the ass." But Chet pointed out that he'd been working with the actors, and that he really knew the material. They could cover him with the best cinematographer in the business, who was excited at the prospect of photographing human beings, since he'd been limited lately to robots and computerized creatures from other planets.

Nick was clearly elated to be back on an actual soundstage, though his trademark gruff exterior and the outfit that went with it, the sloppy cargo pants, pockets loaded with pens, small tape recorder, cell phone, and what appeared to be a hammer, a T-shirt covered by a fishing jacket similarly loaded, were unchanged. But there was a fierce light in his eyes, a happy one, that Louise could not remember having seen in his studio, for all the successful New York actors on his wall.

The kids, as she could not help thinking of them, though she was careful to address them both by name when she spoke to them directly, were dressed for their first scene together. Rita, as Anna, the name they'd kept from the script that had starred Sophia Loren, was wearing a mail-order dress. The clever costume designer had copied it from an old Sears Roebuck catalogue that an assiduous researcher told her was not accurate, since the play was set in 1850, and the catalogue hadn't been started till the turn of the century. Nick had settled it by asking the researcher if she'd rather go back to USC Film School or be working on a movie, so she shut up.

"The point is she looks great in it," Nick said. "And it's obviously old-fashioned and simple. Being made of…"

"Calico," said the costume designer.

"Yeah. What could be more 1850 than calico. So when Eben sees her for the first time, even though he's ready to hate her, he has to be moved by her simple beauty."

That had not been so easy to achieve. The make-up woman had had a hard time downplaying the exotic cast of Rita's features. The pale green of her slightly slanted eyes had a tendency to flash yellow on film, so the lighting director had a real challenge. As did everyone on the project, really, as Nick had made it clear that they were dealing with a masterpiece, and he wanted nothing less on the screen. That he had derided O'Neill to Louise seemed to be forgotten, so Louise did her best to forget it, too.

They were incredibly beautiful together, the kids. Rita's spectacular eyes taking in his youth and strength before he even turned to see her, his stunned realization at first glance that she was lovely, not what he had expected as the enemy, the woman who had come to take away his rightful inheritance, replacing the mother that Cabot had worked to death, all of it worked.

The old man had been their biggest problem. Nick had wanted Al Pacino, but he was not available. Di Niro was too New York to be believable as a New Englander, brilliant as he was, and too big, physically, to seem really vulnerable in the part. Harvey Keitel was mannered. There was no one on the scene anymore like Burl Ives, who'd played the part in the Perkins version, except maybe Willie Nelson, and he didn't want to do it.

In the end they had hired Jesse Prudehomme, an old, reliable actor from the Studio who'd been giving acting classes in New York that were more or less the east Coast equivalent of Nick's, in the absence of great roles, or even mediocre ones for anyone seventy. He was ruddy-faced and slightly bent as a New Englander would have been from tilling the soil all those years. And it was easy to understand why his mail-order bride would back away on finding out they would share a bed, even though he was giving her a 'hum.' And why she would have been drawn against her obviously strong will to Eben, as played by Tyler McKay, who would have given—it embarrassed Louise, she who was embarrassed by nothing, to think about it, with all the history there was around the recollection—a statue a hard-on.

Tall and long-legged in skin-tight jeans, his wide shoulders buffed up as was his chest, with all the exercise his personal coach had had him doing the past many weeks, lifting weights, swimming in Louise's pool to smooth it all out, Tyler was as striking a young man as she had ever seen, golden curls capping his skull. If she had been fifteen or seventeen or even thirty she could have fallen in love with him herself. As it was, who she loved was both of them. And maybe, in a strictly non-sexual way, she was sure, Rita.

No one had ever looked up to her quite like that. With all she had had in her life of actors and actresses she'd found when they were just starting out, of those already arrived that she pirated from other agents who couldn't talk or think as fast, of men and women at the top of their game and their place on the Hollywood ladder, none, not even the one she'd had as the shiniest client on anyone's list, and, for a while, as such things went in Hollywood, best friend, long before there were BFFs that weren't really F, none had ever looked at her with such obvious admiration. And affection, really. Like she adored Louise for believing in her. Grateful. Dazzled. Loving.

It was that last look, one of affection so real and overwhelming Louise saw when she closed her eyes, just before she went to sleep at night. That was the most amazing thing of all. She was actually able to fall asleep without struggling, or pills. Something had settled on her so foreign she was unable to recognize, much less label it. And then one night, just as she was drifting off, the word danced through her still busy brain what it was. Peace. Was it possible?

She had never been happier in her life. And with that realization came another: she had never in her life been really happy. Elated, yes, on occasions when things worked out for her, exultant when she triumphed over adversaries, relieved when the hard work she'd had to do to close a deal was over, or an orgasm was finally there. But the quiet calm that came when you were being carried on a tide of everything seeming perfectly in tune, when the universe seemed to approve of your place in it, had never been hers before. And now it was.

Peace. She could hardly believe it.

CHAPTER EIGHT

AS WE KNOW, there are only ten people in the world. Maybe not even. The brilliant playwright who wrote that there were six degrees of separation had it right. We are all connected. Everybody of interest that I might have wanted to meet, and many I didn't, has come to my hotel. Not because it's chic or central, but because in life you meet all the people you are supposed to. And one of them is your mother.

Who happens to be the dialogue coach they brought in to work with Rita. So even though La Favorita was gone from the hotel, I was still sort of connected, through Mamma. As noted, I had bought her the trades long ago as a birthday gift so she would not need to fish them out anymore from someone else's garbage. She had acquired over the years a fine reputation as a dialogue coach, but aside from that, is incredibly Gung-Ho about going after work based on news she reads in those trades. I don't know that I did her any favors, as she is now well into her sixties, and should be retiring if it wasn't for a sky full of Republicans.

So she has been working with Rita for the whole many weeks of preparation for this film. She tells me very little as she feels that her post is the equivalent of a parish priest's, and that all information is privileged if that word is right for a priest. I wouldn't know, as it has been three quarters of a lifetime since I went to confession. Most of what I had to confess I told to Wilton, imagining that he was my Great Love, which indeed he might have been. I still think of my mother as Mamma, which I call her, because while my father was present he told me to show respect the way sons did in his native Italy. I guess they don't remember it when they grow up or he would have come back or sent us the fare to join him as he'd promised. Oh, well. You have to get over parents who disappoint you at some point in your life, just as they should get over children who disappoint them, which is almost all of us. That doesn't include me, though, as Mamma still tells me I am a good boy—embarrassing at my age.

I took Wilton over to meet her once, and she was polite, but a little removed. I don't think it occurred to her until then, even after my wife left me, that I wouldn't be giving her any grandchildren. Although at the point when both Wilton and I thought this was 'it,' we did talk about getting a surrogate. Never materialized, though, as that was when he started going to AA, and decided, I guess, that the Higher Power he turned himself over to didn't really want us to be a family. Oh, well.

Anyway, Mamma's visits to Chez Louise have been only sketchily described to me, as too much information I think she would have regarded as a breach of etiquette if not confidentiality. She went every afternoon at five as though to high tea, which lessons in fact she did give over some childlike sociable thing, like cookies and juice. 'Rita Favorita goes to finishing school' we might have titled the documentary. Rita resisted sitting in a chair as she recited her lessons, preferring to recline in her personal sun bed, bought from a local tanning parlor, so she could keep up her Mediterranean glow. There she would be lying with those little black plastic cups over her eyes, pronouncing, as Mamma fed her cues. I asked Mamma how smart she thought Rita was, fishing of course for 'stupid,' but she insists that Rita is quite bright. She would say that anyway, as her priest.

"I wish to lose my accent," Rita told her about six weeks into their sessions. That conversation Mamma apparently didn't mind repeating, as I suppose it proved her point, that Rita was no dummy.

"You don't want to lose it. It's part of your charm. You just want to get it under control."

"Like a bad boy," Rita said, smiling through her Bain de Soleil.

I would imagine having experienced so many bad boys on the yacht—and there are no badder boys than men of a certain age who know they are losing it, trying to pretend that they are young—it is like waking up in a Shirley Temple movie to have all this gentle attention. My mother was a toddler in the era of Shirley Temple, when all of America seemed to believe a little child would lead them-- out of the morass of the Depression, and the depravity of Mae West. It was a time when there were no open discussions about sex, which seems to me now, of course, pitiful, because perhaps if Mamma had known more she wouldn't have been so easily won or undone by Papa. But according to her recollection and personal experience which she is pretty open about sharing, as opposed to what goes on in someone else's home for work purposes, in the film business just before Shirley burst across the scene, sex seemed as forbidden in Hollywood as it was in the women's clubs that were trying to close down the movies, since those involved appeared so wicked, the morals they depicted on screen so corrupting. My mother's mother had worked in movies when they were first becoming popular, as an extra. So I guess you could say I come from an actual line of movie people, though unfortunately not the Selznicks or Mayers or Skourases. Grandma told my mother she could actually feel the fear coming with the formation of the Hays Office, panic that movies would lose their popularity so more people would lose their jobs. Fear is the easiest thing to pass on to a child, so from that point of view it is a shame that Wilton and I didn't have a baby, as I am fearless. Or so I like to consider myself. And so I think I genuinely am. Of course it is easier to be fearless when nothing to which you are connected is in real jeopardy, except, lately, your country.

My mother, as a child of Hollywood, came from a unique time in American history: religious leaders of all denominations were united in their loathing. The New Christian Endeavor at its convention had asked for greater tolerance to all mankind, "with the exception of the film industry." That is a direct quote, and makes me laugh. Shirley Temple must have come onto the scene like a curly-haired Jesus, not to be disrespectful, radiantly innocent, spreading a tap-dancing message of non-carnal love. On the Good Ship Lollipop-- better suck that than something else.

"You just need to remember to take a breath before you start to speak a line," Mamma reminded Rita at her lesson.

"Mi piaggi," Rita said, taking off her black plastic eyesavers. "I like."

"What?"

"To take a breath," she said, smiling. Taking one. Stretching with the joy of it as the oxygen bubbled through her fabulous body. Even my mother, who has no tendencies in that direction—or in any, really, anymore, that I know of—I think was a little smitten with her.

But Rita seemed to have downsized her longings to just being comfortable, taking deep breaths of the California air, enjoying

what has been an unusually smog-free season. I suppose when you
have been the Love Object, (I use the expression loosely) of a
number of old, fat guys, just to walk through a day without
someone pawing you is a breather.

It was when they were about to shoot the first love scene between
Eben and Anna that the costume designer pointed out the mark on
Rita's chest. It was not very big, no larger than an ink spot, but it
was quite dark, just above her gorgeously round and tanned left
breast, conspicuous because this was the first anyone—setting
aside the realities of the past-- had seen Rita naked. If there had
ever been a question about her beauty, it was completely dismissed
at this moment. What Tyler seemed to incarnate as a perfect young
man, Rita embodied as a woman. Slender waist, rounded,
Rubenesque hips, as if that Flemish painter with his generously
baroque style had come into the studio and done a sitting, or in this
case, a lying down. Delicate ribs showed above the improbably
tiny waist, and long, slightly muscular legs, and coppery mons
veneris, a shade darker than her hair, nipples tanned to a deep
honey color, and just enough of a hint of pink as she moved her
legs to satisfy Larry Flynt, had Louise wanted to think in terms of a
Hustler centerfold. Of course she wouldn't even consider such a
thing, though she could entertain in the back of her still changing,
almost evolving mind, as she planned Rita's career, the truth that it
would be the biggest porn event since Jackie O's being caught in
the buff, and the resulting headline, "Billion dollar Bush."

There was a literal hush on the set as Rita slipped out of the
gold-threaded pale peach silk sarong that Celestina, the costume
designer, had given her as a cover-up. As much as everybody
might have known about Rita's past, the energy and commitment

she had shown to the part she was playing, and the entire process of movie-making, had earned great respect, imposing a kind of lobotomy on cast and crew. If Love was blind, Louise thought, this much beauty was blinding. Not just to the eyes. To the mind. To the spirit. All areas Louise herself had never really thought in terms of before.

It was, unmistakably, a kind of rebirth. Not that she was the actual mother, she kept reminding herself. But it spoke to transformation. If there were such a thing as a genie in a bottle, something was rubbing him into life now.

But then: "Hold it a second," Celestina said to the assistant camera man.

It was a very small blemish, and would likely not have been noted at all, were there not in play so much perfection. If Tyler would have given a hard-on to a statue, Rita would certainly have given one to an entire frieze, if its predilection, in spite of the sculpted ranks being Greek, were for women.

"We can just cover it with make-up," said Janine, the make-up woman, bringing out a tube of Dermablend, something that actresses used on their skin to cover any flaws. It was still so dark that it showed, so she brought out a Max Factor pancake she had saved from years before, Sun Tan #2. It was just a little less dark than Rita's own skin, and, with the addition of well-tempered powder, obliterated, or at least covered the flaw.

It was not until a few weeks later that the spot began to bleed.

The only non-stop from Dubai to Los Angeles was on Emirates, where they featured private suites, pleasing Hendrik, comfort aside, as that would get him past some possible pitfalls of his journey. Many of his investors had been Arabs, and so he had kept a lower than low profile while hiding out in Dubai, waiting for the moment he could leave and get back to Karen. Never had he considered even going out to dinner, an actual hardship in his mind, since he did so enjoy good restaurants, and Dubai boasted several. As a Dutchman, even one who had been so long away from Holland, living most of his adult life in the great financial centers, he had a great yearning for fish. Having spent a happy and highly sexual part of his young manhood in Hong Kong, he had developed a particular love for sushi, which tasted to him like a woman, the most delicate part of her.

The popular upmarket Japanese restaurant in Dubai was Zuma, and he felt genuinely deprived at not being able to frequent it. But a greater hardship would have been running into any of the people who considered he had scammed them, which he had to admit if he thought about it honestly, he had done. But they had not, as he put it in his own mind, been Madoffed. No widows or orphans or Holocaust funds had gone down as a result of his actions. The only ones who had suffered were those who could afford it, which he considered not suffering at all, since they were like the banks that had torpedoed America, those who had rewarded themselves with bonuses even as their investors sank. He could not, in all good conscience, or even a fairly bad one, consider himself exactly a Robin Hood, stealing from the rich and giving to the poor, as the recipient of his clever manipulations had been himself. But his investors were, to a man—and occasional woman,-- greedy. And greed was, in itself, an index to lack of character. True, he himself had been a bit greedy, or he wouldn't have had to hide. But at least that flaw in him was not paired with ignorance, which he absolutely abhorred. If they hadn't been so ignorant, he wouldn't have been able to take them down.

It was all, of course, sublime rationalization. But that was one of the qualities in himself he most admired: the ability to- as they said in the old fairy tales, spin straw into gold. He considered himself the Rumpelstiltskin of finance, having made them the fortunes that were subsequently to diminish as a result of his maneuvers. It was all quite moral, he thought, even as he suspended judgment about himself, and just tried to figure the best way to live in and ultimately get out of Dubai.

So subjugating his very social need for sushi as he most enjoyed sushi, sitting at a sushi bar exchanging pleasantries with other diners, and suggestions from the sushi masters for the most cleverly presented and best tastes, he contented himself, his palate and his belly, with take-out from Bento-ya, less chic on its surface than Zuma. But since the surface of everything and everyplace was to be avoided, it was a better choice, really, than the more showy restaurant, and, in truth, the one with the best fish. That judgment was based on the fact that it was always crowded with Japanese. But he couldn't go there either, as some of his investors had been Tokyo businessmen, and they were looking for him, too.

He realized even as he suffered over these decisions, where to send his houseboy for take-out, how funny he was—especially for a Dutchman, since his nationality was notoriously straitlaced and humorless—to consider that he was in any way suffering. He was not a stupid man—on the contrary—or a conscienceless one. But as his investors had gritted their teeth and their guts over which stocks would rise, which companies to buy into, he had perceived in them genuine anguish over their decisions. So he was amused by their earnestness, rather than touched. Few of them, no matter how rich, gave much thought to others, or any form of charity, unless participating in it would give them access to other rich men, gathering in Aspen or Switzerland for conferences where they could learn about making even more money, networking with others who might come up with cash.

So deciding where to get his food delivered from, was a patently frivolous decision. As the time came nearer when he would be able to return to Karen, and set their clever escape plot in motion, there were really no other difficult choices. The airline was settled. Besides the convenience of non-stop to Los Angeles, and the private suite, there was Terminal 3—in itself a kind of Arabian Night. Emirates went to a hundred and ten destinations, most, if not all of them, for people who were dealing in money matters. So there were a dazzling number of Duty Frees for the gifts they would bring their customers, or their wives, often several, or their mistresses, often more. He wanted to bring a slew of gifts to Karen, but not enough to create problems with customs when he arrived in Los Angeles.

A bigger problem, but one he was working out with the help of a friend he had carefully manipulated into thinking was a true friend, with a promise of an actual pay-off at the finale, was getting out of Dubai unrecognized, with a passport that would not get him stopped. To get a fake passport was not that big a problem. The problem was getting through passport control.

The picture he had taken, that would become part of his plan, placed on the bogus passport, was of himself in the national dress of Dubai, a white cotton Kandora, obscuring almost his whole body in its generous folds, a ghurta on his head, the sides of it seeming to change the shape of his face, coming down as it did past his cheeks to his collarbone, revealing the beard and mustache he had grown and dyed black, to cover the graying blond that was his natural color. The igal, in black, a sash wrapped around the crown of his head, was the very best quality of black silk. He had black contact lenses to cover the iridescent pale blue of his eyes. There was no way they would not see, looking at the passport, and checking the man, anything but an Arab. That might have excited a more careful inspection, and suspicion at an airport in Europe or America, but not leaving Dubai.

He called Karen to advise her of the time of his arrival on her cell phone, careful not to go through the switchboard of the hotel where she was staying, because you never knew who might be listening in. Even using the cell number gave him pause, so he hadn't called her as much as he might have liked to. He really did adore her, and admired so much the woman she had struggled to keep herself, still attractive, still appealing, still lithe. So being, in his own estimation, a genuinely generous soul, he did have a little trouble containing himself as he strode through Terminal 3. The shops were such a glittering temptation. He couldn't buy so many gifts as to make himself conspicuous at customs in Los Angeles. since his natural impulses were always to be generous, except, of course, to the people he'd mulcted.

But a little something from Cartier was in order, a modest jewel. Karen liked everything low key. He bought a blazer for her at Armani, something she could wear at a country club if ever they rejoined one, as they would surely be able to once their clever plan went into action. He passed by Hugo Boss. He wasn't in need of any clothes, and had always slightly resented their having a name that was so close to his, without, in his opinion, having the stature, as a German company, that went with such a traditionally fine Dutch name. At least the stature it had had before the scandal.

At Hermes he picked up a pumpkin cut from leather, on the end of a metal chain that served as a keyring, something small, but close enough to a jack o'lantern to be amusing that he could give her for the daughter she rarely spoke of but he assumed would enjoy a gift. Pinkberry was an easy miss, since sour was not his taste in desserts, and Starbucks he resented out of principle, because as a businessman he didn't believe you should be everywhere just to be everywhere. There should be design to a wish for conquest.

Just before passport control he stopped in at Haagen-Daaz. He had always been amused at their choice of a name, trying to sound as if it were a Dutch company, though the founders had completely invented the label. Eating an ice cream cone would make more pleasant the waiting on line. Humanize him. And it would also give his crony, who'd told him to be sure to step on Line #2, a chance to examine his face as if it were not familiar to him.

"What does that mean, biopsy?" Rita asked the dermatologist.

She had been reluctant to go to a doctor outside the studio, even as the staff doctor on the film expressed serious concern. Her only real focus was watching the dailies, seeing happily how good she looked and acted onscreen, thrilled as were the studio people, Chet Sinclair and Louise, especially, with her performance, the great chemistry there seemed to be onscreen between her and Tyler. Her dialogue coach was there every day now, insuring that the passion of her delivery would be matched by her words being completely intelligible. There were already rumbles of Academy Award, the happy whispers that would eventually become tumultuous in Hollywood, waves, an ocean's roar, with the word already spreading on the TV entertainment shows. Diversion

Tonight devoted an entire three minutes to the legacy of Eugene O'Neill, showing him played as a young man by Jack Nicholson in Warren Beatty's REDS, a brief cut of Katharine Hepburn in Long Day's Journey Into Night, a flash of Jason Robards that they didn't keep on the air too long since it was in black and white which researchers had found gave people a tendency to immediately switch channels, even though they'd been promised Paris Hilton "coming up."

The love scenes, the studio publicists promised (and sent out releases about) so burned up the celluloid, they had to keep the rushes in fire-resistant cans. That there had not been an actual affair between Rita and Tyler was constantly underscored, as the danger might have been that he would anger his teenage devotees by losing his virginity to a foreigner.

The screenwriter had made Anna a Mail Order bride, which lent her character an additional poignancy, because people remembered when there had been post offices everywhere, special delivery, and no problem with actual mail, postmen delivering it, being afraid of dogs, giving rise to very funny cartoons. It also gave the thoughtful Sunday morning TV shows a chance to call to mind and become nostalgic about Benjamin Franklin's having started the post office, and before him the Pony Express, and the whole idea of "the mail must go through." A sports company briefly publicized the fact that Franklin had invented swim fins, but dropped the campaign when there was no visible impact on sales. The American Library Association seized on the wave of wistfulness as an opportunity to underscore the fact that Franklin had also founded public libraries, so it had a few fund raisers featuring movie stars who, according to their publicists, read all the time, announcing that each of them had recently made book deals with the print publishers that were still in business, strengthened by the successful autobiographies of rock stars.

The remake of 'Desire Under the Elms' was proving to be a true bonanza in every sense. It was the most highly anticipated film event since <u>Avatar</u>, even though it was not in 3D. The publicity releases said that 3D would have been excessive since Rita was, without anything being added, more dimensional than 3D, the most exquisitely voluptuous, exotic and erotic European woman to hit the screen since… Well, they really didn't have to say who, as by now everybody knew, or thought they knew, or at least had an inkling, or had heard the whispers about who her grandmother might have been. Even if that were not the case, it was FABULOUS, simply FABULOUS, to have such a flamboyantly captivating presence in Cinema. They were calling it Cinema again, since the picture was purported to be lifting movies back into Art.

The only problem was the bleeding.

"It means we have to make a little cut and send the skin to the lab for analysis," the doctor said.

"But it won't show?" Rita asked.

"We have to take a stitch if it goes deep."

"A stitch?"

"A piece of thread."

"Will it show?"

"They can cover it with make-up—or your costume."

"I still have the scene where I…" she hesitated, and teared up a little, apparently already feeling the emotion. "kill my bambino…" She pointed to just above the nipple. "The dress come to here."

"Maybe the costume designer could make it a little higher."

"No! It touch the heart! You see the baby, how much she love it, she hold it to her breast, kiss it many times, cry. Then she kill it. Choke baby with her breast. What word...? No can breathe?"

"Suffocate," he said.

"Si. Suf-fo-cate," she managed, with difficulty. "With breast. Hold it between her breasts, press them together hard. Baby struggle. Try to cry. Can't breathe. The breast must show! Mamma, bambino. She love baby. But she love more, her lover, Eben. So she show him how much she love him by kill the baby."

"I don't know the property," the doctor said, checking his watch.

"He believe she have the baby so it inherit his land. The old man think it his baby. But Eben, son, is real papa. He think—he very angry—she have baby to steal his land. So she show how much she love him. Kill the baby."

"Heavy," the doctor said.

"My breasts have to show." Rita's breath was coming fast now, as she seemed to feel the full emotion of the scene, right there in the doctor's office, with him holding out the flat small scalpel.

"The nurse will give you something to numb you, so you'll only feel a little pressure," he said.

"My breast have to show," said Rita.

"I'll only take a very small piece of skin."

"No stitch," she said.

"We have to see how deep it goes."

"How deep what?"

"Whatever's in there." He already had more than a slight suspicion. The spot was very dark, it had two microdots on it, a telltale sign. She was so gorgeously tanned, he didn't have to ask her if she'd spent a lot of time in the sun. He knew the answer. So young. So vital. So incredibly stacked.

"What could be?"

"We won't know till the biopsy comes back."

"It just a little spot."

"Rita..." He looked at his watch again. He was due to speak on a Television show about the benefits of freezing fat as opposed to liposuction, and was still working out in his own mind an inoffensive way to explain that you peed the fat out. 'Peed' was so juvenile. But he hated the word 'urinate.' One winter in New York the hit on Broadway had been 'Urinetown,' and the mere sound of the word 'urine' repeated over and over again was enough to make him wish he hadn't come to the theater. "You're not taking this seriously. This could kill you."

"A little..." She struggled for the word. It was hard without her dialogue coach, or the script. Words, even in her own language, did not come that easily to her. But this was her breast.

"Dot," she managed. For a moment she looked very proud at having come up with it. That was all it was. A dot. What could happen?

It was back in a couple of days. Usually a biopsy took a week, but this was a rush and they knew at the hospital the powers involved, particularly since Chet Sinclair had had regular Botoxing from the dermatologist, and they were Spago friends. That meant once a month or sometimes more frequently they would bump into each other at Wolfgang Puck's restaurant, and say that it had been too long since they'd gotten together, have a drink at the bar, and Chet would search his sort-of pal's face and ask how the doctor was, meaning really "How do I look?" and the doctor would study Chet and say he looked a little worried, which was Hollywood parlance for 'older' and then add "I can fix that." So the day after Chet would be worked into the doctor's busy schedule and have the frown lines and wrinkles eased from his forehead by the injection of botulism toxin. But the two men were, in Hollywood terms, pretty close, especially now that the doctor's biggest patient had left the scene permanently, so he wasn't on call in case of another accusation where the patient had to quickly have the look of the skin on his penis changed.

"You better bring her into the office right away," the nurse said to Louise Felder on the phone. "It's advanced melanoma."

The most interesting thing about Hollywood, in my opinion, anyway, is how everything changes when something real happens. By real, of course, I mean the Life and Death kind, which always blows these people away, they are so used to drama created in a script, or in their personal lives, some egotistical crap where they don't get the success or the phone call or the relationship they wanted, and they consider that heartbreaking.

In a script the story can always be changed. That is to say if killing off the lead might hurt the numbers at the box office nobody cares that the story might become less effective if you keep the star alive. That this unexpectedly radiant young talent, Rita Adona, a name that was already on so many lips, with all the buzz about her performance circulating through the town, should be suddenly diagnosed with something so grave was unthinkable.

The news—and it got out really fast in spite of all attempts to keep it quiet-- of Rita's cancer sent a shock wave of terror through just about everybody in the Hotel Royale, where she had begun her American journey, whether or not they had known her or even seen her when she was here. Those who had met her, or just brushed by her flagrant, noisy voluptuousness, had been impacted, if only for a moment, by how pushily alive she was. So the fact that she was possibly... what? ..these things are hard to filter as it frightens our unconscious, so words are hard to come by... mortally ill, was unthinkable.

According to Mamma, who insisted on being around every minute they would let her be there, since she'd been married to an Italian so understood better than anyone the drama of real life, and genuinely loved Rita, excited by her progress as an actress, feeling especially proud of her steps forward in language, Rita refused to have the bad spot taken out till she had done the scene with killing the baby. So she put aside her own what must have been incredible anxiety, until the moment was captured on film.

Now we know about Nick Papadourus, or at least those who are interested in directors know, that he was one of those extremely sensitive but brutal New York types from the Method days, who had his students use everything they were feeling or had ever felt of a painful nature and make it a part of their performance. So it was, from Mamma's reports, as emotional and brilliant a scene as anyone involved had ever witnessed. The way the scene was behind the scene, for openers, with Nick holding back tears, not all that successfully, as he, too, had become completely enchanted with Rita, had just about torn the whole cast and crew apart.

"Quiet on the set." Nick had called out. But you could still hear the sound of weeping. Tyler was having to ice his eyes as he watched it being shot. He could not afford to look swollen, as he still had one more take to do, of his reaction to Anna's telling him she had killed the baby, which scene, in the curious rhythm of moviemaking, they had shot before the one they were doing now, of

the murderous act itself. But they had all come to love her. She had thrown herself into it with such obvious joy, Rita Favorita, and even as she faced the heinous act she was about to pretend to perform, the real act of real death lay before her. And just about everyone on the set, Mamma felt, realized that that was what lay ahead of them. Because that was the hard truth about life: at any moment it might end. But sooner for Rita.

The breasts Rita had kept so beautifully honey-colored, and carefully unmarred at what turned out now to be such terrible cost were almost completely bare, only the nipples covered as the studio was trying to avoid, in advance, an R rating, so they could count on the attendance of his tweenie fans. The whole film was laced with vibrant erotic play between Anna and Eben, but Nick had been meticulous in the way it was shot, so nothing flagrantly sexual or graphic was onscreen. Mamma said, there was nothing that could be interpreted as tasteless, because of the intellectual roots of the project. Eugene O'Neill, after all. Even those who objected to Huckleberry Finn and Mark Twain would have a hard time questioning a Nobel Prize.

She was telling me everything quite openly now, setting aside her usual aura of confidentiality, because like everyone working on the picture, and, indeed, most of the town, she was in shock, needing soothing herself, and I am, after all, her son. Diversion Tonight had put at the top of their "news" the rumor that the brightest new young star to come to film in many decades was rumored to be suffering from a deadly disease, leaving her name unmentioned, in case it proved untrue, but not taking the chance of being second in line with the bad news in case it was. Annie Charm had alluded to the preparation of a special program to be shown soon of what happens to a brilliant new talent when represented by someone 'toxic.' That was, of course, yet another swipe at Louise Felder, of whom I had never been overly fond. Or fond at all. But she had done a hell of a job, Brownie, of building up and moving along to what could have been glorious heights this strangely remarkable little refugee, which she really was. I mean, had she come in a few generations before she would have been just another greenhorn, seeking sanctuary in what had still been the land of the free, where anyone could become anything they set their mind to even if they were from poor beginnings, if they worked hard enough and there wasn't a Tea Party.

So her achievement, as short a run as she had had so far, and looked to be the one she might have in total if the sad rumors were true, was monumental, and there was no taking away from the truth that Felder had made it possible. Put it all together, in fact that was actually fact, and not just press releases. In truth, Felder had kept a comparatively low profile through all the preparation and actual shooting of the film, though it was bruited about that the entire project had been her inspiration, because of some old romance she had never really had, part of the fantasy life she had conjured up for herself in the town before she evolved into the powerful toughie she had become, the one that most people knew. A romantic. Who would have imagined it.

Apparently she was having an actual romance with Rita. Not a sexual one, my Mamma was quick to tell me, even as she wept over what was happening. But that tough, too-fast-mouthed bitch (not Mamma's word, mine, and I choose it carefully based on my observations) had seemed to soften into an actual human being, the affection and caring and pride she showed for Rita before the horror was discovered, seemed almost maternal, according to Mamma, who is a good judge of what maternal really is. Except for her lack of visible joy when I introduced her to Wilton, because she was probably thinking of herself and how there would be no grandchildren, she has always kept my interest in the front of her mind before her own, which I believe is what real maternal feeling is.

What Louise was showing now was grief of the monumental kind. Her eyes, which she was too self-conscious to ice on the set as Tyler had to, were sealed almost shut with, one assumes, weeping she must have done out of Rita's sight. And when the time came to shoot the actual scene of the baby's murder, the last Rita was to be present for and part of before her actual surgery, Felder hid so no one could actually observe what she was going through. Feeling for someone else before herself was apparently new for her and it embarrassed her as real emotion can when the most extreme emotion anyone has demonstrated publicly is rage.

They had already shot the finale, where Eben, the baby's real father, finding out the truth of what Anna had done, to prove her love for him, shares the blame of the baby's murder and goes off with her, one presumes, to be hanged—O'Neill was not exactly a Spirit Lifter. So it all came down to the last shot Anna would be part of. Rita's own eyes, those jeweled peridots in the dark golden setting that was her skin, thick auburn lashes, only lightly mascared since so little enhancement was necessary, her natural beauty was so compelling, were shining with unshed tears. Mamma said that the wonder of what had occurred was that the gifted newly realized actress had seemed to meld with the blossoming of actual love—for the infant, for Eben, for all she had learned to feel and engage in herself of her own past, with Nick's tutelage. And with the sorrow. Sorrow for what she was about to do, sorrow, maybe, for what she had been, before she had come to this land of what had really presented her with true opportunity, sorrow for the loss of the world that might have been hers were the prospects of her diagnosis not so dire.

The dermatologist had made it painfully clear that in someone so young and healthy the disease could feed on that very youth and strength to eat its way through the body, at a more accelerated rate than it might in someone old. So as she took the child to her beautiful breasts, all that there was in her of sadness and longing, regret at what she was about to do, torment at all that would be lost, showed on her exquisite face, as she began to weep. But weeping that was truly agonized.

Grief, as we all find out, is the one emotion for which we are not prepared. To live fully is to lose. Sooner or later all of us lose people we love, and eventually, ourselves. So even as we grieve, we do not just mourn for the one we have lost, but for our own mortality.

Mamma said that Louise was hiding out in a booth offstage, but the sound of her muffled sobbing could be heard on the set. Nick had to stop the shot for a minute, holding up his hand, because he could not speak either, he was crying so hard. He signaled to Tyler to go into the booth with Louise, as Nick's instincts, in spite of his having spent all those years in Hollywood, were still infallible-- the young man who had come to town feeling everything, loaded for bear, knowing how and doing his best to fix it.

Nobody saw what went on in the booth once Tyler went in there, but the sobbing stopped. Mamma imagined he had his arms around her, and from my take on Louise, which I imagine is pretty accurate-- I have never disliked anyone more, but learned to see her through my Mamma's eyes, which are much more compassionate than mine—it had been a really long time since anyone embraced her with true caring. Mamma peeked in after the scene was finished, and they were just hugging, his big, worked on muscles cushioning that no longer nasty (my word, not Mamma's) cunt. But enough judgment. According to Mama, Louise was truly feeling. And that's the most any of us can do in this life. Is learn to really feel. And for someone else. That's the hard part.

As for the scene of the infanticide itself, Mamma had made a video on her Iphone while it was being shot. Those gorgeous golden globes—not the ones they give out for performances so everyone in Hollywood can have yet another opportunity to get a Goody Bag and walk down the red carpet and be interviewed on Diversion Tonight wearing great albeit dead designers (my favorite is Alexander McQueen), were pressed against the baby's chubby little cheeks. It struggled to seek out the nipple, but instead Anna, tears streaming from those gorgeous eyes, snot from her nose-- this was not to be a pretty scene, but a real one, and the nose will run when you are genuinely weeping, and hard—pushed the infant mouth between those spectacular breasts, and with her palms closed them tight around the little face, as he squealed and squalled and struggled and resisted, and finally--- they had to cut away for a moment, of course, as Anna was so into it there was some panic on the set by the infant's mother she might actually suffocate the baby—breathed, or rather, did not breathe its last. They had a very lifelike doll to replace it. The mother had all but snatched her baby away, the intent to murder looked so convincing.

Close to collapsing, staggering, Anna put the dead baby back in its little wood-carved cradle, tears pouring down her face, and covered it gently with a crocheted white blanket. She leaned over to kiss it. Sitting down on the bed next to it, she started to rock the cradle. And on her face was blank, empty madness, and loss.

There was a stunned silence on the set. Finally Nick called out "And cut!"

A sudden, tumultuous burst of applause. Some shouts of wonder and praise. Rita stood, wiped her eyes, and hearing the applause, turned slowly, bowed her head, and smiled. But nobody spoke, except for a camera man who whispered to his assistant, "I wouldn't mind going like that."

CHAPTER NINE

A FEW TIMES during her long sojourn at the Hotel Royale, Karen had seen the tragic gentleman swathed in bandages, but only fleetingly, as he was obviously hiding, not only inside the gauze that covered almost every area of his skin, but inside himself. His eyes, one of the few parts of his body that was not obscured by gauze or tape, were always averted, or at least they were on those rare occasions when she chanced on him, usually on the back stairway, as he did not use the elevator, for fear, she imagined, of someone's seeing him. It felt almost like an intrusion, a violation, her trying to keep herself in shape by using the stairs as well as the gym in the basement, as though the staircase were his private domain to ensure his not running into anyone. And then, there she was.

She, too, would avert her eyes, feeling almost guilty that she was still in one piece when he had obviously been through so much. She knew a little of his history, but not too much, as she felt that being too curious about that would be yet another intrusion. But she was aware of the sad fact that his wife had perished in the crash off Pacific Coast Highway past Malibu, that their car had gone off a cliff, and it was a miracle that all he had been was burned over so much of his body. But she also knew about survival, that he may not have considered it a miracle, that he probably often wished he, too, had died with his wife. She remembered from her own early girlhood how often she thought, darkly, of wishing that her mother had taken her with her, slit her throat, too, so she wouldn't have had to face the anguishes and disappointments that life, at its best, subjected everyone to. Whether it was all a test to build character, or a curse on some, or a blessing on those who did not suffer as much, or Karma, some debt from a previous life (which she didn't really believe in, but how could you know for sure?) was almost beside the point. Life at best was a puzzle, and the lucky ones may have been the stupid or the silly or the inane, who did not pause to try and put it together.

But all of that seemed beside the point when she encountered him, which she did more often, now that she was walking the Marquesa's dog. She still thought of the fluffy little animal as the Marquesa's, even though the news from the hospital was grave, the word down at reception, although they did not mean to gossip, but people would ask, as there were many at the hotel who cared about other people, even though it was Beverly Hills, was that the Marquesa was failing, and would likely never return.

Karen had still not accepted in her own mind that the dog was becoming hers. Oh sure, it loved her. Dogs were like that, she knew from the time in her twelfth year when she had begged her father for a dog, and he had given her one for her birthday. But then the dog peed and shit on an important memo from the corporation that was negotiating for his studio, and he had gotten rid of it. She had never found out what he'd done with Oliver, exactly, but she'd prayed he hadn't had it put down, though she didn't trust him enough to believe he'd only given it away to someone, he'd said, who didn't have important documents lying around, or a dog they could not train properly. In truth, the dog, a beagle, had been extremely smart, completed obedience school with a puppy equivalent of honors, and had loved her so much and understood her so well that she thought it had simply been expressing an opinion she shared about her father's fixation on business. It engaged him so completely they spent almost no time together, and that made her sad. And, she supposed, now that she was old enough, past old enough to see more clearly the things in life that had once seemed opaque, with the language that came along with some darker aspects of maturity, pissed off. Right. She was genuinely angry with him and Oliver had simply put her feelings into better than words.

Oliver. She wondered now, remembering the little beagle, the creature she had loved most in life after her mother until she met the best of her husbands, Charley, if that was why she had named their daughter Olivia. Olivia. What would she do about Olivia, when her plan with Hendrik went into action? Where would Olivia go? What would Olivia do? Wasn't Olivia too old to have a mother who still considered her a mother's concern? But had she ever been concerned enough? Olivia certainly didn't think so.

The worst thing about guilt was that you couldn't go back to the moment you had messed up and do it over, make it right. A friend of hers, another movie star of the same vintage as Karen, who spent a great deal of time talking about pursuing enlightenment, but even when speaking from the top of her personal inner mountain expressed bitterness and resentment about people who hadn't made her life easier sooner, though she had been a star for years, her career and life going, as far as anyone could see, really well. She spoke all the time to everyone she thought had offended her, which many had, about "making things right." How could you make them right, when the moment they happened and you first did it wrong was over? Work for charity? Try to illuminate a world shadowed in darkness? Write songs even if you weren't Bono?

All of this went through her mind as she passed the poor gentleman on the stairs, and both of them averted their eyes. The little white dog, apparently understanding not much of human mortification and nothing of judgment sniffed at the trousers of the bandaged man, and leapt with enthusiasm, trying for a lick at his hands, which had no more bandages on them. Karen pulled at the dog's leash, attached to a rhinestone collar the Marquesa had overdressed her in, from which dangled a bright red heart, trying to hold her back.

"I'm so sorry," she said.

"Not your fault," he whispered, his voice a sorrowful rasp. "No one's fault. Succede."

Suuuuu- shay- day, it sounded like to Karen. Such beautiful resonance to the word, wrapped as it was in softness so it sounded almost like an invitation to dance, to a buggy ride in the country, to a costumed ball where a little girl stood on tiptoe outside and peered in through the window, watching. Such a lovely word.

She hadn't known before even what nationality he was. A tragic figure was a tragic figure. No real place of origin besides their tragedy. You asked few questions because the answers might have given you too much information, and then you might feel connected, and connection made you more responsible.

"Where is he from?" she asked the manager, Riccioni, when she passed his office, coming out of the stairwell. "The gentleman who had the accident?"

"I'm not really sure," he said. "I believe he lived in California many years before the crash, and doesn't say very much. But I think Italy."

"You're Italian, aren't you?"

"Half."

"What does that mean, 'succede?'"

"It happens."

"What happens?'"

"Life happens. Stuff happens. If I may, shit happens."

"You may indeed," Karen said. "I like the sound of that. 'Succede' Lends a certain poetic elegance to the expression."

"Well, that's the thing about Italian. It makes a lot of things sound elegant that are really shit."

She looked at him hard and saw him really for the first time. And both of them laughed.

Cancer was not one of the things that Italian made sound better. Even as the doctor explained to Louise what was going on in Rita's body, and the translator Louise had engaged to give her the words to pass it on to her beautiful little girl, which she had come to think of Rita as, much as she tried to stop herself from stepping into that trap, there was nothing in the diagnosis or the softer language that could ease the ugliness of the facts. The virulent cells, opportunistic as the oncologist tried to explain they were, had already feasted on the youth and energy of the girl to make it too late for surgery, having made their way to her lungs, and parts of her brain. The disease could be slightly slowed, but at terrible cost, the available procedures simply retarding the progress by also killing the healthy cells, so she would likely lose her hair, her appetite, and all that was in her of vital energy.

Even as Louise heard, she could not take it in. "But she isn't even nineteen years old," she said when she could pull her breath together enough to allow her to speak. "Her birthday is next May."

"Would have been," the doctor said.

"You gotta be kidding."

"I wish. It's probably been present in her for months. When someone is as vibrant and healthy as Rita, as young, the disease really has a party. Even if we had caught it sooner the prognosis can be as short as six months to a year."

"But you can't just give up. You can't just let her go." He was, she knew, after doing assiduous research, after using all of Chet's resources and connections to investigate, that this was the best man in the field, that changing doctors would change nothing.

"We can try some of the newer experimental procedures, but they're all highly invasive. There's always the unfortunate probability they'll make her even sicker. Destroy whatever she has of quality of life."

"Cancer," she said, hating the sound of it. "Even the word is disgusting. They ought to find another name for that fucker."

"'Fucker' is good," the doctor said.

"And there's nothing that can be done?"

"Well, sure. We can cancel our weapons program, take all the money we spend on potential methods of destruction and defense, bring back our troops from everywhere, use all those funds for research and probably find the cure within a year. Money buys talent, and the greatest brains in the world harnessed to a program of research could in all likelihood do it. If there hadn't been means to back Jonas Salk children would still be dying of polio."

"There has to be something," she said, still unable to fully take it in.

"Prayer?" he said.

"Oh, come on," she said. "You've got to be smarter than that."

"I didn't mean it would fix it, or make it better. I just meant it might give her something to focus on that could make it less painful to deal with. The idea, I mean. That she's coming to the end of her run."

Louise took a very deep breath. "I still can't process it," she said, tears of fury in her eyes. "Would you mind if I kicked you in the balls?"

He managed a smile. "Well, it might make you feel better, but it wouldn't change anything."

"There must be something or someone I could get back at. My usual M.O. is revenge."

"That's the worst thing about this disease. There's nothing you can get back at. No visible adversary. Nothing you can punish in return."

"Fucker," she said. "Fucker fucker fucker."

"I'll bring that up as a suggestion for a word change at our next convention," he said. "I'm really so sorry."

"Cosa ha detto?" Rita asked Louise as she came out of the inner office. "What he say?"

"Nothing to bother your pretty little head about," Louise said. "Or your pretty big head, I should say. You're going to be the biggest star in the world. Bigger than Marilyn Monroe. We just have to make sure you don't get too conceited."

"What that mean, conceited?"

"Vain," Louise said. "Puffed up. Full of yourself. Hollywood."

"What it mean?" she asked the translator.

"Is it all right if I tell her?" the translator, a recent graduate of UCLA asked Louise, her face drained of color. Louise had told her to be sure to tell Rita nothing of what had transpired in the doctor's office. But the woman was so rattled by what she had heard she had lost what little composure she had. Riccioni's mother, Rita's dialogue coach, had recommended the girl, and Louise was sorry now that she had taken the suggestion, because one of the things they apparently didn't teach at UCLA, at least in the language department, was duplicity. And as Louise was to tell Riccioni the next time she saw him, she was sorry she had listened to his mother, because she had come up with one of few people in town who had no deceit in her and everything showed on her fucking face, and would he mind if Louise kicked him in the balls.

"You can tell her what 'conceited' means," Louise said, all but gritting her teeth.

But Rita had learned to read Louise, as well as she had learned to read her lines. "I'm going to die," she said, turning pale, beneath her resplendent, and, as it had turned out, lethal tan.

"All right, now I've waited just about as long as humanly possibly without losing my cool," said Annie Charm, having demanded a face-to-face meeting with Bunyan, sending a car for him when he had found too many excuses not to come to her office.

"You might be misstating it, in your particular case, calling it 'humanly possible'" Bunyan said.

"Don't you try and smart-mouth me, you faggot! You took the money. I paid off your debts, got your creditors off your sagging ass. You give me what you promised to give me or I swear I will hang you in the Galleria on Rodeo Drive and whip you to death in public."

"As opposed to private?"

"Don't you hear? Do you have ears, or just a bung-hole that half the world was in before you got old and repulsive?"

"I wish I had worn a wire so your legion of fan could hear this."

"I have more than a legion of fans. I have the whole world paying attention to me."

"I said your legion of 'fan.'"

"How long do you think you can keep up this pansy patter. You owe me. You owe me big time. You're her oldest friend. You know everything about her. The only thing you don't know is what she'd do when she finds out you took money to spy on her inside her own house. Tell me something about her that only a queer 'friend' like you would know. Tell me. NOW."

Bunyan sat down. The truth was his legs wouldn't hold him. The woman genuinely terrified him. More than the prospect of losing Louise, whom he genuinely loved, he feared Annie Charm might be capable of killing him. He already felt urine dripping down his leg, and was afraid he might lose his stool. He was old, and physically weak, and sometimes incontinent, and she would have scared the shit out of somebody young and strong. It was what happened to men on the battlefield or on the gallows, and he felt, rightly, he imagined, that that was where he was.

"All right," he said, defeated. "She lied."

"About what specifically?"

"About her relationship with Harry Bell. That she was with him the night before he died. The most that happened between them was he took her to a couple of dinners and a premiere. She never even slept with him. He did try to rape her once, the only way he could get a hard-on. But she wasn't really engaged to him."

"Oh, for crap's sake. That story is so old. Half the world knew she was lying when she said it a hundred years ago. Exaggerating her relationship with him to open important doors."

"But there were certain legalities," he said. "His estate was settled based on what she said were his wishes. Monies that went to a phony foundation. All of the things she said he wanted and swore to in depositions. She perjured herself."

"There has to be a statute of limitations on crap like that," she said, not having quite gone to law school but enjoying playing around with the parlance. "Nothing that could nail her."

"An entire career based on a falsehood?"

"Jesus man," she said. "This is show business!" She took a piece of chlorophyll gum from her desk drawer and angrily started to chew, the green of the gum punctuating her words. "Give me something I can use."

"She took money from his attorney to lie. He set her up in California where her real career began. He paid for her move and got her an apartment in Hollywood. Bought her all her clothes so she could start going to parties and cultivate people, and become an agent."

"And Darryl F. Zanuck had an affair with Bella Darvi whose name was a combination of his and his wife Virginia's because they both were in love with her, and they're all buried together under an Eternal Flame at Westwood Memorial, and do you feel the world stopping because of that?"

"You better damned well come up with a real piece of information I can use to bring her down and get that darling boy out of her grasp, or I will tell her myself what YOU did. That you took money to spy on her."

"That's the most I can tell you," he said.

"If that's the best you can do, go ahead, go home. I can't stand to look at you."

"The feeling is mutual," said Bunyan, and taking his pants down, turned his back to her and farted.

The flight to Los Angeles on Emirates, non-stop though it was, was going to be very long, sixteen hours and forty-five minutes. Hendrik knew himself better than to imagine he would sleep, private cabin, interior designed with pale tan leather you could smell like the inside of a new Mercedes and luxurious bed notwithstanding. There was too much to be anxious about waiting at the other end: the plot he and Karen were putting in motion— she had made all the arrangements and there would be only hours between the plane's landing, getting through immigration and customs, and the procedure itself. Afterwards, he imagined, there would be plenty of sleep, with help.

So to pass the time with as much pleasure as possible he had equipped his computer with DVDs of Karen's entire career, starting with the bright-eyed, fresh-faced, genuinely adorable (not just his opinion) girl/woman she had been, doing mostly comedies, through the actress she had become, to almost the remarkable woman she was now. He had seen some of the films, of course— she had been genuinely famous—which, to be completely honest with himself, had been part of her dazzle, a word he had learned and truly believed she had. There was a clarity in her eyes even now, as you looked into them—he could hardly wait—but the fact that she was known to just about everyone had factored into his attraction to her, as he had never felt all that wonderful about introducing his less than animated first wife—to his friends and investors. Not that he considered a woman a decoration, but it didn't hurt when you were trolling for millions, sometimes billions, to have a luminous figure on your arm. And face it, (an expression he had picked up from Karen,) people, no matter how high, how mighty, or how rich, still gawked in the presence of movie stars. How else would Elizabeth Taylor (poor thing) have become such a hit (no matter how temporary) in Washington, D.C.,

where everyone in power—which they really thought they were—
was so full of themselves they could hardly see what the country
that had been so gloriously conceived was becoming.

So even as Hendrik cozied down in his private cabin, trying
not to anticipate what ruts might be in the road ahead—he had
made what was to have been his last visit to New York before the
scandal about him broke, and although he might miss the
occasional Broadway musical which he very much enjoyed,
particularly revivals when the songs were still singable, he would
not miss the potholes in the streets, the noise of the jackhammers,
or the monstrosities they were continuing to build (especially
Donald Trump) in spite of how overcrowded the city already was.
Not to mention how frightened everyone was about money. Had he
not been himself a kind of swindler—face it!—he could have
written a few treatises on the folly of materialism. But looking
around the private cabin, larded as it was with sensational extras,
everything for the comfort of the man who had everything, which
he did, except for freedom, and that now lay ahead because of
Karen's cleverness and the arrangements she had made, he realized
he also had the solace of rationalization. And why not. He had
thought really hard for most of his life, never really hurt anyone
except those he had cheated, and all of them could afford it so they
hadn't been genuinely wounded. Not a blow to the heart, the only
one that was really fatal, since love was the answer to it all, Karen
told him all the time. As long as you had money, he could not help
whispering to himself in the secret chambers of his being, which,
now that he was posing as an Arab, he saw as kind of Ali Baba's
cave, where all he had to do was rub the lamp, if he was wasn't
mixing up his stories, and the genie would appear. Karen would
say the genie was love. Amazing woman, to have that kind of
certitude that life was a precious and positive thing, even after all

those years in Hollywood. To have so left her ego behind, in a place where the streets were lined with ego, as once immigrants had imagined America's streets lined with gold, and money grew on trees. In fact, if you thought about it, which he did now that he had so much time,-- the plane about to take off, his seat belt fastened, the flight attendant sticking his head in the cabin to make sure his charge was comfortable and prepared—it was not trees that money grew on, it was the trees themselves it was made of. Paper. So convincing. So seductive. Offering so many promises that only God could deliver. He really believed in God, especially now that he was going to get away with it all.

The room that Rita had been living in was decorated now in magenta, her favorite color, the set designers and art director for the movie that was being edited having come together as one gifted and efficient force to put it all together for her, and Louise, who had gone before the cast and crew of the finished film and told them, trying not to weep as she did so, what the story really was. Time was clearly of the essence, so they had whipped Rita off to Disneyland, a place she had never been but really wanted to see, in the cool hours of the morning when the heat of the desert would not be unbearable. The studio had given her an air-conditioned limo and driver, Chet had called the head of Disney Studios and made sure she would be VIPed through all the rides she wanted to go on, shaded by an umbrella to walk along Main Street, and hugged, but not too hard, by Mickey Mouse.

Few of the Fairy Tales known to Americans were familiar to Rita. But she reveled in Fantasyland, and enjoyed what might have seemed at another time dangerous rides. But there was nothing to be afraid of anymore. She knew where it was all going, and, unbelievable as it still seemed to her, and everyone who knew her and thousands who didn't, as they said in Australia, where Rita had wanted to go one day but there wasn't time or energy to go now, it was how it was.

Tyler had opted out of going with them, as he was devastated by the news about her, and there was the raucous probability that little girls and not so little girls might swarm him, and he didn't want to subject Rita to that, or take a moment away from what he hoped would be the joy of her experience. She was not yet in a lot of pain, but because the disease had gotten to her brain, she kind of floated in and out of her usual sharpness, sometimes not even remembering where she was. She enjoyed whirling round in the cup that was part of The Mad Tea Party, though she had never read or known Alice in Wonderland.

"I promise to read it to you when we get back to Bel-Air," Louise said.

"Read what?" asked Rita, having already forgotten what they were talking about.

So in order not to just fall apart, Louise hustled her onto the Peter Pan ride, where part of it was in the dark, so she could wipe her eyes and blow her nose, the noise of the music obscuring one sob she could not hold back. "Goodbye, Mother!" went the voice on the track, as the Darling children flew out the window with Peter. The entire story was, like Alice, unknown to Rita, who had really never had a childhood, Louise understood. Now she would not have a womanhood either.

The doctor had given her some meds for the pain. But the disease had already rampaged so wildly through her system that her nerves were also affected, and she wasn't all that aware of hurting. Louise got her a hot dog, even though she wasn't hungry.

"Taste it anyway," she said. "You need to experience a hot dog. This is America."

"But I like dogs," Rita said. "I no want to eat him."

"It's not really a dog."

"Then why they call it dog?"

"I haven't a clue."

"Funny language, English." Rita suddenly grew pale. "Need to lie down," she said.

So they took her home to Louise's, where the room had been finished in less than a day. All bright colors and fresh flowers, with a heart spread on the bed made of dark red roses, in the best part of their not-quite-fully bloomed bloom, and her name spelled out in magenta bouganvillea: RITA. She wept as she saw it. "You make me star."

"You _are_ a star," Louise said. "When this picture comes out you will be as great a star as has ever been, or will ever be in movies."

"You talk like you my Agent," Rita said. And they laughed and hugged, before she collapsed in Louise's arms, and had to be carried to bed.

Tyler carried her. He was all finished shooting—the film was being edited, so he no longer had to hide what he was feeling, or ice his eyes. They were swollen almost shut, as Louise's were. As were Mimea's, who had been moved from being Louise's personal maid to care for Rita. They spoke to each other in a kind of garbled Romance language, Spanish on Mimea's part, Italian on Rita's. But they understood each other, and Mimea, being very full of heart, understood how Rita needed to be treated.

"You are not to act sad," Louise instructed her when they were out in the hall. "It is not a hospital room. She is not a patient. She is a princess."

"Entiendo," Mimea said.

"What does that mean?"

"I understand."

"I'm glad somebody does," Louise said, and went into her bathroom to cry. She cried directly into the sink. She ran the water and splashed it on her face as she wept. That way she could just wash all the sadness down the drain, without leaving wadded up Kleenex.

She had just thrown cold water onto her eyes and wiped them with a towel, when there was a knock on the door. "What is it!" she said, angry at everyone, no matter who.

"There's someone downstairs to see you," said the butler, whom she hated personally now.

"Who?"

"Her card." He handed it to Louise as she opened the door. It was the producer of 'Diversion Tonight.'

"How did she get onto the property?"

"The chauffeur forgot to lock the gate on his way out."

"Fire him," she said.

"He doesn't work for you."

"Fire him anyway," she said, and went downstairs.

The producer was a woman, not that easily distinguishable from the announcer on the show. Everyone who worked on it was a cookie-cutter blonde, some with dimples, all with apparently the same hairdresser, so their identifying factors, such as character or eyes with something behind them like thought, were hard to differentiate.

"I'm sorry to intrude," she said, holding out her hand, which Louise didn't take.

"Then why are you?"

"We are all really moved by the tragic circumstances surrounding the film."

"You need a better writer," said Louise. "Your dialogue is a little arch."

The woman did not seem flustered. Bad manners and rejection were a part of the menu when you had the job she did, Louise understood, without feeling a particle of compassion.

"We understand that Rita is absolutely brilliant in the film."

"And?"

The woman looked around, taking in the décor. "May I sit down?"

"No."

"Then I'll come straight to the point."

"Good idea."

"This is the biggest woman's story since Farrah. Of course the full impact of that drama was mitigated by the shocking and much more dramatic death of Michael Jackson."

"Mitigated," Louise said. "You must have gone to college."

"Berkeley," she said, standing up proudly.

"And yet you found your way to Lotusland."

"We had a film department. But I majored in Media. I'll come right out with it…"

"I beg you."

"We heard that she's going to go very fast, but still looks beautiful. So we'd like to cover her passing on our program."

"You got to be fucking kidding."

"We are prepared to pay the funeral costs at the cemetery of your choice, though we would prefer Westwood, as Marilyn is there, and we see Rita as the new Marilyn. We will of course make a sizeable donation to your favorite charity. Or Rita's if she's compos mentis enough to make a decision."

"How about a million dollars to the Church of Go Fuck Yourself," Louise said. "The butler will see you out."

"Think about it," the woman said. "The merchandising. Bigger than Farrah. Marilyn Monroe. Posters! Maybe even a Forever Stamp if there's still a Post Office."

"I'll see you out myself," said Louise, opening the door. "Out!"

"Think about it," she said again, as Louise slammed the door hard, hard as she'd ever slammed anything, catching her on the buttocks.

"Are you okay?" Bunyan asked from the recesses of the entry hall.

"Can you believe these people? As the old lawyer Joe Welch said to Senator McCarthy, 'At long last, sir, have you no sense of decency?'"

"No," said Bunyan. "None of them do. And not me either. I need to talk to you."

"Not now," said Louise. "I have to go throw up."

Mimea, too, had been close to the entry hall, and heard the exchange. Her grasp of English was not much improved since she had worked at the hotel. But she had acquired some of the curse words that Louise threw off with the same unthinking ease she tossed around her undergarments, all of which Mimea was quick to put into one of the double-sinks off the bedroom in lukewarm water and soap flakes that would not make her patron itch. Too many commercial products contained irritants, as life did. She could think thoughts like that in her own language, but understood without anyone's having to tell her that too much thinking in a servant was confusing to those who hired them, so kept her more insightful perceptions to herself. Especially as she still could not express herself well in English.

But she understood enough from Louise's reaction to the cardboard lady she had just slammed the door on that the woman had been really offensive. As moody as Señora Felder was, she generally saved her rages for stupid people, as at heart, which Mimea could see into very easily, since her own eyes went as deep as did her feelings, the señora had love in her. More now than she had when Mimea had first met her at the hotel. So busy since then doing things for other people, not simply out of selfishness, selfish as she was, but because she had in her charge two young souls she obviously cared about, so seemed almost to have forgotten herself.

Mimea knew from her own experience that was a step on the escalator to God. Escalators were Mimea's favorite thing about America, as the town she had come from in El Salvador was very hilly, and even in her childhood the climbing had tired her. So stairs reminded her of the hard times she had in her village. She was not so lazy as to want always to take elevators, but she did enjoy department stores where they did your ascending for you, once you put your foot on the first moving piece of machinery. That in itself was a little bit of a challenge, as if you stepped unwisely, without paying attention to where your foot was going, you could get caught and stumble. She knew it to be the same way with God, who was waiting always at the top, but wanted to see with what grace you started your journey, before true Grace was given to you. And from then on, it was effortless.

She also was wiser than to speak of any of this to Señora Felder. The one thing she had understood immediately at their first encounter at the hotel was the truth that the lady's wounds were partially self-inflicted, like the craziest of priests who flagellated themselves in the cold of their cells in the mountains, because they did not feel worthy. She had told Mimea then that what she wanted was to be feared, a word Mimea understood completely, since so much of her experience had been directed by fear, until she learned how that feeling slowed you down, because you were always looking over your shoulder to see if someone was after you, and that way you tripped getting on to the escalator. But then the señora had confessed that she wanted to be loved, and that was the truth about almost everybody, even or maybe especially those who were angriest.

And she loved now, that was clear as the well-polished (by MImea, even though that wasn't her job) pale green glass in the front hall that sided the great wooden double doors she'd slammed on the lady. The señora loved the boy. But even more she loved the poor young woman, the beautiful child in the bed upstairs, lying on pale pink satin sheets, her coppery hair spread out on the pink satin pillow, as her lovely eyes closed for moments only before she opened them again. She was so frightened they might stay closed forever, Mimea was sure, she had to keep checking.

So rather than leave her alone and in doubt for too long, Mimea climbed the great, wide staircase, holding on to the carven banister, and went into Rita's room. She looked to be dozing. The trip to the play park had worn her out. Rita had told her a little about it in the almost-alike-language they used to communicate, and made her promise one day she would go there and have a hot dog which was not really a dog at all so she shouldn't be afraid to eat it.

Rita tried to sit up, and asked in their personal <u>patois</u> what had happened downstairs, as she'd heard the slamming of the door. Mimea told her with the full magnitude of the great gestures they used in her country and, she imagined, in Rita's country as well, how Louise had thrown the woman out, and actually closed the door on her 'ass.' She actually used the word 'ass' because it seemed particularly funny to her, as it also appeared to for Rita. She laughed.

Her laugh was nowhere near as robust as it had been, and her teeth were starting to look a little gray, as though life and health were already being drained out of them. Mimea tried not to notice. If you saw things and acknowledged in your mind that you had seen them, they became more real.

"But what did she want, this woman?" Rita asked.

Mimea brushed the question away.

"Tell me," Rita insisted.

"No importa."

Rita had been to a cocktail party very early in her Hollywood sojourn where a very clever man,—everybody there spoke of how clever he was—had held court, and she remembered especially what he had said when someone suggested something was really funny. "I'll be the judge of that," he had said, and everybody laughed. So Rita remembered the words and "I'll be the judge of that," she said now, in response to Mimea's saying what the woman had said wasn't important. The words did not come easily out of her mouth or off her tongue, but she did manage to say them.

"Perdoneme?"

"If is important, or no important. I decide. I want to know what she want," said Rita. "Tell me."

"No me recuerdo."

"Yes you do. You see, you hear, you remember."

Mimea colored.

"Per favore," Rita said. "Por favor. Non che tempo per bullshit. No have time."

"She want put you on television," Mimea managed.

"If you're through vomiting, I have to talk to you" Bunyan said, going into Louise's room after knocking tentatively, and hearing her say 'Come in.'

"Okay, what is it?"

"You better sit down," he said.

"I am sitting down," said Louise from behind her desk.

"Then I better sit down," he said, and came near her, but not too close. "I have a confession to make."

"You're gay," said Louise.

"Please, my darling," he said, trying to lose himself in the silk cushions of the settee. "Let me speak."

"That's all you've been doing for the past few years. You should make better use of your time. We could use a few more paintings."

"Which nobody buys," he said sadly.

"If this is going to be about feeling sorry for yourself, can it. There's a beautiful young girl dying next door, so unless you have cancer, you have nothing to feel bad about."

"Fear is a cancer," he said. "Failure is a cancer. Regret is a cancer."

"Give me a break," Louise said.

"I wish I had. I wish I could. But I was terrified. She had me by the short hairs."

"Who are we talking about?"

"Annie Charm," he said.

"What could you possibly have to do with that telegenic piece of shit?"

He hung his head. "I betrayed you."

"I hope you got thirty pieces of silver."

"Don't joke."

"I'm not. If you're going to go for a story that's already been done, you might as well go for the big one.

"I owed everybody. My creditors were after me. I haven't made any money in years."

"And?"

"One of her sneaks showed up at the hotel, and heard that I was coming here. So they had me spy on you."

"What did you see?"

Nothing," he said, and his eyes started to well with tears, "There's nothing you've done since I've been here that was anything other than kind. I hardly know who you are anymore." He let out a sob.

"Stop it! I already puked once today. I have nothing left. Don't be maudlin."

"I had to go and report to her," he wept. "When I had nothing new to offer I told her about Harry Bell. That it was all a lie. Everything you said about the two of you."

"For God's sake, that was a century ago. How could it hurt me now?"

"I don't know. But I'm sure she'll find a way."

"And what did you get in exchange for this betrayal?"

"She paid off my creditors. Bailed me out.

"You should have let me negotiate for you. I would have gotten you a better deal. More on the back end, which is where I know you like most of your action." She smiled.

"You don't hate me?"

"How could I hate you? You're my oldest friend. I know you're weak. No balls. A coward. We all have our faults."

"My God," he said. "Forgiveness? What's happened to you?"

"Well, whatever you think it is, don't tell anybody. I have a reputation to keep up." She handed him a Kleenex from the gold embroidered satin holder on her desk. "Go blow your nose."

CHAPTER TEN

SO SOME ARAB arrived at the hotel in an airport limousine this afternoon about five, and to my surprise asked for Karen Engel. Surprise is hardly the word for it, because as noted, the woman is still pretty fabulous and we're not talking Peter O'Toole as Lawrence standing at the reception desk, but one of those swarthy, heavily bearded types in full Desert Song Sigmund Romberg regalia, the last kind of man I would have conceived in my mind as a partner for her. I realized it could have been a business relationship, some investor in one of her creative projects, or a 'let's make it a better world ' campaigns. But the look in his very dark eyes was absolutely lustful. If there's one thing I've learned it's how to interpret looks. 'If looks could kill' is one of the older clichés but I've always caught the ones that say 'if looks could go down on you.' Frankly, when he heard her voice on the house phone I was afraid he would have sex with it. Right there in the lobby.

When he handed the phone back to me, Ms. Engel herself on the other end said "Send him right up." The excitement in her voice was audible. I don't know. Maybe they have giant schlongs under those things, and she's taking her hormones. One of the things I have learned to give up or tried to lose is 'judgment,' not the good kind which allows you to make sane choices, but the other kind, which narrows your vision so you really imagine you are better or smarter than other people so can come to conclusions about someone, condemn them in your mind, or, in the extreme case of some politicians who imagine themselves righteous, actually condemn them to death and finding out afterwards they were innocent, have no regrets. Honest to God. Sometimes I wonder (not just sometimes, but with increasing frequency lately,) where we are headed and it really doesn't look good. But who am I to judge?

Anyway, Faisal or Nazeem or whoever he was—he didn't give his name, said only she would know who was calling-- took the elevator and pressed the button for her floor and you could see really clearly through the glass and metal front of it, even with that beard and all the hair and the flaps of fabric how impatient he was, and that if he could have, he would have pulled the cables that lifted it himself to hurry the getting there. Takes all kinds, or maybe it just does for old movie stars.

When they had finished making love, with a ferocity that frightened the Marquesa's little dog, apparently made her think Karen was being attacked, so she nipped at the back of Hendrik's bare legs and Karen ended up having to put her in the bathroom, she told him what exactly the schedule was. The surgery was to take place in the clinic across the street the next morning. So though they could spend the early part of the evening together, he was supposed to check in to the clinic by nine P.M. so they could make all tests they had to and get the results before the actual procedure in the morning. Most of the tests that needed time for study had been done in Dubai weeks before, and were faxed to the hospital, the anesthetist and the plastic surgeon. Hendrik knew himself to be in perfect health as he proved himself to be with Karen once the little dog was out of the way.

"You are absolutely brilliant," he said to her as he stood at the sink, afterwards, shaving off the beard. She was sitting on the toilet, lid down, the little dog on her lap, explaining to it that there was nothing to worry about, that this was her great love, the one that she had never imagined she would find at her time of life, and so the dog should be happy for her and relax. "You have thought of everything."

"I gave the surgeon your picture," she said, stroking the soft white fur. "He showed me some of the changes he planned on making so that no one will ever recognize you. He's doing a lid lift to change the shape of your eyes, an implant in your chin so you look even more feisty than you already do…"

'I don't know this word," Hendrik said, wiping the shaving cream from his cheeks with a towel. "Feisty."

"Ready to fight," she said. "Geared for battle."

"As we both are. You brilliant, beautiful woman," he said, and leaned over to kiss her. She pushed the little dog's head further down into her lap, and told it again to relax.

"Did he say how long it would be before I could fly?" he asked.

"A couple of weeks till the stitches come out and there's healing. I have some aloe vera and Arnica and vitamin E cream to help hurry it along. He wanted to break your nose to help change the shape of it, but I love your nose. So he's just going to put a bump in. Make it sort of Roman. Add some Restalyn to your lips…"

"The better to kiss you with," he said, and leaned down again to kiss her, as she held down the dog. "What are we going to do with that creature?" he asked.

"Oh, don't call her that," she said. "She has a very big soul. I thought maybe I'd give her to my daughter. Olivia's having a really hard time. Feeling unloved. You know how that is."

"I did. I don't anymore." He opened his arms.

They were big arms, hairless, except for some faint blond down on his forearms, and well worked on. In the weeks, actual months now that he had spent in hiding, he had not been idle, lifting weights, using gym equipment he had bought and had delivered to the apartment in Dubai, spending an hour a day on the treadmill, strengthening his upper body on the machines. He was in better shape than he had been since he was a boy, and life had gotten easier for him, as he was smarter than most people, especially the ones who thought they were smarter than he was. And Dutchman though he was, with many of their national characteristics, including the strong belief that men should be in charge, he appreciated how clever his wife was, and that none of what had been arranged would have been possible without her.

"How long till you can get the new passport?" she asked him, from the warm fold of his arms.

"We only need the picture," he said. "So we'll wait just as long as it takes my face to heal."

"And then we can go anywhere in the world, and no one will know who we are."

"They will always recognize you," he said. "Everybody in the world will recognize you."

"But my reps sent out a big announcement about our divorce, and how betrayed I felt that you had done what you did, when I believed you to be so honorable."

"And do you feel that way? Even a little?"

"You never betrayed me," Karen said. "At no time did you do anything that in the least hurt me."

"And I never will," he said, and kissed her again. And again. And again.

"Perdoneme," Mimea said, when Louise said a very soft: 'Come in.' If there was one thing Mimea had never expected when she came to work for Señora Felder, it was a soft voice. She had taken the job expecting abuse, and in the beginning of her employment there, she had not been disappointed. But she had come to see that that was just the señora's way, that patience and gentleness were not a part of her character, but that didn't mean she wasn't good at heart. So the harsh tone of her instruction rolled off Mimea's back, and she never cowered before her patron. There was no reason to be afraid of her. She understood even as she understood that, that she was probably one of the few people who understood that.

"What is it?" Louise asked, lying back against the many pillows on he bed, from behind a sleep mask in black satin with false eyelashes on the outside of it, over very big embroidered eyes colored blue.

"She want see you," Mimea said. "Rita."

Louise took off the mask. Her eyes were swollen shut. "Is she very bad? Muy malo?"

"Not so good," Mimea said. "Apurate."

"What's that mean?"

"Hurry." It sounded rude to her, something the señora might say without thinking. "Forgive me," she added.

"I forgive you," Louise said, getting up slowly. "I forgive just about everybody except that cunt from Diversion Tonight." She stepped into slippers. "Do you believe these people?"

"No entiendo," Mimea said.

"Of course you do. You entiendo a lot more than you pretend not to entiendo. You don't fool me."

"Okay," Mimea said.

"Did she eat?"

"Try, " said Mimea. "No appetito."

"I know the feeling. First time in my life." She put on her robe and went down the hall. Stopping to look into the mirror, an antique she had bought at auction when she really thought stuff was important, she tried to pull a smile from her lips, lifting them by the corners. "Grotesque," she said. "I look like a fucking grotesque."

"Look good to me," Mimea said.

"What do _you_ know?" said Louise and went into Rita's room.

"Sweetheart!" she said in a falsely energized voice. "Principessa! What can I do for you?"

Rita tried to sit up. Louise helped her.

"TV lady," Rita said. "Why you no let her come in?"

"What did that bitch do, drop into your room by helicopter?" Louise said, furious. "How did you even know she was here?"

"I know. Know what she want."

"Well, forget about it. Don't let it bother your beautiful head."

"Non voglio... don't want forget about it. Good idea. Say 'Adio' to my Fans."

"Stop it!"

"No. Owe it to my Fans. I 'Star.' You make me 'Star.' Owe it to my public."

"This shit has gone to your brain," Louise said.

"Forza. Maybe. But I want you make poster me. Be bigger than Farrah. Maybe even Marilyn Monroe."

"Oh, my poor baby," Louise said, and started to cry.

"Why you cry? I get my dream. You help me get my dream. Should be proud. Make posters. Make you rich."

"I have enough money," Louise said. "I don't need any more money."

"I need give it you," Rita said. "Say Grazie for make real my dream."

Louise lay down beside her on the bed, and Rita stroked her hair. "Grazie to my mamma."

"Oh, Christ," Louise said, and began to sob.

One of the least well-kept secrets of life in Hollywood, was that nothing remained a secret for very long, even in hospitals. Unproven rumors about movie stars rushed to emergency because strangely inappropriate objects, some of them alive, were stuck up inside male sphincters, circulated freely, sold to gossips by those who worked in emergency rooms and were on unreported retainers. Stars who gave birth to babies with imperfections or serious problems were at risk for blackmail by hospital workers who gave them a choice of paying off for destroying the files or, in the old days, having them turned over to magazines like Confidential, or one of the other scandal rags.

Since the rise of the Internet, and the ascendancy of 'reporters' like Annie Charm, it had become even more of a risk to have something go wrong, or even go right in a hospital, It well might make its way onto the airwaves, via a paid informer.

The reconstructive plastic surgery of Henrick Bos was completed without a hitch. Such was the buoyant state of his health, and his recuperative powers, that even moments after the surgery, before the bruising had time to set in, his new face looked wonderful, and the doctor could tell exactly how he would look when everything healed. And it was in the short space of time between the doctor and the nurses going out to wash their hands, and Henrik's being taken to recovery, that the nurse who needed the extra cash to take care of her aged mother, or so she told herself, took the photo of the new face of Hendrik Bos as he lay on the table, and sent it to the producer of the program trying to outdo the ratings of Diversion Tonight. They had put her on retainer to report what rich and celebrated women were having done to their faces, their necks, their breasts, their upper arms, their inner thighs, their bellies, and their vaginas. The unheralded appearance of Hendrik Bos, notorious ex-husband of Karen Engel, wanted by the authorities of almost every country with citizens who had had money to invest, had been an unexpected bonanza.

His new, altered face was on the air by seven the following evening, on the rival network. It took away a little, though not all, of the thunderclap from Diversion Tonight's announcement that they would soon have exclusive coverage of the great new young star, Rita Adano, dying.

I didn't catch the TV news last night. We had a bit of a brouhaha in the lobby. Stewart, back from wherever he has permanent residence, if a man like that really lives anywhere, came in drunk, holding a cane he jabbed at his pit bull, no leash visible, as if that would keep it in line. The Marquesa's dog was being walked by Naomi, as Karen Engel hasn't been feeling well and is holed up in her room. No sign of the Sheik of Araby, so he must have moved on.

The pit bull went immediately for the little white dog so I snatched her up in my arms. Naomi was clearly terrified as I must admit I was, too. Once more I had to throw Stewart out, but not until after the Pit Bull pissed on my leg. I would have kicked it, but I am fond of my foot.

"Kindly don't come back," I said to Stewart, AND the dog, hurrying them out of the back door to the garage.

Just then, Amber came in from the bar, tears flowing from her pretty brown eyes. Behind her over the bar the TV was simpering news of the entertainment world. Amber told me Rita was dying, which I knew from Mamma, but I hadn't realized it would hit the airways so soon. Then she said something about Engel's ex-husband, a fugitive, having turned up in LA, and his face being on TV. Something about being a face-lifted face so maybe even as a fugitive he caught the local disease of wanting to be young again.

I don't think I'd really like to be young again, although I would like to look that good, because I was pretty stupid about romance which is really your focus when you're young, I think. Romance and sex, and if you are a woman, or have a woman's sensibility which I have to admit I seem to a lot of the time (ask Wilton—he'd give you a smart-assed but witty answer) you do have the tendency to feel that a really great love can fix everything. In spite of Gloria Steinem and how smart and articulate she is, you still probably think in terms of rescue: that a great love will save you. From what? you finally realize as you mature, which I hope I have. From boredom? Well, go inside yourself and see if anybody's home I say, and would like to put whatever you find and measure it against Life with the Kardasians, or whatever manure they're using now to clog up the airways and our mental arteries. I really love my country, or at least I did, understanding Papa's great dream, shitheel that he turned out to be, that he could become something, even though he didn't. I guess you can say that was Rita's dream, too.

Of course hers was on an overblown level, but then, so was Rita. Not a straight man in the world who wouldn't have wanted to fuck her, and even a few of us other guys. I remember an old publicist named Jack Martin, a really clever fellow, friend of Wilton's, who used to hang around the hotel, and tell stories about Hollywood when it was really Hollywood. He said he knew a true queen, another publicist, who was there when Marilyn Monroe came out in that dress, and sang 'Happy Birthday, Mr. President,' and got a hard-on just seeing her. And it was like that with Rita, I think. There was something so ravenously sexual and life-affirming about her that it didn't matter what your tendencies were, you would have liked to stick it into that.

Mamma says that even the hardest studio executive wept at the press screening of Desire, (which they are thinking of shortening the title to, and releasing it as, to stimulate sales when it is released next month.) Wept not just from having lost what fortunes they could have made in the future, since nobody understands how to regret things before they actually happen like Hollywood Brass, except maybe Republicans. But regret because they actually saw what gifts were there, besides the beauty.

As for Engel's ex-husband, the compassionate man's Bernie Madoff,-- they did do a story in Vanity Fair about how he didn't really hurt anybody but jillionaires-- I know Engel's been lying really low, not letting the maid do her room and sending out to the Bagel Nosh for sustenance, apparently not even wanting room service, she is apparently so mortified. She obviously wants contact with no one. She must be really depressed. Bad publicity from a life you're not even having anymore, and a hairy new love vanished overnight. Her daughter arrived unexpectedly, and Karen said on the phone she would be right down, but didn't appear for almost a half hour.

Meanwhile the daughter sat in the lobby drumming her fingers furiously on her knees. When her mother finally appeared, she got the dog from still trembling Naomi, and put it on the daughter's lap. "Why are you giving it to me?" Olivia asked.

"She's a really sweet dog. And very soft, Olivia."

"And?"

"It's comforting. Having something that cares about you with no agenda."

"You think I have an agenda?"

"I wasn't saying that. I just meant that unconditional love is very healing."

"It's good you know that," Olivia said. "Of course it's one thing to know something and another to put it into action."

"Please," Karen said. "I'm going to be leaving L.A. soon. I want things to be better between us."

"So what are you going to do about it?"

"Whatever I can. But I have…"

"… to be at the studio. To answer the other phone. To go to Singapore to make a movie. To do a myriad of things that don't involve taking care of a child."

"You're not a child anymore, Olivia."

Just then one of the blondes that works on Diversion Tonight came in with a guy holding a minicam, and started talking into a hand microphone, looking into the camera with that teeth-whitened smile. "Yes, ladies and gentlemen, this is where it all began. The Hotel Royale, where Rita Favorita came to stay when she first hit Hollywood, literally right off the boat, with nothing behind her but an international scandal…"

"And a really impressive rear-end," said Olivia quite loudly.

The woman stopped talking, glared at Olivia, and switched off her mike. "I'm trying to do something important here," she said.

"Get a life," said Olivia.

"I happen to have a life," the woman said.

"Then get a job."

"What do you think this is?" the woman said, waving the microphone.

"Masturbation," said Olivia.

"It pleases me in a perverse kind of way that you're not just angry with me," Karen said.

"Well, these people are really ludicrous," Olivia said. "They make me sick."

"Then why don't you do something about it?" Karen said.

"Like what?" Her tone, for the first time since she came into the lobby, was free of sarcasm.

"Get your own show. Rant about how empty all this is. Harness all your anger and use it for the good. Rage like Annie Charm, except about things that really matter."

"Yeah, right. Like someone would want to put me on the air."

"I would," said Karen. "Of course you'd have to have your hair done."

"By your hairdresser, I suppose."

"The hairdresser of your choice," said Karen. "Just get it done. You're a really pretty woman. Or you would be if you..." She stopped short.

"What? Don't stop now."

"Sat up straight. Be proud of who you are."

"I'm nobody," she said.

"You are as important as anybody in the world. Everybody is important."

"Easy to say when you're a movie star."

"I'm not a movie star. I'm only a woman who loves you. And wants you to be the best you can be. Go ahead. Do a show. I'll finance it."

"Really?"

"Truly," Karen said and held out her hand. Olivia took it, and Karen turned their joined hands and kissed the back of her daughter's, and the two of them embraced. And wept.

I must say I could have cried myself. But then, I think I was still a little emotional from the news about Rita, and the encounter with the pit bull.

"What are we going to do?" asked Hendrik, when Karen was back upstairs, gently spreading Vitamin E on his scars. "There's no way I can get out of the country now. They'll have my picture at all the ports of exit. I can't even leave this hotel."

"I'll think of something," Karen said.

"Of course you will," Hendrik said, and touched her lips with his finger, tenderly. "You always do. You brilliant, beautiful woman."

"Can't we do something about the morphine drip?" said the producer of <u>Diversion Tonight</u>, from behind the camera. "It's really unsightly."

The tube was taped to Rita's arm, and the bottle to which it was attached was on a metal stand by Rita's bed. The bed was covered with flowers, artfully arranged by Edgar Pildington, the same man who did the reporter's hair, but had always wanted really to be a florist. The wish intensified once he found out the florist Harry Finley had gotten Peter Lawford's place in the wall around the corner from Marilyn Monroe's niche at Westwood Memorial. They had removed Lawford's remains when his widow was unable to keep up the payments. Edgar considered that only just, since many people believed, with all the theories there were, among the many myths and possible truths surrounding Marilyn's death, that the real reason she was in the wall at all was because Lawford had introduced her to the Kennedys.

Edgar had stopped just short of arranging the blossoms in the shape of a heart atop the magenta satin quilt that covered Rita, as that was just a tad too much the honeymoon scene from Sex and the City, although personally, he found it very touching. As it was, he had managed to weave a few of the blossoms into Rita's hair, still thick and lustrous and that wonderful shade somewhere between auburn and actual coppery red, because, thank God, they hadn't given her chemo.

The two hundred and twenty-six flower arrangements that had been sent by Hollywood executives, agents, promoters and restaurateurs, and of course some fans, had been put out in the hall. Rita was having trouble breathing, and the doctor said they robbed the room of oxygen.

She was drifting in and out of awareness from the morphine. The disease had rampaged through her so speedily that it had eaten her nerve ends so she wasn't feeling much pain. But Louise had told the attending nurse that if Rita was allowed to feel as much as a twinge, she would tear her apart.

Still: "I hate the look of that drip," the producer said. "Can't we do something?"

"We could put her arm under the quilt," said one of assistants from the show. "So at least we won't see the tube going in."

"You give her a moment's discomfort and I'll break you in half," Louise said, and headed for the door. "I have to get out of here. Call me if she needs me."

She kissed Rita before she left, and did not say Goodbye. Just looked at her hard, as if she had never seen such a face before, which of course no one had. And probably never would again

"Tyler," Rita managed. "Want to see Tyler."

Louise went to get him.

"Beautiful boy," Rita said, when he appeared beside her bed.

"Beautiful girl," said Tyler.

"We make good love in the movie." She reached for his hand with the hand that didn't have the tube going into it. "Sorry not for real."

"Had it in my head," said Tyler. "All the time. Had it in my dreams."

"Better," she said, and patted his arm.

"I'll see you again," he said. "You'll see."

"Hope," Rita said.

"You have to do more than hope, Rita. Believe. That's what faith is. Knowing with all your heart what you can't really see. Just like you said about becoming a movie star. If you believe something strong enough, then it will be so.

"And now you're a star. A great star. People will see the movie and talk about you forever."

"Da vero? You think so?"

"I know so," he said. "Just like I know there is more than this." He waved his arm around to indicate the room, the fabrics, the flowers. "So…" He swallowed. "Believe in Heaven."

"Was Heaven here," she said. She gave a little gasp. "Can't breathe."

The nurse took the oxygen mask by the bed, and put it against Rita's face. "Do we have to have that?" the producer said. "It really looks awful."

"I think you better leave now," Tyler said, and stood up to his full, handsome, manly height. "I think you all better get out of here."

"But we'd really like to catch the death rattle," said the producer. "I understand that there really is something exactly like that. That at the very end, you can hear a clicking in the throat that's like a rattle."

"Out," said Tyler.

"So, ladies and gentlemen," said the announcer at the end of the show when it aired. "You saw it all here. To protect the delicate sensibilities of young children who might have found it disturbing, we did not let you see Rita's final moment, or hear the actual death rattle, but I understand it was amazing.

"Meanwhile, Rita's representative, Louise Felder, has announced that the half-clad poster of Rita, in <u>Desire</u>, her first, last and only film, to be released in November in time to qualify for Academy Awards, will be available starting tomorrow after the funeral. See details of how to order at www. RitaAdano.com.

The funeral will be private."

I do not consider myself an emotional man. Or, at least, I don't let whatever feminine feelings I actually possess show too often, or to the wrong people. But I have to confess that I wept unashamedly when the announcement came that Rita was actually dead. Wilton was especially kind, and came over to hold me, which is what you really need with grief. Because touch is what they will never have again, the dead. Even if there is an Afterlife, which I think I am a bit too cynical and sophisticated to believe in, but I sort of hope for anyway, the one thing the dead long for according to the psychics I've seen, not that I believe in such things—oh maybe a little—is that as happy as they are in the realms they inhabit, the one thing they long for is touch.

So Wilton and I just held each other while I wept. Because we have all had loss, more than we should have since HIV, so we've buried a lot of friends,-- too many. Even though he didn't know Rita, and how alive she was, he wept with me. We rocked back and forth, and just held on.

Right after that there was one of those stupid emergencies that happen in 5 Star hotels. Stupid because it isn't a true emergency, but guests consider it so because you are five star and their every need should be treated like a nuclear meltdown. So I had to hurry downstairs, and because that wonderful-to-look-at but so-out-of-date elevator is so damned slow, and anyway I didn't want to run into anybody looking as I must have looked, all weepy and fallen apart, I took the back stairway. And who should I come across but Karen Engel, sneaking down the stairs, holding in an absolute embrace the burned guy from the car accident, all wrapped like the Invisible Man, as the visiting Contessa had once noted, holding her heart.

In her left hand, Engel held the Marquesa's little dog, but not as tenderly as she was holding onto the man. The woman must be insatiable. The hairy Arab. And now this man. Honest to God. And all she had asked me for was the meaning of 'Succede," and what nationality he was, not what room he was in. I guess it doesn't take a lot to turn those old dames on.

Still, as I noted, none of this is my business, curiosity killed the cat, etc. etc. So I just pretended I didn't even see as they went out the back door to the garage, and her Lamberghini. We have her credit card on file, so I am not upset that she left the hotel without even checking out. I don't know exactly how old the woman is, but those hormones must be dynamite.

The private yacht left the dock in San Diego at twilight. The sale had been conducted with more than the usual sense of expediency that happened around yachts, especially, the previous owner had thought, one that commanded such a price. The owner-to-be hadn't even tried to bargain a little. The crew, including chef and assistant chef, and all the men who usually worked on board had, because of the enormity of the salaries they were offered, agreed to go along, even though the trip would be long and there were no promises when the yacht would be returning, or if. The announced route was to be across the Pacific, to the Indian Ocean, to the Gulf of Siam. Food was stocked up plentifully before leaving port, by the young Australian chef who knew there would be great produce available again when they reached the little islands off Thailand that they were slated to sail around, like Koh Samui.

None of them got a really good look at the man who was with the woman. But noting her carrying the little white dog, one of the sailors believed he had seen her in the movies. None of them was old enough to know for sure who she was, as she looked, according to the chef who, when not cooking, was easily bored, so had a lot of old movies on his computer downloaded from Itunes, from a very "well- seasoned" vintage.

"I know," said Annie Charm a few minutes into her broadcast, "that I have been accused of being too quick sometimes to rush to judgment. But I can say unequivocally that this is not one of those times."

"We have all grieved over her untimely ending, whether or not we ever met, or even set actual eyes on Rita Adano, which the world will do when her film is released in November to what I understand from my well-places sources, will be resounding praise. But it is never too soon for the buzzards! For the cormorants. The vultures. The birds of prey."

"With Rita not even cold in her grave, the executor of Rita's estate, Louise Felder, her self-serving 'agent', and I use the term in its most insidious garb, released nationally a half-clad poster of Rita that has already outsold Farrah Fawcett's, claiming that that was Rita's dying wish. Yeah, right. Well, this Felder dame gives new meaning to the word 'disgusting.' And a few other words I could use, I gotta tell you, but there may be children watching."

"This actually is not the first time Miss Felder has been engaged in so heinous an act, so great a lie, in circumstances not dissimilar. A lot of years ago the fabled Broadway producer, Harry Bell, had the misfortune to have contact with this Miss Felder. The slightest contact, because even as short and supposedly unattractive as he was reported to have been, he did not want to have that much to do with her."

"But she parlayed the little bit of friendship he might have offered into a giant lie that got her a lot of publicity. She perjured herself, swore that he wanted the money from his estate to be spent in ways that were not really his wishes, to benefit her cronies.

"Disgusting enough. But how much more disgusting to give out the prevarication…" she hit every syllable of the word.. "that poor darling Rita wanted a poster put out so soon and distastefully after her death. And the proceeds to go to… Final Answer: Louise Felder. If I had a bucket here I would vomit into it. But I must consider that there might be some of you watching with sensitive natures."

"So what do you want to do?" Louise's lawyer said on the phone.

"You want me to file suit?"

"No," said Louise. "I think it's funny. Let her keep working herself up. Maybe she'll have a stroke."

She thanked him for calling, and hung up the phone. "Not that you wish her ill," said Bunyan, who sat on the settee near her.

"Ill would be too good for her," Louise said. "Let her just get old."

The doorbell rang. "Oh, shit," said Louise. "They must have forgotten to lock the gate after everyone left. See who it is," she said to Mimea.

Mimea went downstairs into the marbled entry hall, and opened the door. Standing there was the producer of 'Diversion Tonight.'

"I don't mean to intrude at what must be such a difficult time," she said to the maid. "But I wasn't invited to the funeral." She held out a basket of flowers. "And I wanted to bring these in Rita's memory. I'd like to give them to Miss Felder."

Mimea looked at her for a moment. "Por favor," she said. "Go_ fuck youself."

She closed the door.

Two posters of Rita Adano were available: the first by the paparazzo who had caught her sunbathing naked at the Royale, the full-length stretched-out mythic sex goddess she was to become. The other was the one released by Louise, the studio shot of Rita on her lovely haunches, luscious thighs pressed against shapely suntanned calves, in shorts, breasts draped with pale green satin the color of her eyes. Both posters were shortly to outsell Farrah's.

The nude one would eventually outsell Marilyn Monroe's. But not until there after there were three more biopics about her, a musical, an opera, a ballet, two television series, and a comic strip. By that time almost all the cognoscenti knew that Rita was really the illegitimate grand-daughter of Marilyn Monroe and Bobby Kennedy.